MW01702109

A Body on the Flats

ALSO BY MAX MANNING

KANE AND GRANGER THRILLERS
Book 1: A Body On The Flats

STANDALONE
The Killer In Me

A BODY on the FLATS

MAX MANNING

A Kane and Granger Thriller Book 1

JOFFE BOOKS

Joffe Books, London
www.joffebooks.com

First published in Great Britain in 2024

Cover art by Dee Dee Book Covers

ISBN: 978-1-83526-795-0

For my wife, Valerie.

CHAPTER 1

The boy slides the screwdriver into the gap between the door and the frame and wrenches hard. The wood splits and a second forceful twist snaps the lock. Perfect job. More than simple brute force. There's a knack to it, and practice makes perfect. He steps quickly inside and pulls the door shut.

He stands still, waits and listens for a few seconds. Nothing but the gentle murmur of lapping waves. The sea has been unusually calm for days. He takes a deep breath. The air inside the beach hut is damp. It smells of seaweed and rotting crab meat.

He pulls a torch from his pocket and switches it on. The beam of light darts around the room and settles on a pair of binoculars lying on a shelf fixed to the back wall. The boy grins. He'll get good money for those, no problem.

The crunch of feet on damp shingle makes his heart skip a beat. He switches off the torch and freezes. As the sound comes closer, he holds his breath. It's nearly four in the morning. There's no reason for anyone to be on the beach unless they're up to no good. Like him. He nudges the door a fraction and peers into the darkness.

A full moon hangs high in the black sky and his eyes are sharp enough to pick out a figure, arms outstretched, hauling what looks like a roll of carpet wrapped in plastic sheeting toward a rowing boat a few feet from the waterline.

The boy can't see a face but he's certain it's a man because of the figure's bulk and his deep, guttural grunts.

When he reaches the boat, the man releases his grip on the plastic, stands tall, stretches his back and takes a breather. Tugging back the hood of his jacket, he turns his head to scan the row of beach huts behind him. The boy jerks his head back with a gasp. Only when he's sure he hasn't been seen does he take another look.

The man is kneeling now, tugging hard at one end of the plastic sheeting until it unravels. The boy covers his mouth with a hand. His heart hammers wildly against his ribcage. He doesn't want to believe what he's seeing. He doesn't want to watch but he can't stop himself.

The man pulls the plastic down further until the head and neck are fully exposed and swings a leg over until he's sitting astride the body. He pulls something from his jacket and bends slowly forward. The blade glints in the moonlight as it does its work.

The boy turns away and drops to his knees, his stomach heaving, his face contorted in a silent scream. Several minutes pass before he summons up the courage to crawl back to the door. With trembling fingers, he pushes it open and squints through the crack.

The plastic sheeting has been pulled up to cover the head, and the man is stooped over the body, struggling to hoist one end on to the edge of the boat. On his third attempt, he succeeds. He bends low again, wraps both arms around the other end and, with a loud groan, slides it in. He drags the boat out into the water, the waves swirling around his shins, climbs in and starts rowing out to sea.

CHAPTER 2

Edison Kane looks into the eyes of the psychotherapist sitting opposite him and thinks that maybe he's made a mistake. He needs someone to talk to, but this woman looks determined to dig deep.

She gives him a wry smile but says nothing. He suspects she knows exactly how he's feeling and the thought unnerves him. Kane is used to interviewing people who have been coached by their lawyers not to say a word. He's comfortable with silence, but this is different. He's not in control and he doesn't like it.

The consulting room walls are a soft pastel yellow. He guesses it's supposed to soothe the mind. It's definitely not working. The tan leather armchairs they are sitting on are separated by a rectangular steel-and-glass table. By the window is a small wooden desk Kane suspects is rarely used.

As the silence stretches, the therapist tilts her head slightly and fiddles with the top button of her jacket. For a moment, Kane considers walking out. He hasn't come here to play games. Instead, he decides to take charge.

"Are we going to sit like this for the whole session? I thought I'd be getting more for my money."

The therapist doesn't react at first. She stares at him calmly, one eyebrow slightly arched in a way that makes him feel foolish.

"Why don't you start by telling me what you'd like us to work toward achieving."

Her tone is professional and warm. Kane instantly regrets snapping at her, feels he's failed some kind of early test. He shifts awkwardly in his seat and holds up a hand in apology.

"I guess I'm a bit nervous. I don't really know how this stuff works. I'm not even sure how to address you. Do I call you Doctor, or Ms Baxter?"

Baxter smiles. "I'm not a medical doctor. I don't deal with physical ailments. I treat emotions by talking about feelings. You can call me whatever you want. Within reason, of course. Most of my clients call me Rebecca."

Kane is unsure. He's not comfortable with the notion of being on first-name terms with someone he's never met before. All he knows about Baxter is that, according to her website, she's a highly qualified psychologist with a thriving therapy practice.

He shifts in his chair again. "I'm finding this much harder than I expected. I don't know where to start."

Baxter crosses her right leg over her left, props her elbows on the padded arms of her chair and clasps her hands.

"That's better. All I want you to do is be honest about how you're feeling. There are no rules in this room. You can say whatever you need to say. Tell me whatever you want. I try not to lead my clients, I prefer to guide. But I admit I'm a little puzzled. There's no way you would be allowed to return to work if you hadn't passed a psychological assessment, so you must be used to this kind of therapy."

"It's not the same thing," Kane says. "I needed to be signed off to get back to the job. I knew what to say and what not to say. This is different."

"Different because?"

"I genuinely want help. I know I need to deal with what happened. If I can't, then I won't be able to do my job properly."

Kane watches the therapist shake her head slowly, disappointment clouding her face. From the moment he'd booked the session, he'd wondered how honest he should be. Lies breed lies.

"You're admitting that you deliberately deceived your police force psychologist?"

Kane shrugs. "I told him what he wanted to hear. That I sleep like a baby. That I'm no longer consumed by grief. That I've forgiven myself. That the self-doubt and the stress headaches have disappeared."

"And you were lying?"

"Not about everything."

Baxter uncrosses her legs and sits up, her back rigid, her expression stern. Kane's reminded of the time in sixth form when he was called into his head teacher's office to be told his standards were slipping, that he wasn't making the most of his abilities. *This is it then*, he thinks. *She's deciding whether taking me on as a client would be the right thing to do.* He looks directly at her and risks a regretful smile.

"You've just admitted lying to a psychologist. How am I supposed to believe anything you tell me?"

Kane pauses to gather his thoughts. His mouth is dry, his palms moist. This isn't going the way he'd hoped.

"Like I said before, this is different. I needed to get back to work because it's what I do, who I am. I know deep down that it's the right thing for me. I also know that I'm not completely over what happened to me, and I need help to be able to do my job to the best of my ability. I don't want to let anybody down again. I couldn't bear that."

Baxter relaxes back into her chair again. Kane takes it as a good sign. "Well, in the interests of honesty and transparency," she says, "I should tell you that I am also a qualified forensic psychologist and regularly work for the prison service."

Kane shakes his head slowly. This is not what he signed up for. He stands up to leave.

"You don't need to go," Baxter says. "You have nothing to worry about, Detective, I promise. Please sit down."

Kane hesitates for a moment, then does as she asks. "I can't have anything I say getting back to my superintendent. I just can't risk it."

Baxter nods. "My work with criminals does involve liaising with the police, but I assure you anything I hear in this room is confidential."

"Is it really? Things can slip out in conversation."

"Not my conversations, I assure you. The only time I would break confidentiality is if I had good reason to believe that you were about to harm yourself or another person."

Kane takes a moment to consider his options. Walk out and start searching for another therapist, or put his trust in this woman. He needs help. He can't do this by himself. God knows he's tried.

He gives a rueful smile. "Can we start again?"

"I think we should. Go ahead."

Kane decides to go all in. "You asked earlier what I hope to achieve in these sessions. Well, I want to stop blaming myself, stop hating myself for what happened to my wife."

Baxter says nothing. She lets Kane's words hang in the air and he doesn't like it. This time he finds the silence more than awkward. It's painful. He's repeated those words in his head a thousand times before but he's never said them out loud.

"I can see this isn't easy for you," Baxter says. "And, of course, I know your history. You've had a traumatic time, to say the least. I have another question for you and it's important that you answer honestly. Exactly what is it you blame yourself for?"

The question twists Kane's stomach. He expected Baxter to treat him gently, not go straight for the jugular. Nobody has asked him this before, certainly not the police psychologist. He suspects that his answer will decide whether Baxter agrees to see him again.

He takes a deep breath, turning his head slightly to help him break eye contact. When he speaks, his voice is flat, matter-of-fact.

"My wife was murdered and it was my fault. The case has never been solved. That's my fault too."

Kane takes another deep breath and looks down at his clenched fists. *There you go*, he thinks. *I've admitted it. Finally. Now someone else knows the truth.* A familiar ball of pain rises in his chest.

Baxter's expression is impassive. "That's a great start," she says. "Admitting how you feel is important."

Kane's phone buzzes in his pocket. He swallows hard, relieved to have something else to think about. An excuse not to say more. He holds up a hand in apology.

"I've got to get that, it's my work mobile."

He reads the message on the screen. The pain in his chest fades, transforms into a flutter of excitement. He reads it again, to make sure he hasn't misunderstood. He hasn't. His first investigation since returning to work.

"Sorry about this, but I'll have to cut this session short. I've a killer to catch."

CHAPTER 3

Kane walks briskly, his hands deep in the pockets of his suit trousers. He doesn't want to keep his boss waiting too long in case she changes her mind about giving him a murder inquiry so soon after his return.

The morning sky is cloudless. The early spring sunshine is hazy but still strong enough to warm his back, filling him with optimism. He lifts his chin and scans Brentwood's high street. It seems quieter than usual. Some of the storefronts are starting to look shabby around the edges, and there are a few more takeaways and charity shops than there used to be.

He takes a right turn, skips eagerly up a set of concrete steps, enters the office and heads for the lift. A couple of minutes later, he's on the second floor, standing outside the office of Detective Superintendent Helen Dean. He knocks, eyes on the red light above the security door. It stays red. He knocks a little harder, and this time the light turns green.

Dean is seated behind her desk, her back to an open window overlooking the car park. She greets him with a polite smile but doesn't stand. Kane notices that her hair is significantly shorter and a shade or two darker than when they spoke two weeks ago.

"Please sit down, Edison. Sorry to call you in on your day off, but it couldn't be helped."

Kane winces. His wife used to take great delight in pointedly calling him by his first name. She knew he told everyone to call him Ed. He'd been happy to indulge her teasing because it made her smile.

"That's never been a problem for me, Helen. If there's work to be done you can count on me. You know that."

Dean drums the fingers of her right hand on the desk. Kane knows she's taking time to consider what she's about to say. She's always chosen her words carefully, something he'd noticed when they first met as detective constables. It had irritated him at first, but her cautious nature turned out to be one of her biggest strengths, and they'd worked side by side on many murder investigations, her painstaking approach to the job balancing out his tendency to be impulsive. There had been no resentment on his part when she'd been promoted above him. She'd been the best candidate for the post and had gone on to prove herself a natural leader.

"You've been back on duty two weeks now and I'm hoping that you're ready to get your teeth into some proper detective work. I wanted to give you a bit of time to settle back in. But major investigation teams can't carry passengers. You know that."

Kane flinches inwardly at having to show he can pull his weight, prove his worth to the team. It hurts that she might doubt him, but he says nothing. He knows she's not expecting him to. She has a lot more to say.

"What happened to your wife, Edison, well, I wouldn't wish that on anybody. And your reaction, while not ideal, was, maybe, understandable. According to your psych assessment, you're suffering from mild vicarious trauma. Well, I'd guess ninety per cent of detectives in the Essex force are no better off. Crucially, Dr Henson has reached the conclusion that your state of mind is stable and he recommends that you're emotionally fit enough to resume normal duties. What do you think about that?"

Kane smiles. "I think that Dr Henson knows what he's doing. He's the expert. He believes I'm ready to go, and I totally agree. I feel strong now, and doing what I do best will make me even stronger."

Dean taps her fingers on the desk again. She leans forward, narrowing her grey eyes.

"We both know, don't we, Edison, that it's not too difficult to fool any kind of expert if you're determined enough. I'm asking you right now. Has Dr Henson come to the right conclusion?"

For a moment, Kane wonders whether he should tell her that manipulating Henson was a lot easier than he'd expected and that he's paying for private therapy sessions.

He ditches the idea in an instant. Even though he and Dean go back a long way, there's no way she'd put him back on active duty if she thought there was even the slightest chance that he'd be danger to himself or his colleagues.

"It's all good, Helen," he says. "You have nothing to worry about. I've been off for three months and that's long enough. I needed a break, but sitting around doing nothing is mind-numbingly boring. I know I can't change what happened to Lizzy. I've still a bit of grieving to do and a bit of guilt to deal with, but by far the best thing I can do is get on with catching killers. I can't change what happened but I can help the families of other murder victims."

Dean offers him a sympathetic smile. "I'm glad to hear it," she says. "You're taking a trip to the seaside. A body's washed up a few miles west of Southend. You'll find the full report on our online system. Hopefully it'll be a straightforward case and you can hand it back to the locals to deal with after a couple of days."

Kane wants to tell her that he's one hundred per cent ready, that she can depend on him, that he won't let her down. Instead, he nods, gives her a tight smile and stands up. Before he can head for the door, Dean raises a hand for him to wait.

"You're going to need some help. You can take Detective Constable Granger with you. She's new to the team, has a lot to learn, but she's razor-sharp."

* * *

"It's Leigh-on-Sea," Kane says, glancing sideways at the woman in the driving seat. "A small coastal town a few miles up the coast from Southend. Quite quaint, apparently."

Granger, frowning in concentration, her hands gripping the steering wheel tightly, accelerates up the slip road on to the A12.

"I know it," she says, with a chuckle. "Went there for a day out with a friend last summer. Turned out to be a bad idea. I wouldn't call it quaint. Tide was out. Nothing to see except a couple of pubs, old wooden sheds and miles and miles of stinking mud. Still, we had a giggle."

Kane shakes his head. He'd been bright, young and optimistic once, but it's hard to believe sometimes. He's definitely no youngster, and nobody would ever describe him as radiating joy.

Granger's caramel complexion is wrinkle-free. Not a hint of laugh lines, even though it's already clear she laughs a lot. "I looked the place up before we left," he says. "Those 'old wooden sheds' are a big attraction for day-trippers. They're renowned for serving the best seafood fresh out of the ocean. Cockles, winkles, prawns. If you love shellfish, then this place is paradise."

Granger wrinkles her nose in disgust and makes a vomiting noise.

"Don't know how anybody can stomach that slimy stuff. Tried an oyster once. Like a mouthful of phlegm. Disgusting. Don't know what all the fuss is about."

Kane gives her another glance. She's almost as tall as him, her dark hair pulled into a tight bun that adds an inch or two to her height. He wonders if she's ever seen a dead body before, and feels a twinge of sadness at the thought that she's probably about to have her first brush with the reality of violent death.

He'll never forget his first corpse. In uniform, fresh out of training, he was called to attend a suicide at a multi-storey car park in Colchester town centre. Kane was first on scene and had to keep members of the public away from the body until the ambulance arrived.

The poor kid had dived off the third floor. The paramedics said he'd died the instant he hit the ground. Kane lay awake in bed that night, too hyped to sleep, wondering whether an instantaneous death would be as clean and as painless as it sounds. He decided that when you're dying in agony, an instant probably feels like a long, long time.

He found out later that the teenager had been sleeping on the streets. His stepfather had kicked him out of the family home after finding him smoking pot in his bedroom.

Kane felt proud at the way he was able to keep his lunch down when he set eyes on bloodied, broken body. It wouldn't be a good look, especially in public. He didn't throw up until he arrived back at the station. That was the day he decided he needed to create a space in his head, an imaginary document folder. A place to store the bodies. Once in, they never come out. It worked a treat. Kept him safe. Kept him sane. Until Lizzy.

He looks at his mobile to check the time, as Granger slows to pull off on to the A130, heading east. Unless they hit serious traffic, they'd reach the coast in fifteen minutes.

"I'm told you came to us from Harlow. You've done well to get a transfer to one of the major investigation teams at your age. You must have impressed someone."

Granger smiles broadly. Kane likes that she's not embarrassed by praise.

"Thank you," she says. "I'm proud of what I've achieved. I'm not as young as I look, though. Almost twenty-six. Good genes, that's what my mother tells me, and she's living proof of it. Couldn't tell you whether my father deserves a share of the credit. Never set eyes on him. He disappeared, back to the West Indies, a few days before I was born. Harlow was a great place for me to learn the ropes. Plenty of bad stuff going on. This is my first murder, though. Is it wrong to feel like I've won the lottery?"

Kane knows that feeling. The thrill of the hunt never grows old. But the buzz of a murder investigation is always balanced out by the responsibility. The dead can't stand up for themselves. That's his job.

"There's nothing wrong with being excited about an investigation, as long as you keep focused," he says. "If this turns out to be a murder inquiry then you're going to have to work non-stop, and I guarantee you'll learn a lot very quickly. Right now, it's still officially a suspicious death."

They drive on in silence. After five minutes, the road curves, swooping down to sea level. The view that greets them takes Kane by surprise.

Granger's description was accurate, in a way. The tide is out and there's no sign of a sandy beach. A vast expanse of mudflats gleams for miles beneath a limitless sky. Kane can see the attraction. The place exudes a timeless charm.

Granger pulls up next to two white forensic unit vans parked by the sea wall and turns the engine off. Kane gets out first, walks around to the back of the car and opens the boot. He takes out two pale-blue crime scene suits, slips one over his clothes and hands the other to Granger.

When they're both ready, he leads the way down a set of rusty steps to the mudflats and on toward a huddle of more pale-blue figures. Four of them are on their knees in a tight circle, their protective suits spattered with mud. The fifth is standing with his hands on his hips, directing the search for evidence.

As they near the group, Kane recognises the voice of the police pathologist. Martin Carter turns at the sound of their approach and pulls down his face mask.

"Well, look who's come to join the party. This is a pleasant surprise. I didn't know you were back with us. They must have left me off the email list."

Kane's delighted to see Carter. He'd always be his number one pick if asked to choose a pathologist to work with.

"That's probably what happened," he says. "Keep telling yourself that. But maybe they didn't think you needed to know. Now you're fully up with the gossip you must be relieved to have someone on the investigation who knows what they're doing. This is Detective Constable Bailey Granger. She's new."

Carter looks down at Kane's shoes, then across at Granger's sturdy ankle boots and raises a greying eyebrow. He lifts a gloved hand and beckons them both closer.

"Do come and see what we've got, then. The team have almost finished sifting the mud around the body. I reckon it's only been in the sea a couple of days. Unfortunately, as I'm sure you know, the immersion in salt water means there's pretty much no hope of picking up any of the killer's DNA."

In the centre of the ring of kneeling forensic officers, the fully clothed body lies face down, the hips and the right leg twisted grotesquely. The arms are stretched out above the head, the fingers curled, as if clawing at the mud.

Kane gives Granger a worried glance. Her jaw is clenched tight but she keeps her gaze fixed on the corpse.

"Who found the body?" he asks.

"A woman out for an early morning walk with her dog. The last high tide would have been about 3 a.m. When it ebbed, it left the body behind, the downward force of the waves embedding it in the mud. He could have been put into the water anywhere along this coast."

Kane drags his eyes away from the body, breaths in the salty air and scans the mudflats, the sea a distant strip of liquid silver.

"Is the coast all like this along here?"

Carter jabs an accusing finger in Kane's direction.

"You weren't paying attention in geography, were you, Detective Inspector? I bet you were always messing around at the back of the class. What you're looking at here is an estuary. This is where the mighty Thames spews out into the even mightier North Sea. As the waters mix, the flow slows, depositing clay and silt. Further along the coast, away from the mouth of the estuary, you get some decent sand and shingle beaches."

The lesson over, Kane and Granger exchange glances. The detective constable signals her impatience with a roll of her eyes.

"You're certain this is murder?" she asks. "No chance it was suicide, or an accident?"

"No chance at all," Carter says. "You can't see it clearly from here but he's been stabbed in the back. I won't know for sure until I carry out the post-mortem but I suspect the blade penetrated his left lung and then pierced his heart. He would have died within a few minutes."

Kane moves closer, bends and studies the body carefully. The knife wound, below the left shoulder blade, is plugged with mud.

"Can you tell whether the victim was alive when he went into the water? I mean, was he stabbed and dumped into the sea, or killed somewhere else?"

Carter gives an exasperated shrug. "I know I'm good but I'm not a miracle worker. I might be able to give you an answer after the autopsy but I'm not prepared to speculate. I don't deal in guesswork. We'll be finishing up here soon and moving the body to the mortuary. I'll be starting first thing tomorrow. I suppose I can expect an audience?"

Kane has attended more autopsies than he can remember. After a while, it's easy to become desensitised to the sight of a body being dissected, but he always tries to remind himself that he's looking at somebody's father or mother, son or daughter, brother or sister. Only then does he file the image away.

"I'll be there, first thing," he says. "I expect Detective Granger will be too busy to attend. We have a lot to do to get this investigation rolling."

Back at the car, the detectives pull off their plastic coveralls and toss them into the boot. They both turn around, lean on the sea wall and watch the forensic officers raise the corpse from the mud, slip it gently into a body bag and lift it on to a stretcher.

"That was pretty gruesome," Kane says. "How you holding up?"

Granger ignores the question and stares into the distance. After a long moment she asks her own. "What happens now?"

Kane is surprised by the coldness of her tone, but everyone has their own way of dealing with death. Maybe this is hers. On the drive down from Brentwood, she was bright as a button, thrilled by the prospect of being part of a murder investigation.

"We drive to Southend station, get a full briefing on how the inquiry's been going so far. With a bit of luck, they've already made some progress identifying the victim. We need to check if he fits the description of anyone who's been reported missing recently. When we finish for the day, you drive home and I'll find myself a bed and breakfast. I need to be here bright and early for the post-mortem."

Granger glares at him for a few seconds before striding to the car. She climbs into the driver's seat and slams the door. After a few seconds, Kane walks slowly around to the passenger side. He gets in and makes a point of shutting the door carefully. Granger doesn't look at him.

"Seeing your first dead body is always a bit of a shock to the system," he says. "It's nothing to be embarrassed about. It does take some getting used to and I guarantee it gets easier."

Granger shakes her head slowly. "It was a horrible thing to see. I don't know what I was expecting, but it took me by surprise. But that's not the problem here."

"Er, all right, then. What is the problem?"

"It's you, your attitude, and, I'm sorry, I'm not prepared to put up with it."

The words sting Kane like a slap in the face. His mind whirls as he tries to recall their conversations on the drive out, wondering whether he's said anything she might have mistakenly taken as inappropriate or even racist. The thought horrifies him.

"I really don't understand. If I've said or done something that's upset you, then I'm sorry."

Granger takes a long deep breath, releases her grip on the steering wheel and turns to face him.

"Please listen. I don't think you mean any harm or disrespect, but it feels as if you're treating me like a schoolgirl on work experience. Trying to protect me or something. You decided that I wouldn't cope with being at the post-mortem without asking me what I thought about it. Well, I'm going to have to attend one sooner or later, aren't I? You even introduced me to the pathologist as 'new'. I'm definitely not new. I'm a grown woman, and I'm an experienced detective. A bloody good one."

Kane blinks hard. He knows that Granger's right and he's angry with himself for being so stupid. They've been working together for barely a day and he's already managed to make her feel uncomfortable and patronised.

"You're dead right. You don't need protecting, no more than any other colleague. How about we start over? A clean sheet. I promise to treat you as an equal. Well, I'm still your boss, but you know what I mean. What do you think?"

Granger keeps him hanging, her lips pressed tightly together, her eyes stern, then she flashes him a brilliant smile.

"Sounds good to me. We have a deal."

CHAPTER 4

Jack Newman sips his drink and listens to the constant babbling around him. Little people content with their little lives. The Archway Café is always busy first thing and he comes here for two reasons. The coffee is excellent and the customers remind him how humdrum life is without ambition and drive.

His phone rings for the third time in ten minutes. He ignores it again. It can only be one person and she has to be taught a lesson. A crime reporter of his ability and experience doesn't need telling how to do his job.

On the table next to him, a pair of stocky, unshaven men wearing yellow hi-vis bibs are chomping on bacon sandwiches as thick as house bricks. He cringes as one of them picks up his mug and slurps his tea.

Newman's phone rings again. She's persistent, he'll give her credit for that. This time he picks it up and accepts the call, holding the phone a couple of inches from his ear.

"Oh, so you are still alive, then? Where the hell have you been? I've been calling you all morning. You're a bloody reporter. You should have your mobile with you and switched on at all times."

Newman knows that his new boss is good at her job. No, to be fair, she's better than good. Dawn Brady is an excellent news editor. She's energetic, sickeningly enthusiastic, bursting with ideas and angles, and knows how to marshal her team.

The problem, as Newman sees it, is that she left the staff of a smaller newspaper in the wilds of Suffolk to join the *Southend Herald* three weeks ago and is on a mission to make a name for herself. What she hasn't yet grasped is that he's been the paper's crime specialist for five years and the last thing he needs is to be treated like a novice.

"Yeah, sorry about that, Dawn. My battery's started dying randomly, even though I make sure it's fully charged at all times. I'll get it sorted later, I promise. What's the problem?"

"The problem, Jack, is that we have a big crime story breaking and I haven't been able to contact our crime reporter. Listen, if you're not bothered about covering the important stories, then tell me. I could assign someone else. Maybe I should do that anyway. Mix things up. Give one of the youngsters a chance to show what they can do."

A knot twists in Newman's gut. Losing the crime beat would be a disaster. Everything he'd done to make his name, all his hard work, would be wasted, killing his chances of landing that dream job on one of the nationals. He's fast approaching thirty and time's running out.

"Hey, come on now, Dawn. That doesn't make any sense and you damn well know it. I have the contacts and I have the experience. It'll take someone else too long to get up to speed. You'd be taking a huge risk, and I'm not sure the editor would approve. You know he calls me the Mailman, don't you? Because I always deliver. What's this story? Fill me in. I'll get going on it right away."

The phone falls silent except for the faint sound of breathing. A red-headed waitress approaches, pointing in question at his empty coffee cup. He waves her away.

"It's a suspected murder. A body washed up on the mudflats at Leigh yesterday morning. We don't have a name for the victim or cause of death yet. Chase up your contacts and see what they've heard. I'm sure at some stage the police will release a statement, but I don't want to hang around waiting for that. Don't bother coming into the office. Get down to Leigh, try to track down the person who found the body. We need an exclusive angle on this story."

Newman allows himself a smile. There she goes again. Wasting her breath trying to tell him how to do what he does best. She has no idea how lucky she is to have someone like him on her team. But she'll learn.

"I'm on it already, Dawn. Never fear, Jack's in top gear. You've nothing to worry about."

He ends the call and looks around for the waitress. He's going to need that second coffee now. Adrenaline surges through his body. Nothing beats the rush of chasing down a big story.

CHAPTER 5

Kane steps out of the lift and walks to the end of the corridor. Granger is waiting for him. She's standing perfectly still, staring out of the window, her hands clasped behind her back. As he approaches, she turns to face him.

"Good morning," she says brightly. "You get a great view of the pier from up here. Did you know that it's a fraction over a mile long, making it the biggest pleasure pier in the world?"

"Wow. No, I didn't. Thanks for that little gem. I'll store it away until I need to impress somebody with my knowledge of useless facts. Have you had anything to eat yet?"

Granger frowns. "Not yet. I skipped breakfast to get out early."

"If you're ready, then let's get this show on the road," Kane says, leading the way into the post-mortem examination room. It looks exactly the same as every other one he's been in — a hospital operating theatre with one big difference. The patients are all dead before they're wheeled in for surgery.

In the centre of the room stands a steel table. On it lies a body covered by a crisp, white sheet.

Martin Carter, wearing full surgical scrubs, rubber gloves and a mask, is standing over a steel sink scrubbing his hands while humming a cheery tune neither of them can recognise.

"I'll be with you in a second," he says. "Do try to make yourself comfortable."

Kane looks over at Granger. She's staring at the shape under the sheet. He wants to tell her to look elsewhere when the sheet is lifted, to focus her gaze on the wall, but he suppresses the urge.

Carter straightens up, dries his hands thoroughly and walks over to the table.

"I'm afraid I decided to start without you," he says. "I have a busy day ahead. Three examinations in London after this. The city is in the grip of a knife crime epidemic and the Met haven't a clue how to stop it."

He reaches out and pulls the sheet down. Kane has attended dozens of post-mortem examinations but the sight still makes his blood run cold.

The victim has wide cheekbones, a narrow forehead and a narrow chin. The eyes are closed, the facial expression peaceful. You could almost imagine that the dead man is sleeping, if Carter hadn't already made a Y-shaped incision from the top of the shoulders down to the pubic bone and pulled back the flesh to expose the chest and abdominal cavities.

An image of his wife lying on a mortuary slab flashes into his head. This is exactly what he feared. His stomach churns and his legs turn to jelly. He totters to the end of the table and grips the metal frame with both hands. Kane wasn't allowed to go to Lizzy's examination. But sometimes, his imagination plays tricks. He checks out Granger. She's stony-faced, her attention still on the corpse.

Carter throws him a quizzical look. "Is everything all right over there?"

Kane stands up straight and ignores the question. "What age would you estimate?"

"I'd say he's between twenty-eight and thirty-five. His clothes were much too big for him, one of his boots had holes in the sole. He also shows signs of being undernourished, and blood analysis showed he ingested a small amount of cocaine not long before his death."

Kane's breathing steadies and he steps back from the table. "An addict?"

Carter shakes his head. "It's a bit of a mystery. There's no sign that he was or has ever been a regular user of cocaine or any other drug."

"So, the cocaine in his system wasn't the cause of death?"

"Not at all. As I suspected, he was stabbed in the back. The blade punctured the left lung and pierced the heart. The left atrium. Death would have come quick."

"It would have to have been a pretty long blade to reach the heart, wouldn't it?" Granger asks. Her voice is steady.

"Ten out of ten for anatomical knowledge," Carter says. "My best guess would be something like a carving knife — long but narrow enough to slip easily between the ribs. There's also some slight bruising around the neck."

Carter pauses and raises his eyebrows, inviting the detectives to come up with an explanation. Kane obliges.

"The killer wrapped one arm around the victim's neck, pulling tight while stabbing him in the back with the other hand."

Carter nods. "Bravo. Give that man a gold star. I knew you wouldn't let me down." The pathologist steps closer to the corpse and rubs his hands together gleefully. "However, there is one other thing. Something I've never seen before, and I've examined a lot of dead bodies in my time, believe me."

Carter has always been a flamboyant character who enjoys putting on a bit of a show for his audience, but Kane has never seen him this excited before.

"Come on, then. Don't keep us in suspense."

Carter walks slowly over to the body. "I tell you, it rather unsettled me, and you've worked with me long enough to know that I'm not easily shocked."

Kane steps nearer and takes a few moments to study the victim's face.

"I can't see anything unusual."

"Come on, don't be shy. You need to get a lot closer," Carter says. "And I'd advise you both to steel yourself."

Kane takes a tentative step nearer the autopsy table and Granger follows suit. Carter bends over the victim's head and deftly uses his thumbs to lift up both eyelids.

The empty sockets take Kane's breath away, like a sucker punch to the gut. The hairs on his forearms bristle, and a cold shiver ripples down his spine.

"What the fuck?" Granger whispers as she grabs his elbow.

He's not sure whether she's trying to steady herself or holding him up.

"Oh my God," he says, willing his legs to stop trembling. "That's crazy. Why on earth?"

Carter lifts his thumbs, lets the eyelids fall and steps back from the table. The hint of a smirk on his face suggests he's enjoying the moment.

"Why, indeed. However, it's not my job to answer the whys of a death. I'm afraid that's up to you. What I can tell you is that the eyes were removed several hours after death. That's why there was hardly any bleeding. The heart had stopped pumping and gravity will have caused most of the blood to pool. Although it looks a neat job on the outside, there is no evidence the killer has any real surgical skill. There's a fair bit of collateral damage to tissue, muscles and nerves inside the eye sockets. I can also tell you that the knife used to stab the victim would not have been used to remove the eyes. It would have been a much smaller blade. Something delicate and precise, like a scalpel."

Kane shakes his head in despair.

"Have we been able to identify the victim yet?" asks Granger.

Carter shakes his head. "His pockets were empty and he has no tattoos or other distinguishing features. We're running fingerprints and DNA through the national databases. Of course, he might not show up."

"OK. I think I've seen all I need to see," says Kane, meaning every word. "Thanks, Martin."

"The pleasure is all mine."

* * *

Kane and Granger walk back down the long corridor in solemn silence. He waits until they are in the lift and on the way down to the ground floor before he speaks.

"Christ, I've never seen anything like that before and I don't ever want to see it again. How are you feeling?"

Granger gives him a rueful smile. "It wasn't as bad as I expected, at first. But the empty eye sockets, I've got to admit that shook me. I had to keep telling myself that the essence of that person, whoever he was, wasn't there with us. He'd already gone. I was looking at an empty shell. A body. Not somebody. That definitely helped."

Kane nods his approval. Granger has an old head on her shoulders. She's already found her own way of coping and that's going to make a big difference.

As they step out of the lift, the detective constable turns and looks up at him. "And what about you?" she asks. "I know what you've been through. Losing your wife. That couldn't have been easy for you."

An uncomfortable flush of heat rises from Kane's chest to his neck and face. He didn't lose Lizzy. She was taken from him. He doesn't want to talk about it, and Granger shouldn't have to worry about his emotional state.

Someone back in Brentwood, probably Detective Superintendent Dean, will have filled her in on her new boss's recent troubles. He wouldn't be surprised if Dean even asked Granger to spy on him. Was that part of the deal? She doesn't strike him as that kind of person but she's definitely ambitious and, in truth, he barely knows her.

"I'm absolutely fine, thanks," he says, doing his best not to sound rude, while at the same time making it clear the subject is not up for discussion. "We need to identify the victim as quickly as possible, then we can focus on his family and circle of friends. Most murders are committed by someone close to the victim. Sad but true. I want you to find out if anyone has been reported missing in the past few days and make sure the media team has everything it needs to put out a statement. Make it crystal clear that we don't want any mention of the eyes being scooped out. I don't want to start a media feeding frenzy or panic the public."

Granger nods hesitantly. "I know I'm new to this, but this is no run-of-the-mill murder. The eyes, it's some kind of message, isn't it?"

"Whatever the message is supposed to be, we can leave that to the psychologists. Right now, the only thing we care about is putting the killer behind bars."

Kane's gut is telling him that it's only a matter of time before another mutilated body turns up. He wants to be wrong. But he knows, only too well, that once evil shows its face it never rests.

CHAPTER 6

The newsroom falls silent as heads turn to watch Jack Newman walk to his corner desk. He takes off his jacket, draping it over the back of his chair with a theatrical flourish before sitting down.

He loves moments like this. Lives for them. He's the centre of attention again. He's the ace reporter assigned to the big story. The chosen one.

Powering up his computer, he stares hard at the screen, deliberately ignoring attempts to catch his eye and engage him in small talk. People are drawn to success like wasps to a picnic. But he hasn't got time to gossip with the drones. He has more important things to do.

When his colleagues get the message and return to the task of filling the paper's website with their run-of-the-mill news reports, Newman lifts a hand to his face and rubs his eyes. He wasted valuable time that morning interviewing the pensioner who'd found the body.

I was out walking the dog at my usual time and there the body was, just lying there face down in the mud. It was a real shock to the system, you know? My heart's a bit dodgy at the best of times. You don't expect to see something like that so soon after eating breakfast, I tell you. It gave me a really nasty bout of indigestion and I'd run out of my usual antacid syrup. As soon as I called the police I had to go straight up to the pharmacy. I'm sure it was the shock. I've never experienced anything like it before. It used to be so nice around here. That's why we moved out from London all those years ago. For the peace and quiet. What is the world coming to? Youngsters taking drugs everywhere you look, stabbings on the street and all that bare flesh and sex on television. No wonder everything is going to hell. I tell you something, and you should definitely put this in your article — you'd never get away with murder when I was a young woman. Everyone used to look out for one another. Decent people had principles.

Newman searches his emails for the police press release and reads it quickly. The victim isn't named and, as usual, it's about as exciting as a shopping list. *A body found. When and where. Murder inquiry launched. Everything possible being done to identify the victim. Appeal for witnesses and information.*

Reading between the lines, the force's finest brains haven't a clue who the murder victim is and they haven't even got a sniff of a suspect.

Brady won't be a happy bunny when he tells her that he hasn't been able to dig up anything fresh. The press release was issued several hours ago, which means the story will already have been published on several internet news sites, aired on local radio stations and broadcast on TV. The *Herald* desperately needs a new angle to splash across tomorrow's front page if it wants to avoid looking like it's playing catch-up.

He looks over to Brady's glass-partitioned office on the other side of the newsroom. She's too busy to notice that he's back at his desk. Leaning forward and squinting at her computer screen, she's typing and speaking on her mobile at the same time, the phone wedged between her jaw and her right shoulder. Brady's no slacker, there's no doubt about that. But

Newman believes a smart worker trumps a hard worker every time.

His thoughts on how best to break the news that he has nothing fresh on the mudflat murder are interrupted by his desk phone. It's Tina on reception downstairs.

"Sorry to trouble you, Jack," she says. "I know you're on a tight deadline but there's a woman here who says she wants to talk to someone about the body in the mud. She claims she has some important information for us and insists on speaking to a reporter."

Tina has worked in the front office for seven months. The two of them clicked straight away. They have something going but he's not sure what. He's never been great at reading women. There's been a fair bit of flirting and they've bought each other a drink in the pub around the corner a few times. Nothing more than that so far, but Newman thinks she has potential.

He's told her several times that she has more to offer than standing behind a counter all day. She's quick on the uptake, with more common sense than some of his fellow reporters. She wouldn't be wasting his time unless she thought there was something in it.

"Thanks, Tina. Tell her the paper's top reporter is on his way down."

He hurries across the newsroom, pretends not to hear Brady calling out as she beckons him over to her glass box, walks past the lift and heads down the stairs.

Tina is busy on the telephone. She smiles warmly and points at a woman who's squatting near the door, stroking the head of a black-and-white collie. Newman walks straight over, bends down and runs a hand gently along the dog's back.

"What a beautiful dog you've got there. I'm jealous," he says, and he means it.

As a child, he spent a lot of time around dogs. If you show them affection, they'll love you back. No complications. No expectations.

The woman rises to her feet with a groan. She's wearing a grey woollen hat, a long dark coat buttoned up to her neck, green tracksuit trousers and grubby trainers. She tips her head back and looks up at Newman.

"He's a lovely fella, right enough, but he ain't my dog. I been minding him for someone. Doing a favour for a pal, like you do. We have to look after each other on the streets."

The woman sounds younger than she looks. Wisps of wiry, grey hair poke out from under her hat. She's not wearing any make-up, her lips are thin and pale, the skin on her cheeks dry and flaky.

Newman gets straight to the point. "I understand you know something about the body found on the mudflats at Leigh?"

The woman stares into space for a few seconds, blinks hard and sniffs, then wipes her nose with the back of a hand.

"I've a horrible feeling it's him. No, I'm sure it's him. My friend, I mean. I said I'd look after his dog for a couple of hours and he never came back. I ain't seen him for three days."

Newman's mind races. He has a strong feeling that he's on the brink of an exclusive that will keep Brady off his back for months.

"I tell you what we should do," he says, taking the woman firmly by the elbow and guiding her out of the door on to the pavement. "There's a café next door. Why don't I buy you a hot drink and a slice of cake and we can have a nice long chat?"

The woman's eyes light up at the mention of cake. It's a chilly afternoon but Newman sits her at one of the outside tables, the dog curled up at her feet, while he goes inside. A few minutes later, he returns with a large cup of hot chocolate and a blueberry muffin for the woman, and a shortbread biscuit for the dog.

"Can you tell me exactly where you last saw your friend and what he said to you? Try to remember as much detail as you can. You never know what's going to turn out to be important."

The woman cradles her drink in both hands, blows on it and takes a sip.

"We were both dossing in the high street. The bookshop doorway is one of our favourite places to sleep. It's a deep alcove, you see, gives you a lot of shelter from the wind. It was the middle of the night but he suddenly stood up and asked me to look after Tyson. That's what he calls her. Even though she's a bitch. He said he'd something important to sort out. Something that was going to make him some money and he'd see me right. I didn't have much choice really. Didn't mind, though. Cuddling up to a dog's a good way to keep warm. The trouble is, I can't keep her much longer. Can't afford to feed her and she's already just skin and bone."

"Have you any idea where your friend was going, who he was going to meet?"

"Never asked him. Not my business. The thing is, I haven't set eyes on him since. That's why I'm worried, see. Something must have happened because he'd never dream of leaving Tyson for so long. He's had her for years, he told me. Obsessed with her, he is. I've seen him go hungry and give food he's fished out of the bins to the dog. When I heard about the man in the mud this morning, well, I just knew. I feel it in my bones. He's always getting into trouble, upsetting people, getting into bother."

Newman is struggling to suppress a smile of satisfaction. Her story makes sense. The murdered man is a rough sleeper. That explains why no family or workmates have reported him missing and why the police are struggling to identify him.

This is perfect. He can upstage the police by revealing the identity of a mystery murder victim. On the back of that he can probably persuade his bosses to launch a campaign calling for action to tackle the town's homeless problem. To top it off, he'll tug even harder on his readers' heartstrings by appealing for a loving family to adopt the dead man's pet. Everyone loves a good 'dog in distress' story.

"Don't worry yourself, dear," he says. "Let's hope it isn't your friend, but we'll do our best to find out. What did you say your name was?"

The woman narrows her eyes and gives him a sly look.

"I didn't say. The thing is, I think I need to be careful. If you're going to put this story in your newspaper, am I going to get some kind of reward? I should get something for my trouble, don't you think? This is important stuff, ain't it? Someone's been killed. On second thoughts, perhaps I'm being hasty. Maybe I should tell the police about my missing friend first. I don't want no trouble with the law."

The crafty old girl is after cash, Newman thinks. No surprise there. He's the only person he knows who doesn't care about money. He's in it for the glory. Glory over everything. He suspects she's almost certainly bluffing. Rough sleepers usually do everything possible to avoid contact with the authorities. But he's not willing to risk it. The police will know everything he knows when they read his story in tomorrow morning's paper.

"I know you want to do the right thing and I respect that. But there's no need for you to waste time bothering the police. They're always short-staffed and stretched to the limit. We'll make sure they get all the facts they need to help their investigation. I guarantee it. And you're right, of course. You deserve to be rewarded for being a public-spirited citizen. I promise you'll be paid for your trouble. Paid well, and in cash. You can trust me, I'm a journalist."

Newman is confident the old girl will think she's won the lottery when he slips her fifty pounds for her trouble. He'll be able to claim it back on expenses, with a bit extra thrown in.

The woman takes a big bite out of her muffin, catching the crumbs in a skinny cupped hand.

"How much will I get?" she mumbles, her mouth still full.

"We'll sort that out later. But I promise you'll be well looked after. So, tell me, what is your missing friend's name?"

She pauses for a moment, glancing down at the dog as if she's worried it's going to think badly of her for talking to the press.

"Banjo."

"What sort of name is that? Is it his first name or surname?"

The woman shrugs. "It's just Banjo. It's what everybody calls him. What they've always called him. I've been homeless for about seven months now, and he was sleeping rough around the town when I arrived. I think he once told me his real name was Joe. But we all know him as Banjo."

CHAPTER 7

"How the hell has this happened? A local newspaper naming a murder victim before we have any kind of ID. It makes us look like a bunch of amateurs."

Detective Superintendent Dean downs the dregs of her coffee, crushes the paper cup and tosses it petulantly into the waste bin beside her desk.

She doesn't usually resort to displays of emotion, and Kane suspects she's under pressure from above. She's probably already regretting assigning him a murder case so soon. Dark smudges under her eyes suggest she's having trouble sleeping.

"I know it's not a good look," he says. "But there was nothing we could have done. This woman walked into the newspaper office after we appealed for information and the bastards decided to go it alone. It's true we haven't been able to ID the body. There are no DNA or print matches. But the newspaper hasn't really identified the body either. They say he's one of the town's long-term rough sleepers, and he's known locally as Banjo. That's all they have and they can't even prove that."

Dean doesn't respond. Her silence makes Kane more uncomfortable than anything she could have said.

"We're tracking down the woman right now to try to get her to formally identify the body. Unless someone else comes forward with more information, it's the best ID we're going to get."

Dean lets out a long sigh of exasperation. "Regardless, we press on urgently with the investigation. I want this killer caught before the press find out that the victim's eyes were taken. If that gets out, we're going to have to deal with a full-scale media circus. You know how it works. The national press will be watching every move we make, ready to take us down if we fail."

Kane knows she's right but he's having second thoughts. "I'm not sure keeping the gory details secret is the best thing to do. Don't the public have a right to be protected, to know exactly what is out there prowling their streets?"

Dean tightens her lips and looks right at him, blinking in slow motion as if she's been staring at a computer screen for too long.

"I stress: I don't want any of those details released yet. Panicking the public won't do anyone any good. The best way we can protect people is to catch this killer. Please Edison, don't make me regret putting you back on duty so soon. If you mess this investigation up, I'm not going to be able to shield you."

Kane understands what Dean is saying. If he gives the press any reason to question his fitness for duty, she'll have no choice but to pull him off the case.

"I know what's at stake," he says. "Trust me, I won't rest until we get a breakthrough. I'm driving back to Southend as soon as I leave here."

Dean nods slowly. "How's Detective Constable Granger measuring up?"

Kane wonders again whether Granger has been ordered to keep an eye on him and report back to Dean. Does his boss know about his wobble at the post-mortem?

"She's doing great so far. She's a fast learner, I'll give her that. She's not afraid of hard work and, you were right, she's as smart as a whip."

Dean's smile tells Kane that she never doubted that the young detective would step up to the mark.

"One last thing before you go," she says. "I know you don't like dealing directly with journalists, but you need to make an effort to get the local newspaper onside. You need cooperation, not competition."

* * *

Kane's temporary office at Southend police station is a windowless box room, the bare white walls adorned with a solitary, out-of-date calendar. He knows the score. The locals never want to make outsiders too comfortable.

Granger pops her head through the open door. "Everything's set up for the briefing. We're ready when you are."

Kane stands, slips his suit jacket on and tightens the knot of his tie. As they walk side by side along the corridor, Granger fills him in on the strength of their team.

"We have five uniforms, four police constables and a sergeant. We've also been assigned two detective constables. Linda Finch and Sam Miller. I get the impression that neither are too happy about it."

"As long as they all do their jobs properly, I don't care whether they're happy or not," Kane says. "The most important thing is that everyone's putting one hundred per cent into catching this killer."

As they near the incident room, he can hear the buzz of excited conversation. When they enter, the talking stops dead.

"Good morning, everyone," Kane says. He walks across the room to a large whiteboard on which is stuck a photograph of the body face down in the mudflats, a headshot of the dead man taken in the post-mortem room with eyelids closed and another showing the empty eye sockets. Also pinned to the board is the front page of that day's *Southend Herald*.

"I'm sure you all know who I am by now and you've met Detective Constable Granger, so I won't waste valuable time on formal introductions."

He steps closer to the whiteboard and points to the headline: *Herald Solves Mystery of the Man in the Mud.*

"I trust you've all seen this absolute pile of crap. It may well be right that the victim is a homeless man known around town as Banjo but the newspaper hasn't solved anything. That's up to us. There is no mystery surrounding this case. The simple fact is a man has been brutally murdered and mutilated. Make no mistake, we will solve this murder. We will take this killer off the streets. I don't want anybody doubting that."

Kane pauses to study the faces of his makeshift team. The five uniforms are seated in a line at the front, listening intently. Both detectives are further back, one leaning sulkily against a side wall, her arms crossed, short dark hair held off her forehead by a black band, the other perched on a desk, swinging his legs like a bored schoolboy.

"We already have civilian staff manning the public appeal lines and I'm hopeful they're going to come up trumps. But today is all about good old-fashioned police legwork. I'm told that at the last local authority count there were thirty-two people sleeping rough in the town. I want you out on the streets, talking to as many as you can. We need to confirm whether this character Banjo is really missing or has simply moved on."

Kane nods toward the detective propping up the wall. "Detective Finch, I understand there's a night-time soup kitchen in the town centre and a café on the seafront that dishes out free breakfasts to rough sleepers. You and Detective Miller can talk to the people who run the soup kitchen. Granger and I'll take the café."

At the mention of his name, Miller stops swinging his legs and looks up. Kane judges him to be around Granger's age. His untidy mop of sandy hair is close to breaching force guidelines, his youthful features beginning to show the inevitable signs of the wear and tear that come with the job.

"Oh right, so you were paying attention, Detective Miller," Kane says. "I wasn't sure."

Miller's face reddens, he slides off the desk and stands up straight. "Of course I was listening. I heard every word."

Kane instantly regrets embarrassing the young detective. He needs everyone on side, everyone working flat out if they have any chance of wrapping this case up quickly.

"Listen, everybody," he says, "I understand there's a lot of potential for friction when an outsider turns up to run a murder inquiry on your patch. But we haven't time for any of that bullshit. A man's life has been taken. He may have been on the fringes of society, but that doesn't mean he doesn't deserve justice. I need us to work together, to the best of our ability, to make sure he gets what he deserves, that's all."

Miller shuffles uncomfortably and throws a sheepish glance at Finch, who still has her shoulder against the wall, her hands in her trouser pockets.

"There's absolutely no problem here, boss," she says. "I can assure you. Everyone in this room wants the same thing."

* * *

"I knew Banjo, of course I did. We all knew that pain in the arse," says the owner of the Shingles Café. "I threw the bastard out a week or so ago, told him not to come back and haven't seen him since."

Ray Spencer stands in front of the steel serving counter, his hands on his hips, his legs wide apart. He's as tall as Kane and solid with it, built like a tank. Not a man to be messed with is Kane's assessment.

"I'm told you do a great job providing free meals for the homeless here. That's admirable. What did this Banjo do that pissed you off so much?"

Spencer lifts a tattooed hand and runs his fingers across his scalp, ruffling his close-cropped hair.

"I'm a businessman but that don't mean you can't do good things. I own a mobile phone store in the high street, which is my main earner. I'm doing pretty well but it hasn't always been this way. When I came out of the army, ten years ago, I struggled with civvy life. My wife kicked me out and I ended up on the streets of South London for a while. When I sorted myself out, I moved down here and it's gone well for me. I remember how hard it is on the streets and want to help. This place makes a small loss. I'm content with that. But when someone you're trying to help turns on you, then, well, it's not right."

Spencer shifts his weight from one foot to the other, clenching his fists tight enough to drain the blood from his knuckles.

Kane waits a moment, giving him time to calm down. The man clearly has trouble controlling his temper.

The café was busy when he and Granger arrived. As soon as the customers realised that they were police, the place started to empty. A group of four at a corner table, three men and one woman, were the first to go. They grabbed their sleeping bags from under the table and abandoned their half-eaten fried breakfasts. Granger followed them.

"Exactly what did this Banjo do to warrant getting thrown out?" Kane asks. "I can see that you're getting angry just thinking about it."

"He stole from me, the ungrateful bastard. He'd been coming here for months, with his stinking dog, eating my food, taking advantage of my generosity, then he takes cash from the till when he thinks nobody's looking. One hundred and ten quid. The till drawer must have been left open but we didn't notice the money was gone until the end of the day. I checked the security camera and there he was, scooping out a bunch of notes the second Rina's back was turned. The next day he comes and sits down, smiling his stupid smile as if nothing has happened, ready to stuff his face with my food. He was too stupid to work out we'd have a camera trained on the counter."

Kane guesses that Banjo went hungry that morning. It was probably a day or maybe two before he was killed.

"Did you report the theft to the police?"

"What would be the point? I know how you lot work. Some fresh-faced copper straight out of college sent to pat him on the head and tell him to stop being a naughty boy."

A woman emerges from the kitchen area. She looks at least ten years younger than Spencer, her bright red lipstick matching her skirt and the ribbon around the base of her blonde ponytail.

"Is everything okay, Raymond?" she asks, her Eastern European accent as sharp as broken glass.

Spencer smiles at her. His expression reminds Kane of a dog slobbering over a bone.

"Everything's just fine, baby," he says. "Nothing to worry about."

He turns back to Kane, his smile dissolving quickly. "This is Rina, my girlfriend. She manages the place when I'm busy at the phone store."

Kane gives Rina a nod of acknowledgement. "I guess you've read the *Herald*," he says. "It's looking very likely the body that washed up in Leigh is Banjo."

Rina lifts a hand and tugs nervously at her ponytail. "That's sad. I don't wish anybody to be killed."

Spencer shrugs, his shoulders straining the seams of his black T-shirt. "That man was always up to no good. Always upsetting somebody. Ask around. Everyone will say the same. I know it sounds callous, but it really doesn't surprise me that something like this has happened to him."

"Thanks for your assistance," Kane says, not sure exactly how much of a help Spencer has been. He offers up his card. "If you think of anything else that might be relevant, call me on this number."

Spencer gives Rina a sideways glance, takes the card and puts it on the counter next to the bottles of ketchup and brown sauce.

When Kane leaves the café, he sees Granger in the distance, her back to the pier, walking toward him along the concrete promenade. He's impressed that she made the decision to follow the homeless customers who fled the café. He won't tell her that, though. She'd probably call him out for being patronising.

He sits on the sea wall and waits, thinking that his chat with Ray Spencer raised more questions than it answered. He fills his lungs, breathing slowly through his nose. The sea air carries a faint whiff of chip fat.

When Granger arrives, she sits on the wall next to Kane. Eyes shining, she's unable to hide her excitement.

"That was an interesting conversation," she says.

"Glad to hear it. I take it you spoke to that bunch who scarpered as soon as we turned up?"

"I did. Followed them along the prom until they reached the pier and sat under it on the beach."

"And?"

"Well, they weren't too keen to speak to a cop at first. They seemed scared. I eventually got them to open up."

"Used your youthful charm, I suppose?" Kane says with a smile.

"Something like that. I threatened to haul them down to the station and lock them up."

"Did they tell you Ray Spencer threw Banjo out of the café because he stole money from the till?"

Granger looks slightly crestfallen. "You know about that, then?"

"Spencer told me. Said he hasn't seen him since the incident."

"Did he tell you that he really lost it? According to the guys on the beach, he went crazy when Banjo came into the café the next day. Lifted him off his seat, slammed him on his back on the table and tried to strangle him. He only stopped because his girlfriend was pounding his back and screaming at him."

"You're right, that is interesting," Kane says. "That goes some way to explaining why Spencer didn't report the theft to the police."

“There’s more,” Granger says. “And this is the best bit. After Spencer dragged Banjo to the door, he threw him to the ground, kicked him in the stomach and threatened him.”

“Threatened to do what?”

Granger glances around to check she can’t be overheard. “This is word for word, apparently. Everyone in the café heard it. ‘If I ever see your ugly face again, I’ll kill you. You and your mangy dog.’”

CHAPTER 8

"Thanks for fitting me in so early in the day," Kane says. "I appreciate it."

Rebecca Baxter gets up from her desk, crosses the room and sits in the tan leather chair opposite him.

"It's not a problem. Though, I must admit, I've never had a 7 a.m. appointment before. I'm fine with it, though. I've always been an early morning person. I love the idea of being busy while the rest of the world is asleep. It makes me feel like I'm getting a flying start."

Kane takes in her immaculate outfit, her bright eyes and her perfectly groomed hair, and can see that she means every word. He has a feeling that she's someone who's always ahead of the game. As someone who rarely gets a decent night's sleep and often starts the day feeling drained, he wishes he had her energy.

"What about you?" Baxter asks. "Do you have trouble sleeping?"

Kane suspects that this woman is either blessed with an uncanny ability to read his mind, or he simply has a face that's easy to read.

"I do find it difficult to fall asleep, but once I do, it's waking up that's the problem. Fortunately, I have two alarm clocks and always set my phone to wake me up just in case."

Baxter smiles. "Better safe than sorry. How are you handling being back at work?"

For a second, Kane is thrown by the sudden change of subject. Maybe wrong-footing your client is all part of a psychotherapist's armoury.

"It's going pretty well, I think. I'm leading a murder investigation. It's turning out to be tricky but it's good to be back doing what I do best. I'm grateful that they've given me my own case so soon."

"Do you feel they've thrown you in at the deep end?"

Kane shrugs. "Maybe. Perhaps they want to see whether I sink or swim."

Baxter frowns. "I'm not sure that's a good idea. I would have given you a little more time. Eased you in gently."

"That's not how it works," Kane says. "My boss has made it abundantly clear: the force hasn't the time, the manpower or the patience to carry passengers. Like I said, I think I'm handling it well. Apart from . . ."

Kane falters. His natural instinct is not to tell a stranger his secrets. Not to expose his weaknesses. But if he's not going to open up, what's the point of being here?

"Just tell me what happened. It'll help. I promise."

"I had a wobble, that's all. A small one. I was attending a post-mortem. I've been to dozens and never had a problem before. As I looked at the body, I thought of Lizzy — no, more than that, I actually saw her. Well, I imagined seeing her lying dead on the autopsy table. It was weird because I never went to her examination. Never actually saw her."

He leans forward, drops his elbows on to his thighs and bows his head. He waits for Baxter to say something reassuring. Something that will make him feel better. She stays silent.

"My legs went," he says. "Buckled under me. I thought I was going to fall, make a fool of myself in front of the pathologist and a detective constable."

"But you didn't."

Kane shakes his head. "Thankfully not. I stayed on my feet and the trembling passed. I think they both saw it, though."

"Don't you think they'd understand?" Baxter says. "I'm sure they know all about you. They know that your wife was murdered. It was a high-profile case. They would know that you joined the team trying to catch the killer and worked yourself to the point of mental exhaustion."

That's the official version anyway. Kane suspects Baxter has guessed that there's more to it. He's not ready to go there. Not yet.

"Is this going to happen every time I come across a dead body? Because that's what I do for a living. I work for the dead."

Baxter steeples her hands, the tips of her forefingers touching her lips. *She needs a moment to let the words sink in*, Kane thinks. He doubts she's ever heard that before.

"Tell me," she says, "what would it mean if you could see this case you're working on to the end? Solve the crime and catch the killer?"

Now it's Kane's turn to take his time. He's impressed with the question. She's picked up on something that, up until this moment, he hadn't fully grasped.

"I reckon it's make or break for me, probably. If I crack this case, I can prove myself all over again. Not to others, to myself. If I fail, it'd be hard to justify carrying on."

"Even if you know you've done your best?"

Kane doesn't answer. His wife's death changed him for ever, and if his best isn't good enough anymore, then maybe he should quit. He thinks it but he can't bring himself to say it out loud.

"How is the new case going?" Baxter asks.

"It's tricky. A body in the sea for a couple of days. No chance of DNA evidence. It's looking like the victim had been living on the streets. No suspects, and the victim's face . . ."

Kane hesitates. Baxter arches her eyebrows.

"Remember what I told you last time. Everything said in this room stays in this room."

Kane is still hesitant. Normally, he wouldn't dream of talking about the details of a case to anybody outside the force. But he's curious. How will Baxter react?

"The killer cut out the victim's eyes. Took them with him as a souvenir."

Though Baxter fights to keep her expression neutral, her eyes widen, and her lips open and close like a stressed goldfish. Kane guesses she's struggling not to blurt out something unprofessional.

She takes a few seconds to regain her composure, before leaning forward in her seat. "Was the body weighted down when it was dumped in the sea?"

"It doesn't look like it was."

"Then the killer would have known that it would almost certainly wash up somewhere along that part of the coast. He wanted the body to be found. Dumping it in the sea was a charade."

What Baxter is saying makes perfect sense, Kane has to admit.

"And what about the eyes? Why on earth would someone do that?"

"It might mean something important to the killer, or be a message to everyone else. You know as well as I do that serial killers sometimes take something from the scene. A 'trophy', something to help them relive the thrill of the kill."

Kane shifts uncomfortably in his chair. Baxter's observations are confirming what he already knows.

"If it is a message to the world, or the eyes were taken because the killer needs to relive the moment, then it's likely, isn't it, that . . ." He stops talking because Baxter is nodding. The words don't need to be spoken.

"You're going to have to be extremely careful," Baxter says. "You can't let your feelings about your wife's murder become entwined with your motivation for solving this case. That could seriously mess with your head and put your recovery at risk."

Kane understands what she's trying to say but believes she's missing a crucial point.

"I know that the beast who sexually assaulted and strangled my wife and the monster who cut out his victim's eyes have no physical connection. But they do have something in common. They're both infected with the same killing sickness, and there's no cure."

CHAPTER 9

Bailey Granger slows down to turn on to the housing estate, putting her headlights on full beam. Most of the street lights have been smashed, but she has driven up this road hundreds of times and could probably find her way home blindfolded.

She's lived in places like this all her life, and even though she has never feared for her safety, it's time for a change. Her recent promotion and the rise in salary that comes with it means that she'll soon be able to move away from a neighbourhood where women don't generally walk alone at night. She has other people to worry about now.

Granger allows herself a smile. Working on her first murder case means that she wakes up every day with a flutter of excitement in her stomach. The sense of achievement is worth more to her than any extra money she might earn.

She's happy to be working with Kane, even though he clearly has his problems. Granger doesn't want to let herself imagine how she'd feel if someone she loved was murdered.

Her eyes blur a little at the thought of Kane's loss but she doesn't cry for him. Instead, she makes a promise to herself to do everything possible to help his comeback. Being part of the team that solves this case would also be a perfect way to prove herself again.

Since joining the force her rise through the ranks has been meteoric. The jealousy of some of her colleagues has been, at times, difficult to cope with, but she's satisfied that she deserves her success. In her five years as a detective, four of those as a single mother, she has never once been late for a shift, never lied about being sick to get a day off and always volunteered to stay late when needed.

She shakes her head. Colleagues and family assume that she works harder than everyone else because she's a woman, or because of the colour of her skin, or both. They're wrong. She's always pushing herself to achieve more because that's who she is.

Granger recalls that when she first made detective, station gossips branded her ruthless. She prefers to call herself driven.

Approaching a T-junction, she's jolted back to the present by a blood-curdling scream. A middle-aged woman hangs desperately on to the strap of her handbag while a tall, wiry youth, wearing a tracksuit and baseball cap, repeatedly clubs the side of her face with his fist.

Granger jams her foot on the brake and jumps out of the car. The attacker glances at her and throws a vicious punch at the woman's neck. The blow knocks her to the ground and she lets go of the bag.

"Stop, police!" Granger yells, grabbing the youth's right arm with both hands. He turns, swinging the bag at her face. She ducks and he twists his arm loose before sprinting down the side of a house, vanishing into the maze of back alleys criss-crossing the estate.

Granger crouches down on one knee, puts her arms around the victim's shoulders and gently raises her into a sitting position. The woman sobs, struggling for breath, her eyes wide with terror.

"Don't worry, you're going to be all right. He's gone. I'm a police officer. I'm going to take you to hospital to get you checked out and then down to the nearest police station so you can report this crime and make a statement."

The woman places both her hands flat on the pavement, and shifts herself into a more upright position.

"No hospital. I don't want to go to no hospital. I'm fine, and I definitely don't want no police. I just want to get home."

Granger can see that the woman isn't fine. She has an angry red swelling, the size of an egg, on her left temple. Her nose is grazed and bloody, and a bruise is already blooming like a dark rose on her neck.

Granger guesses the woman is in her late fifties, about the same age as her mother. An image of her mother lying bloodied on the pavement flashes through her mind and she shakes her head to push it away.

"What's your name? Do you live around here?"

The woman looks up, her eyes pleading. "I just need to get home, please. I don't need no fuss. I live around the corner. A long soak in the bath and I'll be as good as new, I promise."

Granger doubts that, but then the people living on the estate don't trust the police.

"Let's get you up. Do you think you can stand?" She adjusts her weight and slowly pulls the woman up. "There you go. I'll drive you home if that's what you really want. Maybe in the morning you'll have second thoughts. Can you walk to my car?"

The woman pulls away and staggers back, unsteady on her feet. Granger grips her right elbow to stop her falling.

"Thank you, dear. You are kind. But I'd rather go home by myself. Bill's waiting for me, you see, and he won't be happy if I bring the police to the door. He's been in trouble a few times, you know. Don't like the law much."

Granger sighs. "I really think you should get yourself checked out at the hospital. You've taken a couple of nasty blows to the head."

The woman gives her a feeble smile and turns away. Hunched over and still obviously in pain, she walks slowly away.

Granger gets back in the car and follows at a snail's pace. After rounding the corner, she pulls up again, keeping the woman in her line of sight. She watches her fumble for her key outside her front door before stepping out of the darkness into the rectangle of light.

Ten minutes later, Granger slips her key into the lock of her own front door, more determined than ever to move off the estate and find somewhere else to live. Somewhere her mother can walk the streets without constantly looking over her shoulder. A place where her daughter can grow up safely.

CHAPTER 10

When Kane arrives in Southend, he finds Granger waiting for him in his office. She's sitting at his desk, working on her laptop.

She jumps up flustered, but he waves at her to sit back down. "I'm happy to see at least one of my team working flat out. And you look like you're enjoying it."

Granger grins. "Actually, I am."

"Are we making any progress?"

"Some. Margo Smith has formally identified the body as her friend Banjo. She was a bit shaken up afterwards but a couple of cups of hot sugary tea sorted her out. Unfortunately, the victim has been on the streets for so long, nobody knows who he really is."

"That's pretty sad," Kane says. "Depressing, even. I need a strong coffee."

He ducks out of the office and walks down the corridor to the hot drinks machine, his thoughts still on the fact that Banjo's real identity will probably never be known. No one will mourn his death, except maybe his friend Margo, and his dog.

He returns to the office to find Granger standing, her laptop closed and tucked under her arm.

"I've brought you one," he says, handing the coffee over and sitting down at his desk.

Granger smiles her thanks and takes a sip. "Finch and Miller are doing the rounds of hardware stores and craft shops trying to trace the scalpel used on the eyes. Of course, it could have been purchased online."

"What about Raymond Spencer? Did you check him out?"

"I did. And interesting it was too. He was a bit economical with the truth yesterday. He came back from Afghanistan with PTSD. Ended up on the streets, like he said, but he didn't just pull himself together and suddenly become businessman of the year. He landed in prison. Two years for GBH. Broke a busker's jaw when he refused to stop singing while he was trying to sleep on the pavement nearby. It seems he did a lot of thinking while inside, turned his life around when he got out. I've emailed you my full report."

Kane isn't surprised about the conviction for violence. The man radiates menace. "We're going to have to speak to him again soon. Put a bit more pressure on him and see how he reacts."

Granger turns to leave but Kane calls her back. "Wait a second. I have a meeting with Jack Newman, the local paper's crime reporter. I'm supposed to smooth things over, get the press working with us rather than against us. This might surprise you, but I'm not known for diplomacy. I want you to come along. Rein me in a bit."

* * *

"I'm all for working with the police," Newman says, lifting his pint of foaming beer and taking a gulp. "The *Herald* and its readers fully support and appreciate the work you do."

The Dolphin, an elegant Victorian pub close to the train station, is filling up with lunchtime drinkers. Kane wants to get the meeting over as quickly as possible. The longer it lasts, the more likely he is to lose patience and snap.

The reporter is saying all the right things but there is an undeniable edge to his demeanour that makes Kane feel uncomfortable. He's a smart guy. No doubt about that. In danger of being too smart for his own good.

"That's good to hear," Kane says. "But it would have been useful if you'd shared your information about the victim's identity before you decided to splash it all over your front page."

Newman turns to look at Granger, eyebrows raised in mock surprise, his lips curving into a smirk.

"The perils of working to a deadline, I'm afraid. We didn't have time to think about anything other than getting the story out. We're always looking to get the edge on our competition. I can assure you we had no intention of undermining your investigation. Can I get you another orange juice, Detective?"

Kane feels himself rising to the reporter's bait. He picks up his empty glass and examines the residue of juice to give himself time to calm down.

"The reason you didn't tell us is because you knew we'd either ask that you hold off printing it, or get our press office to release the information to other media outlets."

Newman's eyes widen. "I'm sure you understand that we have to do what we think is best for our readers. We didn't set out to keep information from the police. I'm genuinely sorry if we made you look incompetent. That wasn't our intention."

Kane clenches his jaw. He darts a glance at Granger. She gets the message.

"I'm sure you didn't, Mr Newman," she says, smiling. "It would be a shame if you and your paper were to fall out with us, because a good relationship with the police must be vital for a crime reporter. It's all about give and take. Now, why don't we call it a little misunderstanding and move on in the spirit of cooperation?"

"There's nothing I'd like better," Newman says. "And you can call me Jack, by the way. Mr Newman makes me sound ancient. As we're sort of working together now, I'm looking for a fresh angle for my next article. I know this sounds bad, but readers are always fascinated by the gory details of a murder."

Kane glares at the reporter, appalled by his lack of sensitivity. At the same time, he knows that Newman is right. Everyone, even the most innocent, ordinary people, have something in their psyche that draws them to the dark side.

"Our last press release contains all the relevant details," Kane says. "The victim was stabbed in the back and the blade punctured his heart, causing his death. Sorry if that's not gory enough for you or your readers."

Newman shakes his head slowly and smiles.

"I've got to say I'm still sensing a little hostility but I'm only trying to do my job. Can I ask one more question? Have you been able to fill in the gaps around Banjo's identity? We'd love to start working on a bit of background."

Granger looks to Kane, who nods for her to go ahead. He's done with talking.

"Unfortunately, it's looking like we're never going to get a proper name. The victim has been living on the fringes of society for too long. He doesn't feature on any DNA databases and we can't link him to any dental or fingerprint records. Our press office will be putting out a statement later today."

Newman takes a moment to let the information sink in.

"That's so tragic," he says. "It's almost as if the man never existed. Homeless in life, anonymous in death."

Picking up his glass, he downs the last of his beer. "That's it. Cracked it. My new angle with a ready-made headline. It's been great to meet you both but I have to shoot off. Important editorial meeting and all that."

Kane and Granger watch as he walks quickly to the door, his head bent, his eyes on the screen of his mobile.

"What do you think?" Granger asks.

Kane considers telling her that he thinks the reporter is an unbearable, self-serving prick but decides against it. He doesn't want her telling Dean that he's anti-press.

"I think this is going to be a very long day. It might be easier for you to stay in town overnight."

Granger shakes her head. "I'll be driving back home whatever time we finish."

A stab of envy surprises Kane. Unlike him, she has someone waiting for her. Someone to go home to.

"I take it your boyfriend will wait up for you?"

Granger gives a rueful smile, tilting her head. "It's a girl, actually."

Kane keeps his expression casual. He doesn't want her to think he disapproves. Because he doesn't.

"Her name is Daisy and she definitely won't been waiting up because she's only four years old. My mother looks after her when I'm at work and I want to be there when she wakes up. It's just the three of us."

The more Kane finds out about Granger the more impressed he is. He can't imagine how difficult it must be to do this job as well as she does and be a single parent. He's saved from saying something stupid when Granger's mobile rings. She answers and listens.

"Right, thanks for letting me know," she says, tucking her phone back in her pocket.

"An anonymous caller says he saw someone dragging a body down to a boat on Thorpe Bay Beach in the early hours of the twentieth of March. That's three days before the body washed up."

CHAPTER 11

Kane clicks on the play icon and listens to the recording for the fourth time. The caller's voice sounds male, young and nervous.

"Hello, thank you for calling our inquiry helpline."

"Well, right, the other night, you know, I saw a man put a body in a boat."

"You saw a body?"

"Well, no. Maybe. Yeah. I think it was wrapped, you know, in some kind of plastic stuff. When he pulled the wrapping down, I saw the head."

"You're saying that you saw a head?"

"Yeah, that's what I'm saying. That's what I said."

"Was this head you saw attached to a body?"

"Er, yeh, I guess so. It must have been. It was wrapped up. Are you not listening?"

"And where exactly did this happen?"

"Er, I, er, on the beach. Obviously on the beach. I already told you. He put the body in a boat. He rowed out to sea. At Thorpe Bay."

"That's great. Thank you. Can you tell me when this happened?"

"Yeah, that's why I'm ringing, innit? I'm trying to help. Last Friday morning, between three and four."

"Good. And can you tell me what you were doing on the beach at that time?"

"Yeah, well, no. What's that got to do with anything? Why you grilling me?"

"Please stay calm. We do appreciate you making the effort to call. I'm just trying to get the whole picture. Can you tell me your name?"

"No, I can't. Don't have to. Why do you need my name? I've told you what I saw. I'm trying to do the right thing here."

"Do you know the man you saw putting the body in the boat? Can you describe him?"

"Look, it was dark as shit. I don't know nothing else. I didn't do nothing wrong. I saw something scary, that's all."

"It would be useful if you gave us your name."

"Not happening, though, is it? I told you. No way. Bye."

Kane leans back in his chair, puts both hands behind his head and stretches his legs. The boy is adamant he's not going to give his name. He doesn't want to be traced. What would he be doing on a beach a few hours before sunrise? Nothing legal, that's for sure.

Granger appears at the open door.

"The whole of Thorpe Bay Beach has been sealed off and a forensic team are on their way. I'm heading off now to meet Finch and Miller there."

Kane jumps to his feet. "I'm coming with you. I could do with a bit of sea air to get the brain cells working."

The early evening traffic is light and the drive from Southend town centre takes no more than ten minutes. Kane and Granger work their way through the noisy crowd that has gathered to watch the forensic operation. A uniformed constable guards the concrete steps descending to the beach to keep rubberneckers away. Kane acknowledges her with a nod and flashes his warrant card.

The gently sloping beach is a mixture of sand and shingle strips. Four powerful spotlights stand along a stretch of beach between two wooden groynes, ready for nightfall. The two detectives walk past the forensic officers crawling close to the waterline and head toward a row of candy-striped beach huts where Finch and Miller are waiting.

Finch is wearing a smart trouser suit as dark as her hair. In contrast, Miller is dressed in black jeans and a casual jacket. Kane wonders whether he should have a word with the detective constable in private.

When leading a murder inquiry, he likes his team to project a clean-cut, formal image. It's a matter of looking professional. Showing the world that they're serious about what they're doing.

"We've come up with a strong lead on the witness who called the information line," Finch announces. "Well, it was Sam who thought of it, actually."

Kane turns to Miller, who scowls, drops his head and paws at the sand with the point of his right shoe.

"Go on, then," Kane says. "Tell me what you've got."

Miller buries his hands in his jacket pockets and looks up. "When we got down here, I remembered a report on a break-in a few days ago. I left it to the uniforms to sort out because it was minor. A little damage done and a cheap pair of binoculars stolen. It was here though, the blue-and-white beach hut at the end. I've checked, and the break-in took place just when our anonymous witness says he saw the body."

A familiar tingle, like a weak electrical current, flows from Kane's gut up to his throat. It's always been the same feeling. Since his first breakthrough on his first case.

"That's why the kid was so jumpy," he says. "He's worried about being done for the break-in. We need forensics to check the hut. If we get lucky with DNA or prints, we can pull him in and interview him properly."

"I don't think we need luck or DNA or fingerprints," Miller says with a grin. "About a year ago we had a spate of beach hut break-ins. More than ten, along the coast from Leigh to Shoeburyness. They were all the work of one offender. A thieving little scumbag called Harry Cannon. He pleaded guilty, got twelve months, was released on licence after six. I reckon he's slipped back to his old ways. Beach huts are easy targets."

There's something about Miller's approach to life that gets under Kane's skin but there's nothing wrong with his reasoning.

"We need to contact the probation service right away. They'll have an address for the kid."

Miller grins again. "Way ahead of you there, boss. Already made the call."

CHAPTER 12

It's almost midnight before Kane steps into his first-floor room at a budget hotel on the town's seafront esplanade. He stayed on at the station for a couple of hours after sending his team home for the night.

Most of the time was spent listening to the recording of Harry Cannon's call over and over again. It's not clear exactly what he's seen but he sounds pretty shaken up. They'll be pulling the boy into tomorrow. A detailed account from him could be the key to solving the case.

Kane takes off his jacket and drops it on the double bed. The room is clean if a little shabby. He sits on one of the chairs, puts his feet up on the other and switches the television on. After few minutes channel hopping, he turns it off and places the remote control back on the corner desk.

Too tired to think straight but too wired to go to sleep, he leans his head back and stares at the peeling paint on the ceiling. This is always the time of day when his thoughts turn to Lizzy and how he could have, should have, saved her. He'd seen a report that colleagues in Chelmsford were investigating two cases of abduction and sexual assault they suspected were linked. The women's drinks were spiked in different town centre nightclubs two weeks apart.

Lizzy wanted him to join her night out with work colleagues. He dodged it by claiming that even though it was his day off, he needed to oversee a suspect interview. Lizzy simply raised her eyebrows and smiled. Her perfect, indulgent smile. Why didn't he just do what she'd asked and go out with her that night? He didn't even think of warning her to take special care and keep an eye on her drinks. He was too keen to make his getaway before she changed her mind.

Kane eyes the mini fridge. Perhaps a drink will help him relax, maybe even get some proper shuteye. Before he can decide to go for whisky or wine, his mobile rings. He stands up, lifts his jacket off the bed and fishes his phone out of a side pocket.

He doesn't recognise the number but accepts the call anyway with a curt "Kane."

The caller is breathing heavily, as if he's been running.

"Thank God you're still awake, it's Jack Newman."

Kane shuts his eyes and shakes his head.

"How did you get my personal mobile number? Our media office opens at eight tomorrow morning. You need to go through them."

"This can't wait until the morning. It's urgent. Believe me, you'll want to know what I've got."

The reporter still sounds out of breath, his voice shaking with excitement or fear. Kane's curiosity gets the better of him.

"So, what is it?"

"About an hour ago someone sent a message to my work email. I think it's from the person who murdered Banjo. No, strike that. I'm sure it is."

"How can you be so sure? It's probably a hoaxer. Some weirdo craving media attention."

"You need to see it. I'd bet my life on it being genuine. I'll send a screenshot from my laptop right now. Call me back when you've read it."

Gripped by a sense of dread, Kane sits on the edge of the mattress. People admitting to murders they didn't commit are not that uncommon. But they usually confess to the police, not to a reporter.

Inside he's praying the email that's got Newman excited is a hoax. If not, then he's hunting a publicity-obsessed killer with an ego the size of a planet.

Kane's mobile pings. He opens the file, enlarges the image and starts to read:

> *Murder was easier than I thought it was going to be. So much easier.*
>
> *When I was a kid, my father told me I could do anything I put my mind to, and even though I later found out he was a useless lying scumbag, he was at least telling the truth about that one thing. The proof is in the killing.*
>
> *I'd be surprised if most people didn't have someone in their life that they could imagine killing. The difference is most people, ordinary people, don't have it in them. Guilt, shame, fear of being caught and even the wrath of God, these are the emotions that hold them back. Limit their possibilities. My victim was an innocent man who didn't deserve to die. But who does? He didn't suffer for long and his death will serve a higher purpose.*
>
> *I'm still feeling the buzz. But it's not the act of killing I'm most proud of. It's the eyeballs. Once I'd cut through the muscles and the optic nerve, they popped out like a couple of juicy grapes.*
>
> *See No Evil.*

Kane's heart sinks. There's no doubt this is the real thing. Poison drips from every word. He doesn't need to read it again. He calls Newman. The reporter answers immediately, his voice loud and eager.

"Do you think it's genuine? Is it really from the killer?"

Kane hesitates. The email is not a hoax. The details that haven't yet been made public prove that. Even without them he would still have been convinced. The triumphant tone.

The cold-blooded arrogance. These are things that can't be faked.

He says nothing. His silence says everything. Newman doesn't need an answer.

"Oh my God. It's true, isn't it? This is a message from the killer. The sick fuck took the eyes. Cut the bastards out."

"We need to think about this," says Kane, careful not to confirm or deny anything. "Is there really anything to be gained from making this email public? The killer has sent you this message because he wants recognition. He wants to be in the news. Why give him what he wants?"

"No, no, no way. There's no chance I'm not going to write this story. I'm keeping you in the loop but that's as far as it goes. This is way, way too big. The biggest story I've ever landed. And what about that sign-off? This guy might be crazy but he's given me a brilliant headline. The See No Evil Killer."

CHAPTER 13

Stepping out of her front door into the half-light of dawn, Isabel Anderson jogs across the road, pausing by the sea wall to take in the view.

The light of the sun bleeds over the horizon, painting pink and purple stripes across both sky and sea.

She takes a long deep breath, turns to face east and starts jogging toward Shoeburyness. For most of her adult life, Isabel took her regular exercise after work. It was a great way to smooth out the tensions of the day. But since moving from London to the coast she's become addicted to her early morning runs.

She feels privileged to be able to watch the sun rise over the ocean, a sight that always fills her with joy and energy. It's such a shame her boyfriend disapproves. He doesn't like the idea of her running on her own along a deserted coastal path. Worse still, he hates her alarm going off at such an unearthly hour. She smiles to herself at the thought of Darren still curled up under the duvet, his eyes closed tight as he wills himself back to sleep.

A wave of heat flows through her body as her breathing becomes faster and deeper with exertion. On her left, the landscape drops sharply to Gunners Park Lake, its surface untouched by the sun's rays, still and slick, a dark mirror.

Isabel slows her pace a little as the path takes her past the squat Coastguard lookout station. On the beach below, a young couple walk to the water's edge. They're holding hands, their heads tilted toward each other as they speak. She wonders if they've stayed up walking and talking through the night. How romantic. She wishes Darren was with her to share the moment. The thought makes her determined to convince Darren to get out of bed before dawn at least once next week. It would be great if they could watch the sunrise together. He'll take some persuading but she'll do her best. He loves her. She knows that. She just wishes he'd make more effort to show it.

The unlit sea wall path stretches ahead to the grey concrete hulk of the old Shoeburyness coastal fort. The derelict gun battery marks the halfway point of Isabel's run, where she usually stops for a breather before jogging home.

She slows down to a gentle jog, then a walk. In the half-light she glimpses a hooded figure leaning against the fort wall, watching her approach. She fights a sudden urge to turn around. Instead, she runs on, speeding up as she passes the figure, keeping her gaze straight ahead.

Puffing hard, her heart thumps heavily as she takes a quick look back over her shoulder. The man has vanished as quickly as he appeared. After a couple of minutes Isabel stops running and leans back against the sea wall. She feels sick in the stomach, her legs a little shaky.

She's sure this is the second time she's seen the same dark figure while out running. The first time she noticed him looking up from the beach as she passed the Coastguard station. She grabs her mobile and searches for Darren's number. Her finger hovers above the screen for a few seconds before she slips the phone back into her pocket.

If she asks Darren to come and get her, she'll have to admit that she was frightened and he'd insist that she stops her dawn runs. She needs to pull herself together. More than likely it's a coincidence. She's being silly, she tells herself. Maybe the man in the hood is simply out enjoying the sunrise too.

She stretches her quads and then both hamstrings before starting her run home. Out to sea, the sun edges over the horizon, shooting golden rays through the pink striped clouds. The sight lifts Isabel's spirits, and by the time she reaches the old fort, she wonders how she'd let herself get so spooked.

After half a mile, she leaves the path to jog down to the lake, where the first weak rays of sunlight have encouraged a pair of swans to glide out of the reeds and head toward her across the water.

Standing on the edge of the lake, her back to the sea, she doesn't hear the footsteps softened by the lush grass. She sees the swans stop, turn quickly and head back to their nest. She hears his breathing, quick and shallow. She feels a muscular arm encircle her neck from behind, a hand clamp over her mouth. She can't breathe.

Even then her mind doesn't allow her to accept that these are her last moments. That here and now, this is the end of her.

CHAPTER 14

Kane leans back in his chair, takes a gulp of his third black coffee from the station canteen and screws up his face in disgust. It's bitter and leaves a nasty aftertaste, but he lifts the cup to his mouth and takes another drink. He desperately needs the caffeine to get through this day.

He had zero chance of sleeping after reading the email sent to Newman. Every time he closed his eyes the twisted words of the killer whirled around his brain.

His mobile rings. He doesn't bother checking the caller ID because he knows it's going to be Detective Superintendent Dean. He steels himself. He has to sound more confident, more in control of events than he feels.

"Good morning. I take it you've seen the *Southend Herald*'s front page."

Dean ignores the question, launching straight into a rant.

"What the hell is going on? This is fast turning into a nightmare, Edison. If I'd known how big this was going to become, I wouldn't have given you the job. We're in danger of becoming a laughing stock. You need to get a grip on this case before the shit hits the fan and we both get covered in it."

Kane's boss must be truly worried. She wouldn't normally waste her breath stating the obvious.

"They've gone over the top with the headline. I asked that reporter to treat the story sensitively."

Dean falls silent. Kane takes this as a bad sign and prepares himself for another rant.

"I don't give a damn about the headline. The contents of that email are dynamite. A killer who's so confident he won't get caught he's sending emails to the newspapers is not a good look. And what's all this 'See No Evil' shit. He's taunting us, Edison. It's giving the impression that he's in charge — that you, me, the police, are ineffective and feeble. The national media will be on it like a pack of wolves, ready to pounce if you mess this up."

She's not spelling it out but Kane knows what she's thinking, what she really means. Can you handle what's coming your way? If I think that you can't, I won't hesitate to take you off the case and dump you back on sick leave.

"Rest assured I'm quite capable of handling the situation," he says. "You should know that. I've successfully dealt with high-profile murder hunts before, haven't I? You don't have to worry."

"But I do have to worry. It's a big part of my job. Probably the most important part. I have to make sure that the team is fit for purpose. And yes, I'm fully aware of your record, but that was before. Before, well, you know what. Now, please tell me you have a plan."

Kane sighs. A year ago, he would never have been treated like this. Treated like a liability. He would have been left to his own devices, expected to report back to Dean only when he thought it necessary.

"The reporter's laptop is being examined to try to trace the source of the email. But according to the tech team that is not going to be easy. There are so many ways you can cover your tracks. Granger is out right now bringing in a potential witness. And when we've finished here, I'll be talking to the unruly mob of newspaper and television reporters gathered outside the station."

"For God's sake, Edison, is that wise? They're going to be baying for blood. Yours in particular. Why not leave it to the media team?"

"Like I said before, I'm confident I can handle this. I want to face them. It's my responsibility."

Dean falls silent again. Kane can hear her breathing, can almost hear her mind ticking over. He imagines her trying to come up with something to boost his confidence. A few well-considered words of encouragement and support.

"I hope you're right," she says finally. "I really do. Because if you slip up, I'm afraid there's nothing I can do to protect you."

* * *

Kane unbuttons his jacket, pushes the door open and steps out, flinging up a hand to shield his eyes from the camera flashes. The reporters surge forward, firing a barrage of questions.

Kane shouts above the clamour: "You need to be quiet — now, right now, unless you want me to turn around and walk back into the station."

The rabble falls silent immediately. "I mean it. I'm not having this turn into a free for all. The way this is going to work is I'll take one question at a time, and tell me who you are and who you work for if you want an answer."

A smartly dressed woman in her late twenties, with shoulder-length brown hair and blonde highlights, takes her chance to get in first.

"Jane Fielding, *Daily News*. Can you confirm that the murder victim's eyes had been cut out, surgically removed?"

Kane's dealt with national newspaper reporters before. They like to get straight to the point.

"The victim's eyes were removed, that's correct. To say it was done surgically would be stretching it a bit. They haven't been found so it's likely they were taken by the killer."

"Why on earth would anyone do that and whose decision was it not to make that information public straight away?"

"That's two questions. I'm not going to speculate on the killer's state of mind. I'm the senior investigating officer in this case. The decision to hold back that detail was made by me."

"Lester Bryant, *UK Today*, is it possible that the email published by the *Southend Herald* purporting to have come from the killer is a fake? Could it be some sicko messing about?"

Kane shakes his head. "We're working on the basis that the message is genuine. As I have just told you, I initially chose not to go public with the full details of the way the killer mutilated the body. There's no way a hoaxer would know the eyes were cut out."

"It can't be too hard to track down who sent the email. Have you got anywhere with that?"

Kane is suddenly aware that he's looking down the lenses of at least three television cameras. He's certain the killer will be watching, gleefully basking in the attention, while at the same time assessing the resolve of the detective given the task of hunting him down.

"We have a team of experts on the job doing all they can. I want to assure the public that we will do everything necessary to solve this case. One thing this message tells us is that this person has an inflated ego, an exaggerated sense of self-importance. I will not rest until this barbaric killer is brought to account."

While the journalists murmur their approval, Kane notices a familiar figure shove his way to the front of the pack.

"Jack Newman, *Southend Herald*."

All eyes and camera lenses turn to focus on the local reporter who's suddenly found himself at the centre of the story.

He holds up a hand and waits for the crowd to fall silent before he speaks. "I can't explain why the killer chose to send that message to me but I want to assure you that the police have the full support of my newspaper. We will do everything possible to help them put this evil person behind bars."

Kane wants to say that maybe Newman and his colleagues should stop glamorising a brutal murder, that they should have accepted the senior investigating officer's request that the email not be made public.

"That's good to hear," he says. "Of course, I wouldn't expect anything else from a responsible journalist such as yourself. I want to stress that it's vital that we are informed immediately if the killer contacts you again, or anyone else at your newspaper."

Newman nods thoughtfully as if he's agreeing but he doesn't commit himself to anything. He's clearly loving his moment in the spotlight.

"Maybe you can you tell us, DI Kane," Newman says, putting extra stress on the detective's rank and name, "and at the same time reassure the public, whether you are getting any closer to catching this killer?"

There's nothing Kane hates more than feeding the press information unless it's part of a public appeal that will benefit the investigation. But he knows that sometimes, when you're backed into a corner, you have no choice. You have to throw the wolf pack something juicy. Some red meat.

His mobile phone vibrates against his hip. He takes it out and glances down at the screen. It's Granger. He ignores the call but keeps hold of the phone.

"I can tell you today that we have traced a witness. I can't give you any more details right now but it could turn out to be a significant breakthrough in the case."

The crowd edges forward again, several reporters shouting questions about the mystery witness at the same time.

Kane's mobile vibrates again. This time he answers it, turning away from the noise.

"Have you picked up the boy yet?" he asks.

"No, not yet. We've, er, been a bit side-tracked."

Kane is puzzled. He steps further away from the reporters and lowers his voice.

"What's going on? What are you not telling me?"

"There's been a development."

"Well, spit it out, for pity's sake."

"Another body has turned up. On the beach."

Tension tightens Kane's throat. He swallows hard.

"Is it the same? The eyes?"

"The eyes are still in their sockets. But it's the same."

"What do you mean?"

"There's a knife wound in the back that seems to match the other one. This time the ears have gone. Both hacked off and taken."

Kane looks over his shoulder at the red-faced, news-hungry men and women all still shouting questions at him, some jabbing microphones in his direction.

He turns his back to the crowd and sprints up the steps into the station.

CHAPTER 15

Sheltered from the murky drizzle, Harry Cannon tugs his hood down over his forehead, leans against a concrete pillar next to one of the shopping centre's exits and waits.

He watches the stream of shoppers heading home, their bags bulging with items they don't really need. His eyes are drawn to a slim, middle-aged woman who totters out of the door in high heels, her shiny white raincoat belted at the waist. She's holding a shopping bag in one hand, her mobile in the other. If he has to pick a target, Harry always chooses women, preferably in high heels. It means he doesn't have to worry about being chased.

As the woman passes by, he falls in step behind her. His heart jackhammers. This type of work has never been his forte. Frightening people who've done nothing to deserve it isn't his thing. He prefers the easy pickings from empty beach huts but has to stay away from them, for now.

The woman is jabbering into her phone, oblivious to the world around her, the danger closing in behind her. Harry glances around. Nobody near, no witnesses. It's now or never. He jogs, then sprints, and as he flies past the shopper, he flings out a hand and snatches her mobile.

For a fraction of a second, he sees her eyes widen, her mouth gape in surprise. She spins off balance and tumbles. Before she hits the ground, he's away, running to the end of the alley and around the corner. Breathing heavily, he slows to a fast walk and weaves his way through the shoppers milling around the pedestrian precinct.

Ten minutes later, Harry's inside his tiny ground-floor flat. It's sparsely furnished, always cold, and the interior walls are damp. Still, as his probation officer points out, there's a shortage of suitable accommodation. For now, it's his home, not-so-sweet home, and it's more comfortable and a lot safer than sleeping on the streets. He's been there, done that.

He takes the woman's mobile out of his pocket and examines it. It's a smartphone and looks new. There'll be no problem selling it on. He'll get a fraction of its value but it'll be enough to keep him supplied with burgers and beer for a week.

Harry goes to the kitchen sink, runs himself a glass of water and drinks it down in one go. Stealing phones is thirsty work. Gives him cotton mouth every time.

He lies on the sofa that doubles as his bed and closes his eyes. The trick to going straight, turning his life around, his probation officer tells him, is finding a steady job. He should be so lucky.

He did try, at first, though it soon became obvious that nobody in their right mind wants to employ a kid with no work experience who's fresh out of a young offenders' institution. Especially one who's not naturally inclined to accept being bossed around.

His benefit cash is just enough to pay the rent and buy basics. But, in his opinion, that's not living. That's barely surviving. He wants to do more than simply exist. It's hard, though, and stressful. Stealing for a living isn't as easy as people think.

A double knock on the door makes Harry sit up with a start. Crouching low, he moves to the window and looks through one of the many holes in the plastic curtains. Two uniformed police officers are crowding his doorstep, tight expressions on their faces. Harry grimaces. He always makes a point of checking for CCTV cameras. He hasn't stolen a phone for a while. Maybe he's getting slack because his heart's not in it. Anyway, he thinks, even if the phone snatch was caught on film, how did the Old Bill recognise him and find out where he lives so quickly?

He decides not to hang around to find out. He runs back into the kitchen, clambers on to the worktop near the sink, opens the window and slips out. The tiny yard is crammed with junk. He runs past a mildew-stained mattress, clambers over an upturned bath and heads toward a rusty fridge propped against the back fence.

Harry pulls the stolen phone from his pocket, jams it under the fridge. First rule of robbing: never get caught. Second rule: if you do get caught, don't have the goods on you.

He climbs on to the fridge and hauls himself up and over the fence, into a narrow alley. He stops dead at the sight of a uniformed police constable blocking the only exit. As the officer steps forward, pulling out his handcuffs, a young woman appears behind him.

"I think you can put the handcuffs away," she says, smiling broadly. "I'm sure he's not going to give us any trouble. You're not that stupid, are you, Harry?"

Harry's not sure whether to take that as a compliment or an insult. Either way, he thinks the woman looks way to cool to be a copper, but the constable does as she says, slipping the handcuffs back into his belt pouch.

"What's this all about? I swear I ain't done nothing wrong."

The woman steps forward. "Nobody's suggesting you have done anything, Harry. I'm Detective Constable Granger and I'd like you to come down to the station to answer a few questions for us. We believe you have information that could help us with a murder investigation."

The detective sounds nice. And looks nice. A bit glam. Like one of those pop singers on the TV. But Harry considers making a run for it. If he can get past the officers, he's confident he can outrun both of them. His problem is he has nowhere to go and nobody to run to.

"I don't know nothing about no murder. I don't hurt people. That's not cool. I'm doing good now. Keeping out of trouble. You can ask my probation officer."

The detective smiles at him again, and it's a struggle not to smile back. He can usually tell if people are faking being nice. She's definitely not.

"We know it was you who made the call to our information line the other night," she says. "We want to talk to you a bit more about what you saw, that's all. Nothing more than that. I bet you'd want to help us take a killer off the streets if you could. That's why you made that call in the first place, isn't it?"

Harry shrugs. He's not admitting anything if he can help it. Once you start admitting stuff, they've got you trapped. Caught in web of your own lies.

"I don't know what you're talking about. I'm not lying. I didn't call anyone. I definitely wouldn't call the police."

The detective edges closer, her smile gone.

"You have a simple choice to make, Harry, and I'm trying to help you make the right one. Or if you prefer it, I can ask this officer to get his handcuffs out again."

The police constable edges forward. The bastard looks as if he'd relish a scuffle. Brighten up his boring day no end, it would. Harry's been handcuffed a few times. It hurts like hell. The bloody things rub your wrists raw. Apart from the pain, it's humiliating. Makes you feel like a proper criminal.

Maybe a trip to the police station won't be that bad. The coffee's usually passable and if he's clever about it, he might be able to get some free grub for his trouble.

"No need for all that," he says. "Let's all chill out. I'm ready to go."

CHAPTER 16

Harry Cannon is short, wiry, dark-haired and pale-faced. He's seventeen but Kane thinks he looks a lot younger. A lost boy.

"We know it was you who called our information line, Harry. There's nothing to be gained from denying it. You did a good thing. You were trying to help us and I appreciate that. I'd like you to tell me exactly what you saw that night. Every tiny detail you remember can make a big difference."

Harry, sitting in the centre of a large, three-seater sofa, darts a nervous glance across the room to where Granger is standing, her back against the pale-green wall.

"I've never been in one of these rooms before," he says. "This is a bit of luxury, this is. It's even got a carpet. It's making me nervous. If you think all you've got to do is be nice to me and I'll cave in, then you're wrong. I ain't that stupid."

Kane has made the effort to personally check out the boy's history. Kicked out by his stepfather at fifteen, he spent a short period in foster care before fending for himself and falling into a life of petty crime. No education to speak of, no family support. No chance. Life is a constant struggle for a kid like Harry.

"This is one of the rooms we use to talk to people who aren't suspected of any crime. You're not under arrest. Far from it. You're helping us with our inquiries."

Harry doesn't look convinced. He folds his arms tightly across his chest and chews his bottom lip. Kane considers threatening to charge him with the beach hut break-in unless he cooperates but dismisses that idea. For now. He needs him to let his guard down.

"We know you called us, Harry. We have a recording of the conversation. I can play it back to you right now if you want. It's definitely your voice. I know you made the call because you felt it was the right thing to do. You deserve credit for that. No one wants to see a killer get away with murder, do they?"

The boy lifts a hand to his mouth and chews at his fingernails.

"Maybe I was there that night," he says. "If I was, it don't mean I did anything illegal, does it? Because I didn't. I don't do that stuff anymore." He nods at Granger. "I told that to her before. Ask her. I'm trying to get a job and everything."

"Nobody is suggesting you've committed any type of crime, Harry. We're not trying to trap you. We simply want to know what you saw."

The boy stops chewing, and studies his fingers to assess the damage.

"I reckon that's how you found me though, weren't it? Someone breaks into a beach hut and you lot automatically assume it was me. Just because I've been done for it before. That's discrimination. What about innocent until proven guilty? Like I told you, I've given that stuff up. Crime doesn't pay. Not much, anyhow."

Kane exchanges a look with Granger. They both know the boy's lying, but they want to give the kid a break. The problem is, if he drops himself in it, they won't be able to ignore it. They'll have to charge him and notify the probation service. He'll be back behind bars in a matter of days. Kane has always believed that every criminal should be brought to account for their crimes but he knows that Harry Cannon is a victim too.

"You don't need to admit or deny anything. There are lots of possible reasons for being on the beach that night. Maybe you were unable to sleep and went out for a long walk. That's entirely plausible. I'd certainly have no difficulty believing it."

The boy's gaze shifts warily from Kane to Granger and back again.

"Well, weirdly, that's exactly what happened," he says. "I don't need a lot of sleep, you see. Never have done. Legs get restless if I lie down for too long. Can't keep them still and I have to get up. I did go out for a walk along the seafront that night. Yeah, it's sort of coming back to me now."

"And saw something, didn't you, Harry?"

The boy hesitates, lifts his hand to his mouth and gnaws at his fingernails again. It goes against the grain for him to open up to the police. Kane understands that, but decides it's time to push a little harder.

"I'm running short of patience now. This person you saw has already killed again. A woman's body was found on a beach at Shoeburyness. I haven't got time to waste going round in circles here, Harry. You saw the killer, didn't you?"

Harry shrugs sulkily. "Maybe I did. Maybe I didn't. I'm starving, you know. Haven't eaten all day. It's not easy to think straight when you're hungry."

Granger steps away from the wall and sits on the sofa next to the boy.

"It's being sorted. A pizza actually, and a hot drink. You can relax, Harry. Whatever you think you have or haven't done, we're not after you. We're trying to catch someone who's murdered two people. That's all we care about."

"I'm getting a pizza? No bullshit?"

Granger nods. "It's on its way."

The boy slides away from her until he's resting against the arm of the sofa.

"I'm not a snake, you know. Nobody likes a snake. But maybe I seen something. Like I said on the phone, I saw a man dragging something down the beach. I didn't know it was a body though, not until he pulled down the plastic. That shook me. I won't lie."

"Were you able to get a good look at the man dragging the body?" Kane asks.

"Not really. It was still pretty dark. But he was tall. Solid. There was something about the way he moved. Something scary."

Kane is reluctant to interrupt because for the first time the boy is talking freely, but he takes the risk.

"What do you mean by that? What was so special about the way he moved?"

The boy pauses for a moment, raises a hand and scratches the back of his head.

"I wouldn't say it was special. I can't think of the word. It's hard to explain. He moved like he knew exactly what he was doing and nothing was going to stop him. There was something weird about it. I had this horrible feeling that if he saw me, that would be it. He'd know exactly what he had to do and he'd do it. And it wouldn't be nice. He creeped me out."

Kane pictures the boy crouched behind the door of the beach hut, too terrified to breathe.

"I know it was dark, Harry, but do you think you'd recognise this man if you saw him again?"

Harry hesitates. "I don't want anybody to know about this."

"About what?"

"Me seeing what I saw. Me talking to you. Because if he finds out, I'm—"

"If who finds out?"

"I saw it all on the news, the message he sent to the newspaper. Cutting the eyes out, 'See No Evil'. What's all that shit about?"

Kane wishes he knew the answer. What he does know is that when details of the second murder are made public in a couple of hours, the media circus is going to get even crazier.

"I saw him pull the knife, you know. I just thought he was cutting him up a bit. How crazy must this guy be? What if he finds out I saw him? What if he comes . . ."

The boy falters as he struggles to catch his breath. Kane gives him a moment to calm down. Whatever happens, the boy is going to need help coming to terms with the horror he witnessed.

"I appreciate this is difficult for you, Harry, but you didn't answer my question. Do you think you would recognise the man if you saw him again?"

Before the boy can answer, the door opens and Sam Miller enters, a pizza box in one hand and a coffee in the other.

"Did someone order a large pepperoni?" he says grinning.

Kane holds up a hand. "Not now," he snaps.

Miller eyes Harry and gives him a sympathetic shrug. "I was given the impression it was urgent. Apologies, boss."

Kane doesn't think Miller looks the slightest bit sorry, his grin now an irritating smirk.

"We're in the middle of an interview here. You should know better than to interrupt."

Miller opens his mouth to speak, thinks better of it and leaves with a childishly loud sigh.

When the door closes, Kane turns back to Harry. The boy is fidgeting nervously with the zip of his jacket, his face pale, his head bowed.

"We're almost finished here, and then you can eat. Okay?"

Harry looks around the room, eyes wide with panic, before dropping his gaze back to his feet. "I'm not hungry anymore. I just wanna get out of here, please. I can go home, can't I?"

"I suppose so. You want to help us catch this killer, don't you?"

"Maybe . . . dunno really," the boy stutters. "I didn't do nothing, didn't see nothing. I don't have to say anything if I don't want to."

* * *

Kane and Granger stand on the steps outside the station entrance and watch Harry Cannon walk away, his hands in his pockets, his shoulders hunched against the wind. When he reaches the end of the road, he looks back at the detectives for a few seconds before turning right and disappearing.

"Is it just me or does he look absolutely terrified?" Granger says.

Kane reckons the boy, considering what he witnessed, has every right to be frightened.

"Life must be scary for him at the best of times. I feel sorry for him. His instinct is to help but he doesn't trust anybody. I thought he was ready to give us a full statement, then he shut down."

"When Miller burst in, that's when Harry clammed up. Maybe he thought he wasn't going to get fed."

Kane doesn't believe it had anything to do with the pizza. That might piss him off but it's not going to scare the wits out of him.

"I'd like you to dig around a little, find out what you can about Sam Miller. I'd like to know if he's been involved with Harry Cannon before. Ask around but be subtle about it."

Granger smiles. "I know it might be hard to believe but I can do subtle when I want to."

They're going to have to bring the boy in again, Kane knows it. If he's unwilling, they'll have to arrest him.

"What do you think is scaring Harry Cannon the most right now?"

Granger crosses her arms, taking a moment to think.

"He knows if he's charged with breaking into the beach hut, he'll have breached his probation conditions and will be dragged straight back to prison."

"And," Kane says, "as far as we know he's the only person who's seen the killer."

Granger nods. She understands what he's getting at. "He's terrified that the killer is going to discover who the witness is."

CHAPTER 17

Jack Newman leans back in his chair, stretches his legs and surveys his new kingdom. The room is small, windowless and smells of disinfectant but he loves it.

He smiles to himself as he recalls the look on Dawn Brady's face when she heard he was being moved out of the newsroom and given his own office. The editor of the *Herald*, no less, had decreed that Newman needed to escape the chaos of the newsroom to concentrate on his 'potentially award-winning' coverage of the murders.

Lying on his desk is the latest copy of the paper. Newman picks it up and smiles. Once again, his byline is on the splash. The main front-page story. The headline shouts *See No Evil Killer Strikes Again*. He scans the first few paragraphs, even though he can quote them word for word.

> *The mutilated body of a young woman found on Shoeburyness beach yesterday morning is believed to be the second victim of the See No Evil Killer. She has been named as Isabel Anderson, 26, who recently moved to the town from London to work at Southend Airport. According to the police, her body was identified by her partner, Darren Ellis. The tragic*

couple lived in a flat in Thorpe Hall Avenue close to the seafront.

Last night, the police media office said details of the crime will be revealed at a press conference once the post-mortem examination has been completed. Detective Inspector Edison Kane, who is leading the hunt for the killer, refused to comment.

Newman folds the paper, making sure the headline and his name are visible, and places it carefully back on the desk. Of course Kane won't comment. He's too scared of slipping up, saying the wrong thing. He doesn't want the spotlight on him because people might realise that he hasn't got a clue what he's doing.

Since the first murder and the publication of the See No Evil email, the newspaper's circulation figures, and the number of clicks on its online edition, have soared to record-breaking levels.

This is the big break Newman has been waiting for. In his gloomiest moments, he had wondered whether his time would ever come. As long as he doesn't mess up, the country's top newspapers and maybe even a few TV news channels will be queuing up to offer him a job.

His thoughts are interrupted when Dawn breezes in. It irks him that she didn't knock first.

"Hey, Jack, you must be missing the buzz of the newsroom stuck up here, all alone like Billy No Mates."

Newman detects a tremor in her voice. She has her weaknesses but he admires her fighting spirit. She's determined not to have her authority undermined by his 'star reporter' status. Many people in her position would have surrendered by now.

"Do come in, Dawn. I'd offer you a seat but I'm short on chairs. Can I help, or is this purely a social visit?"

Brady shakes her head. "I'm the news editor."

"I know that."

"You still answer to me."

"Maybe."

Brady steps forward and looks him hard in the eyes. "I lead this paper's reporting team and that includes you."

Newman points at the newspaper on his desk. "Tell me. Who else in your precious team can you trust with a story like that?"

"There's a fine line between confidence and arrogance, Jack."

Newman's phone pings. He takes it out of his pocket.

"Let me know when I cross that line," he says, glancing at the screen.

"You know as well as I do, you're only as good as your last story. I need to know what you're working on next."

Newman is staring intently at his phone now. He puts a finger to his lips to shush her.

Brady's cheeks redden. "Are you even listening to me?"

"Wait a second. It's another message from him. The killer. Sensational stuff. He's talking about the Anderson murder. I don't think he cut out the eyes this time. Listen."

> *'I almost feel sorry for her. She was out running, enjoying the sea view, enjoying life. An innocent destined to die. The truth is, I don't feel in the least bit sorry for what I've done. I can kill but I cannot tell a lie. I don't know when I'll stop. Everyone better hope it will be soon.*
>
> *'Hear No Evil.'"*

Brady's eyes widen with excitement. "You think this is genuine?"

"Course it is. This killer's as crazy as they come but he's obviously loving the attention and the way I'm covering the story."

Newman pauses and scans the message one more time. He lifts his head slowly and looks at Brady. "This is some real scary shit. 'Hear No Evil.' You get what that means, don't you? Fuck. He sliced her ears off."

CHAPTER 18

Kane stares at the *Herald*'s website, fighting an urge to hurl his phone at the wall. He's not angered by the report on the killer's new message, or even Newman's speculation that Isabel Anderson's ears were taken. It's the smaller story, tucked away in the corner of the screen, questioning his competence, that sickens him.

He shifts uncomfortably in his chair. It's all there. A recap of his wife's murder, his subsequent breakdown and the time spent on sick leave. It was never a secret. It's a matter of public record. But it's been dragged up for one reason and one reason only: to question his position as the detective leading the investigation.

He slips his phone back into his jacket and stands, his heart thumping, his face flushed. The consulting room door swings open and Rebecca Baxter steps into the waiting area.

"I'm ready to get going if you are," she says. "Are you all right? I can give you a minute if you want."

Kane doesn't feel like talking to anybody right now but if he has to it might as well be to a psychologist.

"I'm as ready as I'll ever be."

Baxter turns and walks briskly back into the consulting room. Kane follows, closing the door behind him. He sits in his usual chair, while Baxter walks over to her desk, picks up a pen and notebook and starts to write.

Kane watches in silence, desperate to know exactly what she's writing but can't bring himself to ask. Therapy is supposed to be a safe place where you can show your emotions without being judged, isn't it? Hell, what does she expect?

Baxter puts the pen and notebook down and turns to face him.

"How are you feeling today? You seem a bit troubled."

Kane wants to deny that there is anything wrong. He's embarrassed that he lost his composure, and that Baxter noticed.

"Have you seen what they're saying about me in the papers? Questioning my fitness to do my job."

"How does that make you feel? Can you tell me?"

Kane supposes this is what psychotherapists are meant to do. It's drilled into them over years of training. Ask you how you feel. About everything. Get you to talk about your emotions. Analyse your emotions at great length, then help you straighten them out.

The problem is, since he lost Lizzy, he rarely knows exactly how or what he's feeling. Most of the time his mind is a whirl of conflicting emotions.

"That story is utter nonsense," he says. "I'm dealing with everything that's happened. I believe that I'm perfectly capable of running a murder investigation. Not just capable. I'm extremely good at what I do."

"That's great to hear," Baxter says. "It's good to stay positive."

Kane leans forward, rests his forearms on his knees and stares down at the grey carpet. Commenting on his positive attitude isn't exactly a ringing endorsement. It strikes him as a way of avoiding having to agree or disagree with his statement.

When he looks up, Baxter is studying him carefully, her head slightly tilted to one side, her expression hard to read.

He's not sure whether it's compassion or pity but he feels uncomfortable all the same.

"You know, I'm starting to wonder if all this talking is actually doing me any good. I'm finding it hard to justify spending time in this room when there are so many other things I should be doing. It's almost as if I'm coming here to feel sorry for myself, to whine about my problems and all you're doing is holding my hand while I do it."

Baxter blinks in surprise.

"Is that what you truly think is happening here? Nothing more?"

Kane shrugs. "Maybe I do. I don't know. Sometimes I wonder if it would be better never to talk about what happened to my wife. Leave it all in the past. Shut it away and get on with my life. Focus on catching this person who has already killed and mutilated two people."

"Do you believe it's that simple? People often try to block out negative emotions, but it doesn't work in the long term. It's just delaying the inevitable."

Kane knows it's not the answer for him. He'd love to be able to put himself into a state of emotional numbness. God knows, he's done his best. He's tried his hardest to put Lizzy's death behind him, to move on. He's tried telling himself that he can make up for not saving her, for not catching her killer, by catching other murderers, by saving other people. And it works. For a while.

"Lizzy is dead. But in my mind, she's more alive than anyone else I know. She haunts me. Not like a ghost. I don't believe in that stuff. She's still alive in my head. When I hear or read about a suspicious death, or someone spiking someone's drink, she's there. When I see the body of a murder victim, she's there. When I close my eyes at night to try to rest, she's there."

"I understand. You had a successful marriage."

Kane allows himself a half smile. Baxter's observation is such an understatement it's almost funny.

"We met in school, you know. I was drawn to her even then. But she had a boyfriend and I didn't have a clue. Years later we bumped into each other at a party. I was a young police constable and she was, well, she was amazing . . . she just . . ."

Kane shakes his head slowly. The memory is too vivid, too beautiful to bear. Baxter walks slowly to her chair and sits down.

"I appreciate this is painful. Talking this through is the only way you are going to fix yourself. I can't do it for you but I do know how to help. Have you tried to imagine what Lizzy would say if she could speak to you now?"

Lizzy often told him she was proud of him because he made the world a safer place each time he took a violent criminal off the streets. She was a super-smart City lawyer, but he was her real-life hero. A hero who couldn't even protect her.

"Lizzy would be disappointed if she saw me now, if she knew how I'd fallen apart after her death. She'd tell me to keep on doing what I was born to do. Putting bad people behind bars."

"Do you think solving the murders you're investigating now will help you stop blaming yourself for what happened to her?"

Kane closes his eyes for a few seconds and lets himself imagine catching the man who drugged, raped and murdered his wife. He'd make him pay for what he did. Take away his liberty. Cage him like the animal he is. But he knows that's not possible. Not yet.

"It's my job to stop evil people doing evil things. Lizzy loved that."

Baxter sits up straighter and crosses her legs neatly at the knee.

"Do you actually believe that evil exists?"

Kane's aware that many of the world's top neuroscientists now believe that psychopaths are born, not made. That may be so, but when they become killing machines, there's something else at play. He's interrogated several over the years, and the worst of them possessed a cold-bloodedness that always chilled him to the bone.

"From what I've seen, I've no doubt that this killer is an evil human being. A ruthless individual."

Baxter raises her eyebrows. She doesn't look convinced.

"You know, there is a school of argument that there is no such thing as evil. That idea is an obsolete relic of medieval religion. There is growing evidence from studies around the world that psychopathic killers do what they do because of a neurological fault in their brain. I personally believe it has some merit."

"You've read the newspapers, haven't you? You've seen what this so-called human being did. How he mutilated the bodies."

Baxter leans forward, her eyes bright with curiosity. Not for the first time, Kane notices that she appears slightly more animated, slightly less professional when they talk about the murders.

"I'd be curious to know," she says, "if the pathologist was able to tell whether the first victim was alive when the eyes were removed."

Kane hesitates. They haven't decided whether to make these details public yet but he's intrigued to know where she's going with this.

"The pathologist is as certain as he can be that in both cases, the mutilations took place after death. Also, in both cases the cause of death was a stab wound to the back which pierced the heart."

Baxter lifts her chin and gazes at the ceiling while she mulls over his answer. "That could mean the killer didn't intend to torture."

"We don't know for sure that the killer had any idea the victims were dead when he cut them up. To be honest, even if he did, I don't believe he deserves any credit. It doesn't make him more humane or less of a monster. Cutting out someone's eyes after they are dead is not an act of kindness."

Baxter nods. "Also, there's the sign-offs the killer used. See No Evil, Hear No Evil. Part of the Three Wise Monkeys maxim. This must be important, to him at least."

Kane holds up a hand to stop her continuing. It's understandable that she'll have a professional interest in the murders but he's finding the conversation uncomfortable.

"I'm sorry, I don't think we should be discussing this right now."

"No, I'm sorry," Baxter says. "You're right. I can get carried away. The human mind is fascinating, and murderers, even psychopathic killers, are human."

Kane shakes his head. He wonders how scientists and psychologists like Baxter would feel if they had to look at the butchered bodies of innocent people lying on the mortuary slab. If they had to explain to the victims' families the details of what had been done to their loved ones.

"I know why scientists might question the existence of evil," he says. "And I can't describe in scientific terms exactly what it is. But I promise you this: I know evil when I see it."

CHAPTER 19

Jack Newman stands at the end of the pier, his back to the shore looking out to sea. The walk from the entry gate took twenty-five minutes, the brisk pace keeping him warm despite the biting wind.

It's always been one of his favourite places for meeting informants. It's easy not to attract attention if you can blend in with the holiday crowd, and although it's still early spring, the pier is already busy with weekend day-trippers.

As usual, the man is late. He's arrogant, and cunning with it. But he's such a good source of information, Newman is prepared to put up with his boorishness. He glances back over his shoulder at the stalls selling fast food and spots the detective sauntering toward him, chewing on a beef burger.

When Detective Sam Miller catches sight of Newman, he lifts a hand and waves furiously. Newman turns his back on him, and returns to staring out to sea. He's happy to be civil but he doesn't have to pretend to like the man.

"You're fifteen minutes late," he says when the detective joins him.

Miller leans his back against the railings and snorts scornfully.

"You know, you're lucky I made it at all. I'm a busy man. You're aware I'm part of a team investigating two murders, aren't you? Oh, of course you are. That's why you're so eager to talk to me, isn't it?"

Newman grips the top iron railing with both hands and keeps his eyes fixed on the rolling waves.

"I understand that work must be hectic right now. You may have noticed that I'm pretty busy too."

Miller snorts again. "Of course, you're the killer's best mate, aren't you, his little email buddy. Bet you're loving all the attention. Lapping it up."

Newman turns his head slowly and glares at Miller. The detective responds with a grin and waves his half-eaten beef burger at him.

"Fancy a bite? Go on, help yourself."

Newman ignores him. Miller doesn't know it, but Newman spent months gathering evidence that would have exposed the detective for taking bribes from criminals. It would have been a great scoop. A sweet moment. But Banjo's murder killed that story dead. Months of hard work put on hold indefinitely. As it turned out, he now had something much bigger to work on. The biggest story of his life.

"Like I explained, I'm busy too right now. Let's get straight down to it, shall we? Have you got anything new for me?"

Miller takes another bite out of his burger, then tosses the rest over the railings into the sea. A pair of gulls swoop down to fight over the remnants of the bun, stabbing at each other with razor-sharp beaks.

"I don't think there's anything I can tell you at this moment that isn't already public knowledge. I've got to be careful not to leak anything that can be traced back to me."

Newman wonders whether he's wasting his time and his cash.

"I'm not sure this arrangement is working the way I expected. I'm paying you good money and I'm not getting anything worthwhile in return. I get the feeling I'm being taken for a ride and I can't let that happen."

Miller squares his shoulders and grins uneasily.

"Didn't you hear what I said? If my bosses find out I'm feeding the press information, my career goes straight down the sewer. When I have information that I can safely give you, I will. There's no need to go all cold on me."

Newman turns his head away to hide a smirk of satisfaction. The detective has started whining. The prospect of losing out on easy money has unsettled him.

"I suppose that's fair enough, but in that case, I hope you're not expecting anything today. Our arrangement is that I pay you for information. It's a simple equation. You did do maths in school, didn't you? Zero information multiplied by zero information equals zero cash."

Miller rubs his forehand and clenches his jaw. Newman knows the detective is not as stupid as he appears. And if what people say is true, he's definitely more dangerous than he looks.

"I'm not unreasonable," Newman says. "You'll learn that about me if we continue to work together. But I need something. Even if it's something I can't use right now. I need to feel like I'm getting something for my money."

A muscle in Miller's right cheek twitches. Newman takes a quick sideways step, to make sure he's out of punching distance.

"Well, I suppose there is something I can tell you. We're doing a televised news conference later today. DI Kane is going to announce that the murders of the homeless guy and the woman have been officially linked. That they were victims of the same killer. This See No Evil, Hear No Evil guy. Kane's under pressure to be more transparent. To warn the public to be careful."

The news is not worth paying for. The second email makes it clear that the same person murdered both victims, and whatever else Kane chooses to reveal at the press conference, it'll be for everyone to hear. Newman deals in secrets. Little gems of information the police don't want anyone else to know. Secrets are powerful. They give you an edge.

"If you can't do better than that, then I'm going to have to reconsider our arrangement."

Newman starts to walk away but Miller shoots out a hand, grabs his wrist and yanks him back. His desperation is puzzling. Miller has been taking backhanders from local villains for years and must be swimming in cash.

"Look, there is something else," Miller says. "But you can't publish it, not yet anyway."

Newman turns back and leans slowly out on the top railing into the wind.

"Sounds intriguing."

"It's the witness Kane's been talking about. There's a boy who says he saw the killer with the body of the first victim. I could give you his name but you have to keep it to yourself. Personally, I don't care about the boy's safety. I'd love someone to cut the little rat's eyes out."

"I'll pay you for the name, right now," Newman says, trying not to sound too eager. This is a secret he desperately wants. He probably wouldn't reveal it. Not yet. But it'd put him in a strong position if Kane found out that he knew the boy's identity.

Miller sidles up beside him and lowers his voice.

"A baby-faced kid called Harry Cannon. Been inside for breaking and entering. Thinks he's something special, I reckon. But he's drawn to trouble like a fly to pig shit."

Newman doesn't speak. He allows himself a smile, reaches into his jacket and hands Miller a folded brown envelope.

"Don't spend it all at once."

CHAPTER 20

"We now have compelling reasons to believe that the homeless man, known locally as Banjo, and Isabel Anderson were both murdered by the same perpetrator. As of yet, we have not been able to link the two victims."

Detective Superintendent Helen Dean has always been a stellar performer in front of television cameras. Kane is impressed. His boss's voice is steady, confident and oozes authority. He prefers informal press briefings because he can cut them short when he's had enough.

He knows the advice is to look straight ahead but can't resist a sideways glance at Dean, resplendent in full uniform, a look of steely determination on her face.

Kane shifts nervously in his chair. His turn is coming soon and he's not a natural performer in front of the cameras. A colleague once confessed that she always had a good laugh whenever she watched his press conferences because he always seemed incredibly pissed off.

"What I do want to do right now," Dean continues smoothly, "is to reassure the public that we are doing everything in our power to bring this killer to justice. I am confident we have the right team investigating these brutal crimes and that my officers will be working non-stop until the perpetrator is off the streets. I will now hand you over to Detective Inspector Edison Kane, who is the senior investigating officer."

Kane clears his throat, leans a fraction closer to his microphone and blinks hard into a fresh burst of camera flashes.

"First, I want to echo what Detective Superintendent Dean said. We will not rest until this killer is in custody. Second, I need to ask the public, the people of Southend, men and women, to think a little more about their personal safety. Finally, if anyone out there believes they have information that could assist our investigation, I'd urge you to contact us as soon as possible."

With the easy bit over, Kane pauses to scan the faces of the assembled TV and newspaper journalists. This is the part he dreads.

"If you have any, I'm happy to take questions. I'll answer them as fully as I can, as long as I don't feel they compromise the investigation."

In truth, Kane is far from happy, but he grits his teeth and smiles.

A tall woman with cropped blonde hair steps forward. "Anna Blake from News Line TV. From what you've said, and from your warning to the public, can we assume that these were completely random murders and that anyone in this town could be the next victim?"

Kane bristles. This is what he loathes the most. People putting words into his mouth, whipping up panic.

"We haven't been able to establish a link between the victims. There may not be one. That's a fact. I'm suggesting members of the public be careful. That's all. What we don't need is for people like you to make the residents of this town feel too scared to go about their daily lives."

In his peripheral vision, Kane sees his boss shoot him a sideways glance. He gets the message. Don't mess this up. Stay calm.

"Jane Fielding, *Daily News*."

Kane recognises the woman in the dark red, shoulder-padded suit. She was at the informal press conference on the steps of the police station.

"The recently published second message from the killer ends with the words 'Hear No Evil'. Can you confirm that Isabel Anderson's ears were cut off and taken?"

Kane suppresses an urge to smash his fist down on the table and storm out of the room. How can anybody have the nerve to ask such a thing in such a matter-of-fact way?

He considers telling Fielding that her job may be to ask difficult questions, to put senior police officers on the spot, but she should have consideration for the feelings of the murdered woman's parents. A deathly silence falls over the room, and he senses Dean shifting uneasily beside him.

"I can confirm that the killer removed the victim's ears. I won't be saying any more about this particular detail. It's important that we understand the loss the family have suffered and how they must be feeling."

Fielding nods thoughtfully. "We all know what comes next, don't we, Detective Inspector? See No Evil, Hear No Evil, Speak No Evil. Can we expect the next victim to have his or her tongue cut out?"

Kane has been dreading this question. He turns to Dean for help. She stares straight ahead, waiting, like everybody in the room, for his answer.

"I'm not prepared to speculate," he says. "If you lot, you people, let me get on with my job then there won't be another victim. I'm doing my best here. We all are. We need your support."

"You seem a bit emotional, Detective. Is this case getting to you?"

Kane doesn't answer. The reporter smiles at his silence.

"Detective Inspector Kane, do you believe that you are in the right frame of mind to hunt down someone who is clearly a ruthless and extremely cunning psychopathic serial killer? Maybe the people of this town would feel safer if you considered stepping down."

A murmur of surprise and approval runs through the assembled journalists. Kane clenches his jaw, anger gnawing at his gut.

"Did you hear what I said?" Fielding asks with a smirk. "Would you like me to repeat it for you?"

"I heard you. I'm hesitating because I'm puzzled. I'm sure you've done your research, so you will know that I'm an experienced investigating officer, with many successful murder cases under my belt."

"I acknowledge that. Your record is excellent. But past performance is no guarantee of future results. It's a matter of record that you were taken off active duty, and this is your first case since returning."

Kane doesn't try to hide his anger this time.

"Yes, you're right. I have no reason to deny it. My wife was murdered, and I needed time off to deal with the grief and sort myself out. Have you got a problem with that?"

Fielding's smirk fades. "Of course not, we all have great sympathy with you and we also understand that mental health issues can be complex, but—"

"Stop this now!" Dean barks, raising a hand to silence the reporter. "I won't have an officer grilled in public about personal issues. I will answer your question. I have every confidence in Detective Inspector Kane's ability to bring this investigation to a successful conclusion. I have no doubt that he is the right man for this case. Thank you, ladies and gentlemen. This press conference is now officially over."

Kane gets to his feet quickly and follows Dean out of the room. She strides away from him, down the corridor, swinging her arms like a soldier on parade. Kane understands. She doesn't want to stop and talk about what just happened. She has more important things to do.

"Thank you, Helen," he calls out. "What you said in there means a lot."

The Detective Superintendent doesn't slow her pace or turn her head but her words echo loudly down the corridor.

"Do your job, Edison. And don't you dare let me down."

Back in his office, Kane kicks the waste paper bin hard against the wall, scattering its contents across the floor. He puts both hands flat on his desk and hangs his head. Don't these people realise that every word written about his personal situation takes the focus off the investigation?

He takes a couple of deep breaths and sits down. Should he blame himself for the death of Isabel Anderson? An innocent young woman, her life brutally extinguished. Maybe if he'd warned the public to take care after the first murder, she would still be alive.

Granger steps into his office carrying two cups of coffee.

"I thought you might need this," she says, putting one of the drinks down on the desk in front of Kane. He looks at it but leaves it where it is.

"You were watching, then?"

"It was out of order. What that reporter said. Unfair."

Kane thinks unfair is a bit of an understatement. Cruel and sensationalist would be a more accurate description.

"You know, I almost lost it."

"I don't blame you."

"I was teetering on the edge. I was so close to proving her right, that I'm not mentally strong enough to lead this investigation."

"But you didn't. You held it together. And what about Detective Superintendent Dean? She made it clear what she thinks about you."

Kane gives Granger a doubtful smile, picks up his coffee and takes a sip.

"Tell, me something, would you? Has she been in contact with you recently?"

Granger frowns. "I'm not sure what you mean. She has telephoned me a couple of times to ask me how I'm getting on. How I've been coping with my first murder case. Why do you ask?"

"No reason really. I was just wondering whether she's been checking up on you."

Kane picks up his coffee again, blows on it and puts it down without taking a drink.

"Now let's get back to the important business," he says. "How have the house-to-house inquiries been going?"

"We've been assigned extra uniformed officers to knock on doors along the route taken by Isabel Anderson to ask if anyone saw anything strange that morning. So far nothing. We're also checking footage from every CCTV camera in that area. Unfortunately, there's virtually no coverage along the coastal path. Also, we've carried out a fingertip search of the area where the body was found. No luck."

Kane feared as much. He's convinced the killer took the ears with him. A macabre trophy to go with Banjo's eyes.

"What about the other thing I asked you to look into?"

Granger walks quickly to the door and pushes it shut, peering through the glass panel to check if the corridor is clear.

"Sam Miller arrested Harry Cannon for a spate of beach hut break-ins about fourteen months ago."

"Maybe that explains why the boy reacted in the way he did."

"It's possible, I suppose. If he thought Miller turning up meant he'd be locked up again."

It's a plausible explanation but Kane isn't convinced. He has a feeling there's more to it. Cannon had been shaking with fear.

"Was there anything else?"

Granger glances at the door again.

"Nobody I spoke to in the squad room had a bad word to say about Miller. That's no surprise. They're going to close ranks to protect one of their own, especially if it's an outsider asking questions. But one of the uniforms, only after I swore on my life not to tell anyone, said she'd had a few complaints from some of the town's regular offenders. You know, the characters who are in an out of the station for shoplifting and being drunk and disorderly."

"Complaints about what?"

"Saying that Miller has been throwing his weight around on the streets. That he enjoys scaring people who can't fight back. That he's a bully."

Kane isn't surprised. Miller doesn't strike him as a gentle soul. But in his experience, not many villains, even minor offenders, can bring themselves to say good things about police officers. They may be lying, but the best lies usually have some truth in them.

"Okay then," he says. "Let's bear that in mind and keep an eye on him. He may not be a cuddly person, but I wouldn't describe any of the detectives I've worked with as cuddly. And that includes you."

"Thanks. I'd be insulted if you did."

"You've had a long day. Why don't you finish up, take an early cut and get back to your family?"

"Thanks, don't mind if I do," Granger says. Before heading for the door, she hesitates. "What about you? Are you staying in town or going back to Brentwood later?"

Kane hadn't even considered where he was going to spend the night. The thought of returning to the cramped budget hotel room makes his shoulders slump.

"I'm probably going to carry on here for a few hours. Then go back to my flat. Maybe I'll be able to get a decent night's sleep in my own bed."

Granger stretches out a hand to open the door, then pauses again.

"Well, if you're definitely driving back to Brentwood, what about coming around mine for dinner? No talking shop, though. After the day you've had, you'll need to unwind. If you come at about nine, my daughter will be in bed and the food will be ready. I'm not great in the kitchen but my mum is. How about it?"

Kane is taken aback and at the same time touched by the detective constable's kindness. She probably suspects he's going back to a cold, empty flat, and she'd be right. He takes a moment to try to come up with a good excuse to refuse the invitation without hurting her feelings.

"If you have something else on, or if you don't fancy socialising with a lowly detective constable, then don't worry," Granger says with her trademark smile. "I won't take offence, promise."

Kane is still struggling to come up with an excuse. It's been a while since he's had a night out. He's got used to eating alone. Used to feeling miserable.

"All right, why not?" he says, surprising himself with how excited he sounds. "I'll be there. I warn you, though. I can't promise that I won't talk about the job."

CHAPTER 21

Kane stands on Granger's doorstep in the dark, half regretting his decision to accept her dinner invitation. The end-of-terrace house is on the edge of a shabby, seventies housing estate south of Brentwood's town centre. The sort of place where Kane would usually think twice about visiting after dark.

He raises a hand to knock but draws it back. It would be better if he rang the doorbell. A musical chime is probably less intimidating. Before he can press the button, the door opens and he's greeted by Detective Constable Granger's vibrant smile.

Only it isn't Granger. The woman's thick dark hair has a few subtle streaks of grey and a maze of laugh lines around her brown eyes.

"What can I do for you, mister policeman?" The woman holds up a hand, her face stern. "I hope you've got a search warrant. I never let filth into my house without one."

Kane blinks in confusion and the woman laughs.

"My little joke," she says. "Couldn't resist. You must be Detective Kane. Come in, come in."

Kane gives her a sheepish smile and steps across the threshold.

He follows her into a modern kitchen with a dining area and she gestures for him to take a seat at the small, square table.

"Something smells great," he says. "I hope you haven't gone to too much trouble, er, Mrs Granger."

Granger's mother laughs again. "You can call me Naomi. Because that's my name. And no, I haven't gone to much trouble at all. I'm afraid I've been much too busy to cook today so I ordered in three pizzas. Just keeping them hot in the oven. Bailey will be down soon. She's checking on Daisy."

Kane remembers Granger has a four-year-old daughter. That explains why her mother didn't get the time to prepare a meal. The nursery school run, the bedtime routine. He's been looking forward to a homecooked meal after surviving on takeaway pizzas and fried chicken for weeks but disguises his disappointment with a broad smile.

"I love a good pizza. Can't get enough of them."

Granger's mother gives him a doubtful look and sits beside him.

"How are you holding up? Bailey explained what happened to your poor wife. So tragic. I'm so sorry."

"Thank you, but I'm good," Kane says, wondering exactly how much Granger told her about the man leading her first murder investigation. He doesn't want to talk about Lizzy or himself. Not here. Not now. "Have you any other children?"

Naomi's eyes darken. "Bailey has two brothers. One older, one younger. Sterling and Marcus. We don't see much of them. Not anymore."

"Oh, I'm sorry," Kane says. "I didn't mean to pry."

Naomi glances quickly across the room, making sure that they're still alone. "The truth is," she says, "where we used to live, where Bailey was brought up, it's worse than here, would you believe? The police are considered the enemy. You know what I'm talking about, don't you? You don't talk to police. You don't respect them. You fear them. When Bailey decided on a career in the force, it . . . didn't go down well.

Her brothers wanted nothing to do with her and they rarely speak to me because I choose to live with her."

"That must be difficult," Kane says, wishing he'd kept his mouth shut. He wants to say more, something that shows he understands why certain communities consider the police pariahs. And it's true. He does get it. But he knows he can never really know.

Naomi listens to his silence for a while, then smiles. "I can guess what you're thinking. You're assuming that my sons must be shady characters, criminals even."

Kane shakes his head. "I really wasn't."

"Well, that's a good thing. Refreshing. Just in case you were wondering, Sterling is a chemical engineer and Marcus is still at university. He's not sure what he wants to do yet."

Kane doesn't say he's impressed. He doesn't need to. "Sounds like they're doing well for themselves. It's a shame that they can't bring themselves to respect their sister's choice."

Naomi nods. "It's terribly sad. But they didn't have it easy growing up, believe me. You couldn't rely on the law. You were guilty until proven innocent. Forgiving and forgetting is not easy, trust me. I'm proud of my boys. And I'm so proud of Bailey. She's chosen her own path and she's determined to make the world a better place for Daisy. Give her more choices. But sometimes I can't help worrying when she's out there."

Kane understands. Police work can be dangerous. You're on the frontline, and no matter how prepared you think you are you can find yourself in unpredictable situations, dealing with dangerous people.

"From what I've seen so far, your daughter is an extremely capable young woman and damn good police officer."

Naomi smiles. "I believe you. I know how resourceful Bailey can be. And she can handle herself. She had to learn quickly. You've got to survive before you can thrive. That's what I always told my children. But I still worry. I know my daughter better than anybody alive and she's not as tough as she thinks she is."

Kane senses Granger's mother is desperate for him to reassure her, to say something that will help her worry less, but he can't promise anything. The last person he promised to take care of ended up dead.

"In the police we're trained to work in teams. That way we can rely on, support and look out for each other. We can all feel safer if we watch each other's backs."

At that moment, Granger waltzes into the room. "Who's watching their backs?"

Her mother stands up, laughing loudly. "Nobody's watching anybody, darling. I'm just having a very interesting talk with your detective inspector. You're right. He seems nice enough. We were wondering where you'd got to. This man is starving. He needs a good feed."

She fetches the pizzas from the oven and the three of them sit at the dining table to eat, the two women sipping glasses of cold beer, Kane drinking coffee. At first, they're all so busy eating, no one speaks. When the conversation does start, it's banal, light-hearted.

Naomi is the first to clear her plate. "Are you sure I can't get you a beer, Edison? I know Bailey calls you Kane but that doesn't feel right."

Granger and Kane exchange smiles across the table.

"Almost everyone calls me Kane and I do prefer it, but you can call me whatever you want. I'll pass on the beer, thanks, I'm driving. Besides, there's something I want to research when I get back to the flat and need to keep a clear head."

Once they have all finished, Naomi puts the plates and cutlery in the sink, excuses herself and disappears upstairs, while Granger and Kane stay sitting at the table.

"What's this research you mentioned?" Granger asks.

"I thought you didn't want to talk about work."

"I didn't but I'm curious. Detectives are naturally curious, aren't they? It's compulsory."

Kane folds his arms and leans back. "Well, it might not be important, but I want to check the origin of 'See No Evil,

Hear No Evil, Speak No Evil'. It may be that the killer is simply being literal and thinks it's a good way to whip up a media frenzy."

Granger pauses for a moment before jumping off her chair and running out of the room. A minute later she returns carrying a laptop.

"We might as well get started right away."

As she sits down at the table and fires the machine up, Kane can't tell whether she's out of breath through exertion or sheer excitement.

This isn't how he usually likes to do research. He prefers to take a considered, more meticulous approach. But Granger's enthusiasm is contagious and he can't bring himself to shut her down.

Her fingers skip across the keyboard and she bites her lip in concentration as she skims the top few search results.

"Here we go, then. It says that in the West, the Japanese pictorial maxim representing the Three Wise Monkeys — See No Evil, Hear No Evil, Speak No Evil — is generally used in reference to turning a blind eye to wrongdoing, to rejecting responsibility for it. That's what I would have said. Does that help us?"

Kane shrugs. "I can't see how that applies." He's starting to regret going down this route. Granger is showing no sign of being deterred. He appreciates her enthusiasm but it's making it hard for him to think methodically.

"Okay, good, there's more to it," she says. "It's believed the proverb actually came from the works of the Chinese philosopher Confucius, and its original meaning is to teach the importance of being careful to avoid contact with evil because it can draw you in, infect you. What do you think?"

"From what I've seen over the years, that makes a lot of sense." Kane can't disagree with the idea that evil can be contagious if you let it get too close.

Granger shuts her laptop and turns to face him. "That's a pretty depressing way to look at it, and if it's true, we've got to be particularly careful in our line of work. But, hey, let's look on the bright side."

Kane is starting to learn that in Granger's world, everything has a bright side.

"And that is?"

"Well, if evil, cruelty and darkness are infectious, then so are goodness, kindness and light."

CHAPTER 22

The beach is dark and deserted, the sea a foam-flecked vortex. Harry hears the crunch of footsteps behind him. He tries to run but the shingle clings to his feet like thick treacle. An arm encircles his neck and he's thrown to the ground on to his back. The attacker pins him down, so close Harry can feel his hot fetid breath. The face is chalk white. The mouth a blood-red gash. The eye sockets black holes of despair.

Harry cries out, rolls off the sofa and hits the floor with a thud. After a few seconds staring at the ceiling, he pushes himself up and sits down. Wiping sweat from his forehead with the back of a hand, he picks up the half-empty bottle of beer by his feet and takes a swig. It's still slightly chilled. He's not been asleep for long. The hum of traffic outside suggests the early evening rush hour is in full flow.

He grabs the TV remote and starts to channel hop. He pauses when he finds what looks like a promising movie. The scene features an aerial view of a cemetery, the camera panning in to focus on a freshly dug grave. As the discordant soundtrack reaches a crescendo, a single bony hand breaks through the soil, clawing at the air.

Harry's heart hammers so hard he jumps, spilling his beer down the front of his shirt. He switches the TV off and dumps the remote on the threadbare carpet. Horror movies used to be his favourite. Not now.

He's not usually this twitchy but he's hardly left the flat since the police pulled him in. The constant tiredness isn't helping either. The nightmares are making it impossible for him to get any decent sleep. They're always the same and he always wakes up with the shivers.

A loud knock on the front door fills him with dread. Instinctively, he drops on to his hands and knees. *Stay quiet and keep your head down*, he tells himself. A shadow looms at the window, knuckles rapping on the glass.

"You've got ten seconds to open the door before I kick it in. I won't be happy and you know what happens when I'm not happy."

Harry utters an involuntary groan. He recognises the voice and knows the menace it carries is real. He considers arming himself with a knife from the kitchen. What's the point? He'd never have the guts to use it, even if things turn really ugly. He's no saint, but he hasn't got that in him.

He stands, walks quickly to the door and pulls it open. Detective Constable Sam Miller shakes his head slowly as he steps inside and strides into the living area. Harry shuts the door and follows, a sinking feeling in his stomach.

Miller stands with his back to the window, looks around the room and curls his lips into a sneer.

"How do you live in a stinking rat hole like this? I suppose it makes sense because that's exactly what you are. Vermin. A little rat."

Harry has heard it all before. He can take it. If Miller does nothing more than hurl insults at him, he'll count himself lucky.

"What do you want?"

Miller's mouth gapes and his small, round eyes widen in mock surprise.

"That's hurtful, boy. I know we're not friends now but I expect a little respect. I'm your caring neighbourhood police officer."

Harry takes a couple of sideways steps, putting the sofa between himself and Miller. It makes him feel a little safer. He knows from experience that the detective's mood can turn in a split second.

To most people, Miller comes across as a man weighed down by having to deal with criminals on a daily basis. He's doing his best to keep the streets safe but it's a struggle.

Harry knows different. The detective frightens him more than anyone he's ever met, including the bullies he had to deal with while in the nick. It's not the violence that worries him the most. It's the cruelty that goes with it. Harry has never understood how Miller's colleagues can't see the truth. They're coppers after all. They're supposed to be able to spot a villain when they see one.

"I told you, leave me alone," he says, trying his hardest not to sound too frightened.

Miller grimaces, his eyes narrowing into slits. Harry is reminded of a TV documentary he watched about the world's deadliest predators. The detective has the cold-eyed stare of a snake about to strike.

"That's not very friendly, Harry boy. Maybe I need to teach you some manners. Hammer them into that thick skull of yours."

Miller lunges and Harry flinches. His naked fear makes the detective grin.

"Be careful, boy. You know what I'm like. Sometimes I get carried away. I want to make sure you know how important it is that you keep your mouth shut."

Harry wipes his hands on the front of his shirt. He hates himself for being so frightened but he doesn't know how not to be.

"I won't say nothing, I swear. Your boss, DI Kane, doesn't know anything about us. I'm not stupid."

Miller walks to the sofa, sits down and pats the space beside him.

"Sit. Let's have a proper talk. We need to sort this out."

Harry tries to calculate whether sitting next to Miller will be more dangerous than refusing to do what he's told. He sits, and immediately regrets it. The detective swings an arm around his shoulders and grips him tight. Harry tries to wriggle away but Miller is too strong.

"Let's get one thing straight," he snarls. "Edison Kane isn't my boss. He just thinks he is. He and his sidekick are outsiders, glory hunters. Once they get bored with this murder investigation they'll be off."

Harry keeps his head down, his eyes on the floor. He's not going to argue, even though he disagrees. He's had the displeasure of dealing with plenty of coppers since he left school and Kane and Granger seem sharper than most.

"All I want you to do," Miller says, "is show me respect. No shooting your mouth off next time, because I know they'll come calling again soon. You're their star witness."

Harry sits up straight and shrugs Miller's arm off his shoulders. The detective responds by wrapping his arm tightly around Harry's neck and pulling him close.

"I won't say nothing. I'm no snake."

"I hope so. Because if you do, you'll end up in urgent need of medical treatment. And when you come out of hospital, you'll be taken straight back to juvie because I'll make sure you're booked for breaking into that beach hut in Thorpe Bay."

Harry's vision blurs to grey. The pressure on his neck is stopping the flow of blood to his brain. *This is it,* he thinks. *It's all over. Miller's choking the life out of me and he doesn't even know it.*

"I can't breathe," he pleads.

Miller stands, yanking Harry up with him.

"Of course you can't. This is what we call a chokehold. We aren't supposed to use this restraining technique anymore, it's too dangerous, which is stupid because that's the point."

Harry's lungs are burning. A pounding pressure builds in his head. His eyes bulge out of their sockets, ready to pop. He opens his mouth to beg for mercy but no sound comes. He feels Miller's muscular arm tighten around his throat. His legs give way as he's swallowed up by blackness.

CHAPTER 23

Miller pulls up at the kerb outside Ray Spencer's home and gives a low whistle of appreciation.

"Nice place. Not bad for a jailbird, is it? You've got to give him credit, don't you, boss?"

Kane has never liked being called 'boss' and Miller is particularly skilled at making it sound like an insult. The detective constable sulked like a tired teenager when he was told the two of them would be teaming up, but he perked up during the drive out of town.

Kane gets out of the car and climbs the concrete steps to the house, checking over his shoulder to make sure Miller is following. There's no disputing the house, in the Southend suburb of Westcliff-on-Sea, is impressive. Georgian in style, the red-brick facade is rigidly symmetrical, with fluted white columns framing the front door.

"This place must be in the million-plus bracket, boss. It's way out of our league."

Kane is already regretting bringing Miller. He thought it'd be a good idea to get him out of the station while Granger brought Harry Cannon in for another interview.

The boy seems to like Granger and, more importantly, he trusts her, which suggests he's a pretty good judge of character.

Kane lifts a hand to rap the brass door knocker but pauses and turns to Miller.

"Don't forget what I told you. Let me ask the questions. Smile, be polite and watch Spencer very carefully. It'll be interesting to see how he reacts under a little bit of pressure."

Miller grins and gives a mock salute. "You've got it, boss. I think I can manage that. No problem."

Kane cringes and lifts a hand again, but before he can knock the door swings open. It's mid-morning but Spencer's girlfriend looks like she's just arrived home after an eventful night on the town. She's wearing a knee-length silver sheath dress, a chunky chain around her neck and a large, reddish bruise under her left eye.

"I saw you coming," she says. "We have many cameras here. For security, you see. Raymond says it's best to be careful."

Kane introduces himself and Miller. They both show their identification cards but Rina doesn't even pretend to look at them.

"I know who you are. You came to the café the other day."

Kane nods. "I did. But I'm here because I need to speak to Mr Spencer again. I have a few more questions I'd like to put to him. Is he in?"

Rina pauses, lifts a hand to her face, touches the bruise gingerly with her fingertips and winces.

"Raymond is working out in the gym right now. Please come with me."

The detectives step inside and follow her across the large entrance hall. "That bruise looks pretty nasty," Kane says. "It might be a good idea to get yourself checked out at hospital. You could be concussed."

Rina doesn't stop walking but shakes her head. "It will be fine, thank you. Raymond says I drink too much and sometimes he's right. It's easy to fall over and get hurt when you are drunk. It's my own fault."

She leads them to a room at the end of a short corridor and stands aside to let them go through the open door. "He's expecting you."

Spencer is sitting on a low bench surrounded by an impressive array of weightlifting equipment. His tight, grey T-shirt is stained with sweat. As Kane and Miller enter, he turns to face them, wipes his brow with a hand towel and scowls.

"Can't a man exercise in his own home without being hassled by the police?"

Kane scans the room. One wall is covered with floor-to-ceiling mirrors. Another is home to an extra-large, slightly curved television screen, below which is a row of four computers monitors, each showing live footage from security cameras covering the front of the house, the entrance hall, the rear garden, and the front of what looks to Kane like a large flat-roofed outbuilding.

"I hope this isn't inconvenient. If you'd rather, I'd be happy to give you a few minutes to shower and get dressed and then we can drive you down to the station. Your choice."

Spencer wipes his brow again and hurls the towel at the mirrored wall.

"I'm a respectable businessman. This is pure harassment. Tell me, what am I supposed to have done?"

Kane wishes he'd brought a couple of uniformed officers along. It's possible he's underestimated Spencer's volatility.

"We're not here to accuse you of anything. I want to ask you some questions about a feature article about you that was published a few weeks ago. I'm sure you remember it. It had a very flattering headline: 'Zero to Hero'."

Spencer puts his hands on his knees, sighs and stands up. "Oh, yeah, that bullshit. I didn't really fancy doing it but media coverage is good for business. Besides, Rina loves that sort of thing. Makes her feel like she's living with a celebrity."

He twists and glares at Miller. "Who's this? He looks like a frightened puppy."

"This is my colleague, Detective Constable Sam Miller."

Spencer sneers. "Can't he speak for himself?"

Miller's cheeks redden. "I'll speak when I want to, don't worry. I can read you your rights if necessary."

Spencer turns his attention back to Kane. "What exactly is it you want to know?"

"I want to ask you about some of the things you were quoted as saying about your experience of being homeless."

"Get on with it, then. Ask away. I haven't got all day."

Kane takes his mobile from his pocket and pulls up the article.

"Here, you say that once a person finds themselves homeless, sleeping on the streets, they become statistics, faceless, which makes it almost impossible for people to empathise with their plight. I quote: 'Nobody wants to see them, hear about them or speak about them.'"

Spencer nods and sits back down on the bench. "Last time I checked it's not a criminal offence to have an opinion."

Kane notices that the Spencer's demeanour has changed. He's calmer. His lips tight, his expression thoughtful.

He glances the screen of his phone again. "And here, further on in the article, you say that the way homeless people live, how they suffer, day after day, means that many have suicidal thoughts, some feel they would be better off dead and most would welcome death as an escape."

Spencer shrugs. "I was being honest. If you've read the article, then you'll know that I know what I'm talking about. I've been there. I've lived through it. That's why I do what I can to help others in that situation."

Kane is almost convinced. The journalist who wrote the article makes it clear that she feels Spencer deserves to be thought of as a role model for his rise from the gutter to respectability and financial success. But for Kane, something about the story doesn't feel right. He can't explain it. Not yet.

Spencer walks across the room and picks his towel up off the floor. "Is that it, then? Are we done? I'm getting cold. I need a shower, and I don't know about you but I've important work to do."

Kane considers dragging Spencer out of the house in handcuffs. Instead, he smiles.

"I need a few more minutes of your time if you can spare it. We've spoken to witnesses who say that when you threw the man known as Banjo out of your café, you assaulted him. Their actual words were that you roughed him up and threatened to kill him."

Spencer starts to walk to the door, changes his mind and turns back. "What the hell are you suggesting? Why on earth would I want to risk everything and kill a loser like him? Anyway, I thought you'd linked Banjo's murder to that woman killed on the beach. I've never had anything to do with her. Never met her. I told you the truth. Banjo stole from me and I got mad, but that's it. I didn't assault him and never threatened him, and whoever your so-called witnesses are, they're lying."

He has a point. Kane won't rule it out but he'd be surprised if Spencer turns out to be the killer. He's too hot-headed, too emotional. Unless, of course, the persona he presents to the world is fake. Maybe, underneath the fire, an icy poison flows through his veins.

Kane points to the row of security camera monitors. "I see you're taking serious measures to protect your property."

"And why not? I like to be careful. Envy can drive people to do terrible things. Anyway, you can't depend on the police nowadays. They're a bunch of incompetents."

Kane ignores the insult. "In that case, I guess you'd have a pretty good system set up at your phone shop and your café."

Spencer nods slowly but gives nothing else away.

"It would be helpful if I could have access to the footage from your café cameras, especially those covering the entrance on the day you threw Banjo out. It'd help us clear this up. Show us exactly what happened."

Spencer's eyes narrow. His muscular neck flushes red, a thick vein pulsing across his right temple.

"You haven't arrested me and you insist you're not accusing me of anything. What if I refuse? I don't have to allow you access to any camera footage."

"You don't. That's correct. If that's how you want to play it, I'll contact a friendly judge, apply for a warrant and you won't have a choice."

Spencer smiles and shakes his head. "I reckon that'll take at least a couple of days, won't it? What's to stop me wiping the footage before you come knocking on my door, waving your useless bit of paper."

"Why would you do that if you've got nothing to hide?"

"Maybe I'm not naturally inclined to help the police. Maybe I simply can't stand being told what to do. Or maybe I just don't like your face, Detective Inspector."

Miller looks at Kane and raises an eyebrow.

"I'm sure you're aware that tampering with evidence is a serious crime. Do you really want to risk going back to prison? Because if I suspect that's what you've done then I'll do everything I can to bring a perverting the course of justice charge against you."

Spencer puts his hands on his hips and glares silently at Kane. After a few seconds, he turns to face the open door and calls out.

"Rina. Here now. You're needed."

Almost instantly, she's standing in the doorway but doesn't come into the room. She fiddles nervously with the chain around her neck, her head turned at an angle to hide the bruised side of her face. Kane has a feeling she's been just out of sight all along, listening to their conversation.

Spencer lifts a hand and beckons her in. She doesn't move.

"These detectives want the footage from the camera system covering the café. I don't know what they think they're going to find but would you sort it out for me?"

Rina's gaze drops to the floor, and when she eventually lifts her head to speak, she stumbles over the words. "I can't do that, no, I'm sorry. Normally, I could, but no. It's not possible."

Spencer frowns and takes a couple of quick steps toward her. Although there is still at least twenty feet between them, she cowers.

"What are you talking about, woman?" Spencer asks. "What do you mean you can't do it?"

Rina raises a hand and rubs her face. "I'm so sorry. You know I wipe the recordings every few months. I always do that, don't I, Raymond? Well, I did it two days ago. I'm sorry. I didn't know. They've been erased. They're gone."

* * *

Kane doesn't speak during the drive back to the station. He lets a sullen-eyed Miller concentrate on the road while he considers their meeting with Spencer.

The businessman radiates a smug hostility. That doesn't mean he's guilty of anything but Kane suspects that he is. He's definitely hiding something and getting a kick out of it. Kane also suspects that the bruising on Rina's face is the result of something a lot more sinister than a drunken stumble.

He waits for Miller to pull up and switch off the engine before asking the question.

"Tell me, what do you think? Did Spencer know all along that the security camera footage had been wiped?"

Miller turns to face him. "Why didn't you just ask Spencer? Or maybe let me ask him? I wanted to, but you told me to keep my mouth shut and watch."

"That's right. And that's why I'm asking you now to give your opinion on what you saw and what you heard."

Miller's top lip twists and his nose twitches, like someone detecting an unpleasant smell.

"He knew the footage had been wiped, of course he did. He almost certainly told her to do it. He was playing you all along. People like that, they always believe they're smarter than the rest of us. They think they're untouchable. That all police officers are dumb plods."

Kane knows Miller is right. He may be obnoxious but he doesn't miss much. If he applied himself he'd have the makings of a good detective.

"You think I was too soft on him, don't you?"

Miller grunts. "I'd have pushed him a lot harder, let's put it that way. And what about that bruise on his girlfriend's face? We could have used that to pile the pressure on him. I don't get why you didn't even mention it."

Kane hates the thought that Rina may be too frightened to involve the police, but if he's right about Spencer, he'll be behind bars soon enough. For now, he's happy to let him believe that he's too clever to be caught. Any criminal who believes that is not as smart as they think they are.

Miller is waiting for an answer but Kane doesn't feel the need to give one. "As you're such an expert, I want you to take another look into Spencer's background. His criminal record and his business dealings since he came out of prison. See if there's something we haven't picked up."

Granger did the original digging into Spencer's history and Kane is confident nothing has been missed. But he wants to keep Miller busy and out of sight while they have another talk with Harry Cannon.

Miller hunches his shoulders, his upper lip curling into a sneer. "Sounds like a waste of time to me, but if that's what you want. You're the boss, apparently."

Kane leans toward the detective, close enough to see the tiny blood vessels in the whites of his eyes.

"That's right. I'm in charge of this investigation. Do you have a problem with that?"

Miller shrugs sulkily but says nothing.

Kane smiles. "Apparently not," he says, turning away and walking briskly to the car park exit. "Report back to me as soon as you're done."

CHAPTER 24

Kane heads toward the seafront. It's lunchtime and the streets are busy, people wandering aimlessly in twos and threes. He's forced to slow down and step off the narrow pavement to skirt around two women posing for a selfie. The joy on their faces and the sound of their laughter makes him want to be alone.

When he reaches the seafront, he crosses the road and skips down the concrete steps to the beach. To his right, the town's world-famous pier stretches out into the grey, shifting waters of the estuary. He can see the green and cream–liveried train heading out to the end of the pier and remembers riding the narrow-gauge track with Lizzy. They'd taken a trip to the coast to celebrate five years of marriage. Back then, a detective constable's salary didn't stretch far. The train ride to the end of the pier took seven minutes and Kane recalls they held hands the whole way. It wasn't something they did often but that day it felt right, an unspoken promise that they would always be together.

Kane pushes the memory away and walks down the beach, stopping just short of the waterline. He needs to think clearly. To focus. He has a killer to catch. Two lives have been taken and he's damn sure a third body will turn up soon unless he gets his act together.

He crouches down and searches through the shingle until he finds a smooth, flat pebble. A skimmer. Kane edges closer to the waterline, turns his left shoulder to the sea and draws back his throwing arm. If I can get three bounces, he tells himself, it'll be a sign that the killer will be caught before another life is lost. The instant he thinks it, he knows he's being stupid but he can't erase the thought. Not now. He hurls the pebble at an incoming wave and watches as it skips twice before sinking in a swirl of foam. Quickly, he scoops up another pebble and launches it hard, fast and low. Not even one bounce. An epic failure.

Kane strides back up the beach, berating himself for being such an idiot. What the hell was he playing at? He climbs the stone steps to the promenade and starts walking toward the pier. After a couple of minutes, he finds himself outside Ray Spencer's café. The lunchtime rush hasn't started and the place is deserted apart from an elderly couple sitting at one of the outside tables, nursing their mugs of coffee.

Opposite the café, the pink neon sign of the Flash Vegas amusement arcade flickers garishly in the spring sunlight. As Kane approaches the entrance, his attention is drawn to the three security cameras evenly spaced on the brickwork below the first-floor windows.

Stepping into the arcade, his senses are hit by a wall of electronic sound and the acrid smell of burnt cooking oil mixed with stale sweat. He slips past a line of teenagers pumping money into a bank of slot machines and heads for a central kiosk where a young woman, her tightly curled hair dyed bright red, is handing out coins in exchange for folding money.

The woman looks up as Kane approaches, stops what she's doing and fishes her mobile phone out of the back pocket of her blue jeans.

"Don't bother with that," Kane says. "Where's your boss's office?"

"She's not in. Taken the day off."

Kane might have believed the lie if the woman's eyes hadn't flicked nervously to her right. He follows her glance, walks straight to the door in the corner of the room, grabs the handle and enters without knocking.

A woman sitting behind a desk looks up wide-eyed from the screen of her silver laptop. Her short hair matches her chocolate-brown trouser suit and Kane guesses she's in her mid-thirties.

She takes a moment to compose herself before managing a half smile.

"Usually, when a stranger barges uninvited into my office I call the police, but I'd be wasting my time, wouldn't I?"

"Is it that obvious?"

"To me it is, yes."

"Detective Inspector Kane," he says, pulling out his warrant card and presenting it to her over the desk. The woman leans forward and studies it for a few seconds. She takes a closer look at the photograph and glances up to check the faces match.

Kane slips the card back in his pocket. "And you are?"

The woman sits back in her chair and crosses her arms across her chest. Kane gets the impression she's considering her options.

"Kate Steen, the proud owner of this fine establishment. And before you ask, nobody is allowed to play our slot machines unless they can prove they are over the age of eighteen. We do our best to enforce the law, but it's pretty much impossible to tell whether ID cards are genuine or fake nowadays."

Kane is sure that at least half of the youths he saw pumping their money into the slot machines were several years short of eighteen, but he holds his tongue. He needs this woman's cooperation.

"I'm not here to check the ages of your gamblers. I want to ask you about your external security cameras. The ones on the front of the building."

Steen arches her eyebrows in surprise. "Interesting. What's this about?"

Kane doesn't feel like spelling out the detail. He hasn't the time or the inclination.

"Are those cameras working right now? Believe me, if this wasn't important, I wouldn't be here."

Steen pauses briefly, then starts tapping on her laptop keyboard. "They better be working. We handle a lot of cash in this kind of business. Our security has to be tight."

Kane walks around the desk, stands behind Steen and watches as she pulls up the live footage from the three cameras. He points over her shoulder, jabbing a finger at the screen.

"That's the one I want. The middle view. Can you enlarge that one?"

"Of course. This is an expensive system. Top of the range."

She clicks on a file and the live footage fills the screen. The images are as crisp as high-definition TV. Excitement flutters in Kane's gut. The footage shows a steady stream of pedestrians walking past the arcade entrance, and behind them, in the background, the front of Spencer's café.

Kane gestures at the screen again. "Are you able to focus in closer on the café across the road?"

Steen doesn't answer. She taps a few keys and zooms in on the tables outside the café's front door. Kane can see the grey-haired couple still sipping their hot drinks.

Steen turns to look up at Kane. "What's this all about, anyway?"

"How long do you usually store your camera footage for?"

"Usually 90 days. This is a digital system. It's all on SD cards."

Kane allows himself a smile. "Then I'm going to need copies. I'll send someone to pick them up."

Steen stands up to face him. She's almost as tall as he is. Her eyes a rain-cloud grey.

"I don't suppose you have a warrant authorising the seizure of these images?"

"Do I need one?"

"Well, you haven't even asked me nicely, have you? A little bit of politeness goes a long way, Inspector. You barged in here without an invitation."

Kane sighs. She has a point.

"Look, I'm sorry. You're right. I'm investigating very serious crimes and the footage from your camera could be a great help."

"The crimes were committed in that café?"

"Not necessarily. I didn't say that."

"What the hell has Ray Spencer done?"

"You know him?"

"I wouldn't say that. I know of him. I also know that he's not someone you want to cross."

Kane hadn't considered that Steen might be worried about Spencer's reaction if he finds out she helped the police. He doesn't want to add to her fears but decides to be honest with her.

"I'm investigating two murders and your security camera footage could help us make important progress. There's no evidence that Spencer is involved in any way. We're following several lines of inquiry."

Steen steps back, frowning. "The man in the mud, and the woman killed while out jogging? I read about them in the paper. How can anybody do something like that to another human being? You've got to lock this monster up."

Kane nods. "That's exactly what I intend to do. There's no reason for anyone to know that we're viewing your camera footage. I don't even know for sure that there's anything significant on there."

Steen thinks for a moment. "It'll take me a couple of hours to sort things out, then I'll bring the SD cards into the station. I'd rather do that than have someone come here to collect them. I'm not the only one who can spot a plain-clothes detective a mile off. I don't want to get a reputation as a grass. It wouldn't be good for business, or for my health."

Kane wonders exactly what she's heard about Spencer that would make her this nervous.

"If that's what you want, then it's fine with me. I appreciate your help."

He digs into his jacket and pulls out a card. "My mobile phone number is on here. You can call me any time."

Steen hesitates for a moment before reaching out and taking the card. She scans it quickly and smiles. "I've had a few police officers slip me their number over the years but never a detective inspector."

Kane is buzzing on the walk back to the station. He's feeling more optimistic about the investigation, and maybe life in general.

It's going to take two officers several hours to sift through the security camera footage but it has to be done. Most of his past investigation successes have come as a result of what he calls old-fashioned detective work. The boring stuff, the detail, long hours spent in front of a computer screen, often bring that vital breakthrough.

He'd often tell novice detectives in his teams that if they want to believe that murder cases are solved by genius hunches, gut feelings, out-of-the-blue coincidences and flashes of inspiration, then they should stay at home, slouch on their sofas and binge watch TV crime dramas.

Back in his office, Kane is surprised to find that Granger hasn't returned to the station. She went out first thing to knock on Harry Cannon's door and bring him in. He calls her mobile but gets no answer. He drops his phone on to his desk, irritation stinging his throat.

Since Lizzy's murder and his subsequent breakdown, he's become more emotionally erratic than he used to be. Nobody's said as much but he knows it to be true. Before, he'd possessed a stillness, a certainty, that enabled him to cope with any setback. That has gone. It's as if he's shed a layer of skin and with it lost a level of calmness.

He reaches impatiently for his phone to call Granger again. Before he can pick it up his office door swings opens and she walks in, her breathing heavy, her expression grim.

"Harry Cannon's gone," she says.

CHAPTER 25

"What do you mean he's gone? Gone where?" Kane's mind races. His heart is a drum. A witness to a killing. The only witness. They should've kept the boy in custody. For his own safety. Kane stands up. He felt so good, so in control after finding the arcade camera footage. Now a wave of sickness churns his stomach. He sits back down, wiping beads of sweat from his brow with the back of his hand.

Granger steps forward. "Is everything all right? You don't look too clever."

Kane fears he's going to faint but holds up a hand, dismissing her concern. "What's happened to the boy?"

"We don't know that anything's happened to him. Not yet. All we do know is that he's not at his flat. The front door was swinging open when I got there and the place was a mess. It looked like he left in a hurry. He failed to turn up to an appointment with his probation supervisor this morning. He's missing. He could be anywhere."

Kane tugs at the collar of his shirt and loosens his tie. "He can't have vanished into thin air. Are you sure he's done a runner? Maybe someone took him."

Granger spins around and checks that the corridor outside the office is clear before shutting the door. She sits on the chair opposite Kane and puts both hands flat on the desk in front of her.

"Take a deep breath. Nice and easy. Breathe slowly, deeply."

Kane does as she suggests, sucking air into his lungs and exhaling slowly through his nose. It works. His heart rate steadies, then slows, his head stops spinning.

"I'm sorry," he says.

Granger shakes her head. "For what?"

"Losing the plot. For panicking."

"Don't worry about it. You're fine. I'm going out to get us both a drink. I'll be back in a few minutes."

Kane nods and watches her disappear down the corridor. Embarrassing himself in front of a junior colleague is a new and humiliating experience.

What is she going to think about her boss going into meltdown? She's probably going to think he's weak, erratic, not fit for the task he's been trusted with. He drops his head into his hands and massages his scalp with his fingers.

He's pretty sure that Granger doesn't want or need a coffee. She's giving him time to compose himself, a chance to get a grip. Kane stands up, walks across the office to the window and stares out at the four concrete tower blocks dominating the town's skyline. He's praying the kid is in hiding somewhere out there, keeping his head down. Fearful but safe.

Kane knows from experience that psychopathic killers don't feel fear. They can fake it when they need to show vulnerability but they don't experience it. They also, contrary to popular belief, don't lurk in the shadows. They're never social misfits with staring, reptilian eyes. They walk around their neighbourhoods with their heads held high, smiles on their faces. Some have high-status jobs, friends, even families. Kane wonders how many killers he has passed in the street.

The monster who murdered his wife is out there somewhere. He's living his life, laughing, eating his favourite meals, sleeping in his comfortable bed. The thought twists like a knife.

Granger returns carrying the coffee. Kane spins round to face her and she hands him one of the cardboard cups.

"Thank you," he says. "I appreciate it."

"It's just a lousy coffee. I didn't even have to pay for it."

Kane favours her with a rueful grin. They both know what he meant. He walks back to his desk and sits down. Time to get to work.

"We need to get a forensics team into Harry Cannon's flat. See what they can find."

Granger nods. "I've made the call. They're already on their way."

Kane takes a sip of his drink. Granger is proving herself a real asset despite her lack of experience. He has the feeling that he's going to have to be at his best just to keep up with her. No more slip-ups.

"Is it possible that Harry has simply gone off to visit a friend, or even family, and will turn up in a day or two?"

Granger shrugs. "A friend, possibly. But the truth is I'm worried for him. He's a witness who can potentially identify a double killer. That puts him at risk, doesn't it?"

Kane is worried too, but he clings on to the fact that although he told the press they had found someone who had seen the killer, the identity of the witness was never revealed.

"We knew the boy was scared of something, or someone. Maybe he decided to get out of town. Fear can make even sensible people do stupid things."

He picks up his desk telephone and punches in an extension number. "This is DI Kane. I need to speak to you in my office, right now."

Granger opens her mouth to speak, but she hesitates. She looks uncomfortable, as though she wants to say something but is unsure how it will be received.

The office door opens and Detective Constable Linda Finch enters. She glances nervously across at Granger and then back to Kane.

"You said you needed a word?"

"Harry Cannon has disappeared," says Kane. "I need the media team to put out a press release appealing for anyone who might know where he is to get in touch. You know, a mugshot, a full physical description, the usual stuff. Make sure there's no mention that he has any connection to the murder investigations."

If Finch is surprised by this turn of events, she doesn't show it. Kane has a feeling that if he'd told her that Russia had just dropped a nuclear bomb on London, she'd still look only slightly fed up. Over the past few days, Kane has come to the conclusion that sullen is her natural expression and it doesn't mean that she's not a competent, conscientious detective.

"I'll get right on it," she says. "I'll also put the word out on the streets, speak to a couple of my informants. See if there are any interesting rumours going around. I've worked this place for nearly fifteen years now and know a lot of people who hear a lot of things."

Kane nods. Local knowledge and local contacts can prove crucial when trying to track down a misper.

"That's what I want to hear. Report back to me quickly if you find out anything significant."

Granger waits for Finch to leave the office and makes sure that she's out of earshot before she speaks.

"There is one thing we do know for certain. If Harry has run off and left town, then he's broken his probation conditions. As soon as he's picked up, he'll be carted back to serve the rest of his sentence in a young offenders' prison."

The same thought had occurred to Kane. He picks up a pen and taps it on the desk, wondering what could be so bad that the boy would choose to risk being locked up again.

"We need to find him, and quickly. Get one of the team to check the local hospitals, and we also need to put a trace on his mobile."

Granger glances over her shoulder and lowers her voice. "I have an idea how we could help Harry, but you might not like it. I've been thinking that we could have a quiet word with his probation supervisor. I'd be willing to do it. Tell her that even though we're putting out an appeal for information on his whereabouts, we actually know where he is and that he's cooperating with us on a murder investigation. That would mean she wouldn't have to report him for being in breach of his probation conditions."

Kane takes a moment to think. That Granger is willing break the rules to stop Harry Cannon being sent back to prison doesn't surprise him. The fact that she's confident enough to suggest it to her boss does. When he was her age, he'd never even consider bending the rules to help someone out, especially not someone who'd been convicted of a crime. He's not sure that he can do it now. He can't afford to put a foot wrong with the press pack already watching him like a hawk.

"You mean we say that he hasn't run off, that we've put him into hiding for his own safety?"

Granger nods. "I get the impression his supervisor thinks a lot of him. Nobody else needs to know. No one gets hurt and Harry gets another chance."

Kane is regretting his earlier suspicions about Granger. He'd bet his police pension that he can trust her and that she simply wants to do her best to help the kid out.

"If you think you can pull it off, then go ahead and have a word. The boy's had it rough. Maybe it's about time someone gave him a break."

"Thank you," Granger sighs. "I'm sure it's the right thing to do. And don't worry, I'll be careful."

In Kane's mind, Harry Cannon ending up back in prison isn't the worst possible scenario. It beats turning up dead on one of the town's beaches minus a tongue.

CHAPTER 26

Bailey Granger is nervous. Convincing Harry Cannon's probation supervisor not to report him doesn't seem as simple as it sounded when selling the idea to Kane.

She's still trying to work out what she's going to say, when a slender woman in her mid-forties marches across the reception area.

"This way, please, Detective Granger," she says, without breaking stride. Granger jumps up and follows her into a side office. The woman, her long black hair streaked with grey, sits behind a small, cluttered desk and gestures with a flutter of her fingers for Granger to take the seat opposite.

"Apologies if I seem in a hurry but things are hectic today. To be honest, this place is chaotic every day. I'm afraid I have only ten minutes before my next appointment. A drug dealer fresh out of prison yesterday morning. I always do my best for my clients but I won't be surprised if she's back behind bars by tomorrow."

Suri Kumar talks as quickly as she walks. The symmetry of her finely boned face is enhanced by an immaculate centre parting.

"Ten minutes is all I need, Ms Kumar. As I mentioned on the telephone, I need to speak to you, confidentially, about Harry Cannon."

Kumar leans forward in her seat at the mention of Harry. "Please, call me Suri. Harry missed his appointment with me and I understand he's no longer living in the accommodation I arranged for him. Dear Harry, what can I say about him? He's certainly had his problems, but deep down he's a good kid. I had great hopes that he was going to turn his life around. I truly thought he'd set his heart on staying out of trouble."

Granger nods in agreement. "That's why I'm here. To explain why you don't need to report him as absent."

Kumar puts her bony elbows on the desk and leans further forward. "I don't understand, Detective. He's disappeared, hasn't he? I heard on the radio that you're appealing for anyone who might have seem him to come forward. As much as I'm loathe to see him sent back to serve out his sentence, I have no choice."

"But you do. Harry Cannon is an important witness to a serious crime and we have advised him to keep a low profile for a while. I want to assure you we know exactly where he is. He's cooperating with us, not breaking his probation conditions."

Kumar sits up straight. "I've never heard anything like it. Why do you want people to believe he's gone missing?"

"Well, that's the bit that's confidential. It's all tied in with our investigation. I'm sorry I can't give you any more details."

Kumar sits silently, her head tilted as she thinks. After a few moments she stands up, walks to the door and pulls it open. "Well, I suppose that's good news. For Harry, at least. Thank you for filling me in. I'm pleased for him. As soon as he's finished helping you, he needs to come and see me. Make sure you tell him that."

Granger gets up, pleasantly surprised at how quickly she was able to the get the probation officer on board. She supposes Kumar has too much on her mind to question the situation.

"Thank you for your time," she says, with a smile. "I'll let you get on with your work."

Granger is halfway across the reception area when Kumar calls out for her to wait. The probation officer walks purposefully toward Granger. She catches her by the arm and pulls her close.

"One last thing, Detective. How worried should I be about Harry Cannon's safety? Is he in danger?"

Every time Granger's mobile rings, she fears she's about to be told that Harry's body has been found. Kumar doesn't need any extra stress. Her job is hard enough as it is. "No, I don't think you should worry. We're doing everything possible to keep him out of harm's way."

Kumar fixes Granger with her eyes. "And how worried should I be about losing my job when this lie blows up in our faces?"

* * *

The roads back into the town centre are clogged with traffic, and it takes Granger forever to drive the short distance from the probation service offices back to the station.

The atmosphere is tense when she finally arrives back in the squad room. A large group of detectives and uniformed police constables huddle in one corner as they receive a final briefing before setting out on a house raid.

Granger hears the detective sergeant leading the operation tell her team that the suspect is wanted for stabbing his girlfriend. Every one of the police officers is wearing a stab vest. She crosses the room to where Miller is perched on the edge of a vacant desk, his legs crossed at the ankles. Finch sits at the desk opposite, her eyes fixed on her computer.

"Anything new come in on Harry Cannon?" Granger asks.

Finch glances up for a moment, then immediately returns her attention to the screen.

"Nothing at all. Not one single sighting. We've had a few calls from people claiming they know where he might be but none of them checked out."

Granger steps around the desk, curious to see what the detective is looking at.

"Your boss has got me going through this footage from the security cameras at an arcade down on the seafront." Finch clicks on pause and the video freezes. "I'm supposed to be looking for Ray Spencer and Banjo having a scuffle outside the café but haven't even got to that day yet. Kane says he wants every minute of the footage checked. 'For anything that might seem unusual,' he said. What the hell does that mean? It's mainly a bunch of old people sitting at tables outside sipping hot drinks and eating cake."

Granger notes the use of the phrase 'your boss' and considers pointing out that during this investigation, Kane is Finch's boss too. Before she can, Miller snorts, hitches himself right up on to the desk and swings his legs idly, like a bored child.

"The whole thing is a waste of time if you ask me. Kane had me spending half a day looking into Ray Spencer's background. You did that already, didn't you? Either he doesn't trust you, or he wanted me out of the way for some reason."

Granger knows which one of those options is true but she keeps it to herself. She walks around to the front of the desk and gives Miller a hard stare.

"If you have a problem with the way Detective Inspector Kane's running this investigation, I suggest you speak to him about your concerns instead of moaning behind his back."

Miller slides off the desk, lifts his head high and juts out his chin. His eyes narrow, his lips forming a tight, bloodless line. Granger wonders if she's gone too far. She's seen that look before. Murderous.

Finch materialises between the two detectives, a protective arm blocking Sam's path. "Take it easy now, Sam. What are you playing at?"

Everything in Miller's demeanour changes. He even laughs. "I'm just have a bit fun with Kane's happy little helper. I bet he loves her running around, his own personal little gofer."

Granger feels her right leg tremble. A mixture of fear and anger heats her blood. She tells herself to walk away. Be the bigger person. The smarter person. She clamps her mouth shut, trying her best not to rise to Miller's bait. She fails.

"I'm going to give you one warning only and this is it: You need to be very, very careful. I don't tolerate bullies. I never have and I never will."

Miller's smirk twists into a sneer. "What are you going to do about it? Report me to human resources? Play the race card?" Before he can say any more, Finch lifts a hand and pushes his right shoulder hard. He staggers back.

"That's enough, Sam. For God's sake, don't be such an idiot. Get out of here right now before you do something stupid. Go on. Move it!"

Miller stares blankly at her for few seconds, glances across at Granger, then saunters across the squad room and out of the door. Finch sighs loudly, returns to her desk, sits down and restarts the security camera footage.

"Don't take any notice of him," she says, without taking her eyes off the screen. "He doesn't mean half of the rubbish that comes out of that big mouth of his. Once he's cooled down it'll all be forgotten."

Granger takes a deep breath. She's pretty sure she won't be forgetting the confrontation in a hurry.

"Thank you. How's it going?" She nods at the monitor.

"Incredibly slowly and it's mind-numbingly boring."

Granger starts to leave, then hesitates. "I've got a meeting with one of the crime scene investigators shortly but I'm in early tomorrow. How about I lend you a hand checking the footage? Four eyes have got to be better than two."

Finch looks up, surprised. "You'd do that?"

"Why not? We're supposed to be a team, aren't we?"

Granger is halfway across the squad room when Finch calls out to her.

"Hey, wait. Who is it you're meeting?"

"I think his name is Lucas. That's right, Peter Lucas."

"Oh, right. Lucky Lucas, we call him. Enjoy."

* * *

Granger knows exactly what Finch meant the moment Peter Lucas walks into the office. She gestures for him to sit down but he passes. He's a few years older than her, tall, short dark hair, and extremely attractive in a slightly nerdy way. He flashes her a smile and then gets straight down to business. "You said the results from the missing youth Harry Cannon's flat were urgent, so we gave them priority."

"I take it you got something?" Granger guesses Lucas would have telephoned otherwise.

"We did. The place was filthy. The floor, the furniture, the worktops. Everything was coated with grime. How anyone can live like that . . ."

Granger isn't sure where this is going. Lucas is undoubtedly pleasant to look at but she hasn't got time to sit and chat about the potential pitfalls of an irregular cleaning routine.

"Apart from the fact that the kid hasn't been doing much housework, what have you found?"

Lucas smiles again. "We found blood on the floor in front of the sofa. Not much, because someone had given that area of the rug a good scrubbing, which is strange, considering the state of the rest of the place."

Granger has a sinking feeling in her chest. "This was fresh blood?"

"It was. I'd say no more than a day old. I checked the DNA database and a match popped up straight away."

Granger opens her mouth to ask her next question. She doesn't really want to hear the answer so she doesn't bother.

Lucas obliges anyway. "The blood match is Harry Cannon. No doubt about it."

CHAPTER 27

Kane stares across at Baxter. The psychotherapist stares back. Kane knows she wants him to speak first, to tell her what he wants to talk about, without being influenced by anything she might say.

He decides to make her wait a little longer. The hell with it. He's paying handsomely for these sessions. He can sit in silence for a while if he wants to.

Baxter shifts uncomfortably in her seat. She's close to caving in, Kane can see it in her eyes. It would be a petty victory but nevertheless sweet. He waits to the last second. Her chest rises as she takes a breath, and her lips part.

"I almost lost the plot while on duty yesterday. I panicked. Could hardly breathe. It was humiliating."

Baxter relaxes back in her chair. "What exactly happened?"

Kane would rather not go over it but he knows he can't afford to let it happen again. He's a leader. People depend on him. He can't let his team down. He can't betray the dead.

"Like I said, I panicked. I couldn't catch my breath. I couldn't think straight. At one point I thought I might faint."

Baxter takes a moment to consider her response. She clasps her hands together and rests them on her lap. "Can you tell me what it was that brought this on? What was the trigger?"

"I'd just been told that a witness to a crime I'm investigating has gone missing."

"Is this this the case we talked about before?"

Kane is regretting giving so much away last time. "It's the same case."

Baxter waits for Kane to say more. He doesn't. "This missing witness. Is there reason to believe that he, or she, is in danger?"

"I'm sorry. I don't think I should say any more about the case."

A flicker of disappointment crosses Baxter's face. She nods and moves on smoothly.

"Can you remember what you felt when you heard the news?"

There she goes again, Kane thinks. *The woman is obsessed with feelings. Feelings are the problem. Why doesn't she just prescribe me something that will stop me feeling? Then I'd be able to focus on doing my job.*

"I felt useless. Frightened that something bad would happen to the person who's gone missing because I've failed to do my job properly."

Baxter nods again, to show she understands. But Kane doubts that she does. Not truly.

"You feel you've let this person down?"

"I suppose so."

"The same way you feel you let down your wife?"

Kane shakes his head even though he knows Baxter is right. Everything comes back to Lizzy's murder. To his failure to warn her. His failure to catch her killer.

"Listen," he says. "I kind of understand what's going on. What I really want right now is for you to tell me how I can stop this kind of thing happening again. What I can do to keep my emotions under control, so I can do my job to the best of my ability."

Baxter smiles and Kane wonders why. "I'm glad you're finding this funny. Because I'm definitely not."

"That's not why I'm smiling. It's because I can see that this is working for you."

"I'm glad you think so. I'm not so sure."

"It is. Trust me. You talked about controlling your emotions just now, without any prompting from me. Part of your problem is that your emotions are controlling you. Emotions evolved because we needed them to survive. They motivate us to make decisions. Hopefully good ones."

Kane takes a moment to think. Sometimes Baxter makes a lot of sense. "What do I do?"

"You can keep doing this. Talking things through. When you feel a strong emotion threatening to overwhelm you, try to use it to your advantage. Direct it into positive action. I know that's easier said than done but that's how you have to approach this."

An image of Harry Cannon lying dead creeps into Kane's head. Blood trickles from the boy's mouth on to the rug. Kane shakes the thought away. He wonders what he'd do if the next time he sees Harry it's on a pathologist's slab. He'd have no choice but to take the blame. He'd have to accept what his critics have been saying all along.

CHAPTER 28

Jack Newman weaves his way through the commuters pouring out of the train station. Young and old, men and women, they all have one thing in common. They want to get home, eat, drink, relax and zone out.

Newman would have some sympathy for them if he wasn't heading to the top. If he didn't have the opportunity and the ability to carve out a brighter future, perhaps he'd be the same. All the years he's put into learning his trade, his dedication, his drive, has prepared him for this moment.

He steps off the pavement out of the chilly sea breeze into the cosy atmosphere of the Dolphin. The pub is one of Newman's favourite places to hang out. Its mock-Victorian grandeur always lifts his spirits.

The bar is busy, considering it's late afternoon. Across the room, he spots the delightful Detective Constable Bailey Granger sitting alone and looking pensive. He feels a stab of disappointment that Kane hasn't bothered to turn up.

At the bar he orders a beer and a small glass of white wine and carries them over to Granger. He sits and slides the wine across the table.

"What's that?"

"What does it look like?"

"I'm afraid I don't drink when I'm working." Her tone is professionally cordial, which Newman finds both amusing and grating.

"I can get you a soft drink."

"No thanks. You said you had something important to discuss."

Newman picks up his beer and takes a sip. He doesn't like the detective's tone. He's not being treated with the respect he deserves.

"Where's your boss? I was expecting to talk to him."

Granger smiles. He takes it as a peace offering. "Look, I'm sorry but we're rushed off our feet at the moment. Flat out. Detective Inspector Kane asked me to apologise for his absence but he couldn't make it. I'm sure you understand."

Newman understands that she's lying. Trying to smooth things over. She's pretty good at it, he'll give her that. There's no way Kane would send his apologies. He's not the type.

"The last time we spoke we agreed we should cooperate as much as possible. You said you wanted a good relationship with the local press."

"I did and I meant it. That's why I'm here."

"But Kane can't be bothered to show his face."

"It's not like that. He's leading a double murder investigation, he has—"

Newman holds up a hand to stop her. "All right, I get it. He's busy. You've already said. I'm busy too, you know. This is the biggest story of my career. It's my chance to make a name for myself."

Granger nods and smiles again. "I understand that. I do. Perhaps we should get down to business, then. What was it you wanted to talk about?"

Newman takes another sip of his drink. He's looking forward to seeing the detective's reaction.

"It's about that youth who's vanished. You know, the missing persons appeal you put out."

Granger sits up straight. "Harry Cannon, you mean?"

Newman has her full attention now and he's enjoying it. "Yes, that's the one."

"You know where Harry is?"

"No, I don't. But I do know why you're so desperate to find him. He's your murder witness, isn't he?"

Granger says nothing but stares at him for a few seconds. He can tell that beneath the calm exterior her mind is racing.

"You can't publish that," she says. "We'd ask you, officially, not to do that."

It's Newman's turn to smile. "You know you can't stop me writing the story, don't you? It would be a great scoop for my newspaper. *Fears Grow for Missing Murder Witness.* That would sell a lot of copies, generate a lot of clicks on our website."

Granger shakes her head. "You can't do that. Who told you Harry is our witness? This has never been released. Please, Jack, I really need you to cooperate on this. Making this information public could seriously put him at risk."

Newman nods thoughtfully. He wants to give her the impression that he's giving her plea serious consideration. Drag it out a little before putting her out of her misery.

"You know reporters never reveal their sources," he says. "Not the good ones, anyway. But listen, you don't have to worry. Seeing as you asked so nicely and in the spirit of our newly forged relationship, I'm not going to write this story. Not now. I'm expecting something back for this, though. Any developments in the hunt for this killer. I need to hear about them first."

"I'm sure we can sort something out. But we need to know who told you about Harry. We can't have leaks."

"No chance. Forget it."

"When I report back to Detective Inspector Kane, he's going to want to talk to you himself. He won't let this go."

Newman shrugs, picks up his beer and drains the glass. "He'll be wasting his valuable time. I know what I'm doing. I have good contacts, good sources in this town, and I'll never reveal their identities."

He stands up and heads for the door. Halfway across the room, his mobile vibrates. He stops, pulls it out and studies the screen. After a few moments, he turns and walks slowly back to Granger. He sits down and passes the phone across the table, his hand trembling.

"It's another one," he says. "From the killer. I've been sent another message."

CHAPTER 29

Kane walks into the interview room and holds out a hand. It takes a determined effort to keep it steady.

"I'll need to take your phone. We'll return it to you as soon as our tech team is done."

Newman gives a reluctant grimace as he passes the mobile over. "I gather you've had no luck tracing the first email the killer sent. Is this going to be any different?"

Kane stays silent as he slips the phone into a plastic evidence bag. He can't trust the reporter not to quote him.

Newman grins. "Don't worry. Everything is off the record, unless you say otherwise."

"Does that include this new message?"

Newman looks sideways at Granger, who's sitting next to him, her arms folded.

"You know it doesn't," he says. "I have to write this story. The killer sent that message to me because I'm the crime reporter on the local paper. I have a duty to publish it, every single word. We serve the community, and my newspaper's readers have the right to know what's going on. Don't you agree?"

Kane doesn't. Not if it's going to cause a wave of panic. The only reason the killer is sending these messages is to satisfy his out-of-control ego. He's relishing the notoriety, actively building his public image. And Newman isn't motivated by duty, or by the thought of serving the community. The man's clearly a glory hunter.

"You're telling me you don't care that by feeding the killer's hunger for publicity you're possibly encouraging him to kill again?"

"I didn't say that. You're putting words into my mouth. Can I go now? You've not even offered me a coffee and I have a lot of work to do to get this exclusive ready for tomorrow's newspaper."

Kane would love to be able to tell the reporter to get out of his sight. The problem is he needs him.

"I'm afraid I'm going to ask you to stay for a little while yet. I need to know how you found out that Harry Cannon is our murder witness."

Newman shakes his head and glances at Granger again. "I've already been through all this. I'll never reveal my sources. Nobody would ever trust me again. It's exactly like you guys and your underworld informants."

Kane finds it hard to fathom why anyone would trust a reporter like Newman in the first place. He guesses that being handed money helps.

Granger catches Kane's eye and he gives her an almost imperceptible nod. She stands up and turns to face Newman.

"It's obvious, isn't it?" she says. "Your contact has to be someone who works in this police station."

"I'm not saying anything."

"I'd suggest that your source has to be a police officer or a civilian police worker."

Newman sighs. "For God's sake. This is getting ridiculous. I know I'm not under arrest or suspected of any crime, but I've watched a lot of true crime documentaries and this is all you're ever going to get: no comment."

Granger pauses. Kane can tell she's choosing her words carefully.

"At least tell me you're not going to identify Harry as the witness. You said you wouldn't."

Newman holds up a forefinger and wags it. "That was before I got this email. The message refers specifically to your witness. Naming him will make the story even more amazing."

"But you promised you wouldn't."

"I didn't promise anything. I'm sorry but things have changed."

Kane has had enough. "You can go now," he says, heading for the door. "Thank you for your cooperation."

He walks down to the end of the corridor, enters his office and slams the door behind him. On his desk is a printout of the email the killer sent to Newman. Kane picks it up. He's already read it so many times he can recite it by memory. The words still chill his blood.

Death means nothing to me now. It is a game I play and, for me, killing is winning. I watch the news and see the police are losing. They say they will get me but that promise is empty. They say they have a witness. What use is a witness who can't talk?

Speak No Evil.

CHAPTER 30

Kane enters the makeshift incident room, where his team are already seated in front of a large whiteboard. Across the top are photographs of Ray Spencer, Banjo, Isabel Anderson and Harry Cannon.

Kane taps the Spencer mugshot with a forefinger. "He has a history of violence and we know he threatened to kill the first victim a few days before the body was found. That would normally make him a suspect in anybody's book. The problem is, he has no links at all to victim number two, and his girlfriend says he was at home in bed with her at the time our witness saw the killer on the beach."

He pauses, waiting for one of his team to comment. Granger opens her mouth to say something but stops herself. Finch and Miller stare blankly up at him from their seats.

Kane needs a moment of inspiration, a brilliant idea. He doesn't care who it comes from. Time is running out. Newman's new exclusive is whipping up a fresh media frenzy, with the killer's new message featuring on every national TV news bulletin, many of them even running interviews with the reporter himself.

"Anything from the amusement arcade footage yet?"

Finch shakes her head. "Nothing unusual so far. I'm about three hours from the end so I'm guessing the Spencer Banjo row will be somewhere on there."

"Where are we on Harry Cannon?"

"We're still drawing a blank," Granger answers. "Camera footage at the railway station has already been checked and he doesn't appear to have left on a train. We have uniformed officers checking empty properties in the town but there are a lot of them and it's going to take a while."

Kane wants to find Harry quickly. Find him and keep him safe.

"I'm thinking we should speak to the town's rough sleepers again. It's possible we've missed something about this Banjo character. Let's bring in Isabel Anderson's boyfriend and Ray Spencer too. See what they have to say for themselves."

Miller grunts and shifts in his seat.

"Is there something useful you want to contribute, Detective?"

Miller scowls. "Well, you say that Spencer has no links to Isabel Anderson but does there have to be? We all know these serial killer guys pick their victims at random. Maybe he just got the taste for it. You know, killing the homeless guy gave him some kind of thrill. Perhaps it triggered something inside and he decided he likes offing people for the fun of it."

Kane knows the detective has a point. He's seen it happen before. Most people are repulsed by violent death. A few individuals find it thrilling. They can become obsessed and intoxicated by it. Blood-drunk.

"Like I said, apart from the heat-of-the-moment threat, we have nothing on Spencer. No forensics, nothing. And he has an alibi. But we'll bring him in and squeeze a bit harder. See if we can get some juice."

Kane feels his phone vibrate and fishes it out of his pocket. "Get going," he says. "Let's make this a productive day."

He waits until the detectives have gone before he calls the number back. Detective Superintendent Helen Dean answers straight away.

She doesn't bother with small talk. "The shit has hit the fan. This is getting worse and worse. These messages are making us look completely ineffectual and the press are loving it. This killer is taunting you, Edison. He's making himself a celebrity and that's starting to reflect badly on me."

Kane pauses. For a split second he considers resigning from the case, from the force, from everything.

"I understand things don't look good at the moment," he says. "But I know it's going to turn our way soon. These messages tell me that the killer is getting far too confident and he's going to make a mistake soon."

"You're basing that on what exactly?"

"On years of investigating murders, catching killers and interviewing them."

Kane holds his breath as he waits for a response. He feels like a drowning man clinging on to a raft by his fingertips. Perhaps he should let go and slip under the water.

"Is that really the best you've got to offer me? 'Years of investigating'? What you really mean is you're basing this on gut instinct. A fucking feeling."

Kane winces on the inside at being called out. She's right, of course.

"I just need a little longer to turn this case around." He's trying not to plead. "We're close to the tipping point. If you replace me now, whoever takes over is going to benefit from the groundwork we've done so far. When the killer's caught, it's going to look like he or she made the difference. That can't be fair."

Dean falls silent. Kane can hear her calm and steady breathing as she takes time to think. He knows she's past caring what's fair and what's unfair. This moment will decide his future. Shape his life. Destroy him, or give him the chance to redeem himself. He won't blame her whatever she decides. He'll blame himself.

"You have one week," she says. "That's all I can give you. Seven days, then I'm going to have to pull you out, and it won't be discreetly. Do you understand?"

He understands perfectly. There's no way for him to avoid public humiliation.

"I do, and thank you. You won't regret it, I promise."

Dean terminates the call without another word. He guesses she started regretting her decision the second she made it.

Kane is still staring at his phone, wondering how he's going to deliver on his promise, when Granger bursts into the room.

"It's Spencer's girlfriend," she says, catching her breath. "She's downstairs. She says she has important information but she'll only speak to you, and only if we can guarantee her protection."

CHAPTER 31

"I'm a dead woman if he finds me now. Please, I need protection. He'll tear me apart."

Rina Kroll props her elbows on the table and rests her head in her hands. She's wearing grey sweatpants and a matching sweatshirt. Her make-up is smudged where she's been crying and the bruise on her face has darkened.

Kane edges his seat a fraction closer and ducks his head to catch her eye. "You're safe here. Tell me, what's happened?"

Rina lifts her head and her eyes widen as if she can't believe what she's done. "I've left him. Can't stay in that house any longer. He can't control his rages. They're getting worse."

Kane nods reassuringly. "Don't worry. I'll make sure you're not harmed. Has Ray Spencer threatened you?"

Rina lifts her head, tugs at her ponytail and studies the interview room's pale-blue walls. She spots a camera fixed high in one corner and takes a sharp breath.

"You're filming me? Why is this being filmed? Ray will see this. He has people, he will—"

Kane holds up a hand to silence her. They're not going to get anywhere unless she calms down. He glances at Granger and shrugs. She crosses the room, pulls up an empty chair and sits next to Kane.

"It's normal protocol for us to film interviews like this," she says. "It gives us an accurate record of what was said and protects everybody involved. The footage is securely stored."

Rina sniffs and wipes her nose with the sleeve of her sweatshirt. "But Ray has people inside. You don't understand."

"You're right," Granger says. "Why don't you help us understand?"

Rina sits up straight and glances nervously at the camera again. "Well, you see, it's about Ray's alibi. You know, the night that boy saw the killer on the beach."

"You swore that Spencer was in bed with you," Kane says.

Rina raises a hand and pulls her ponytail again. "I lied. He made me. There was no choice. I'm sorry. He left the house at close to 10 p.m., I think, and I didn't see him again until he walked into the café at lunchtime."

Kane turns to Granger. Her expression is calm and professional. He wonders if her pulse is pounding as fast as his.

He turns again and looks across at Rina. "Do you think Spencer killed Banjo?"

"I don't know. It's possible. Sometimes when he loses his mind, his anger is terrible to see. You need to protect me. Until I can go back to Poland."

"And why would he cut out his eyes?"

"I don't know. Sometimes there's no logic to the things he does. When we first met, I thought he was a strong man. But he is cruel. No, worse than that. He is a savage man."

Kane is desperate to believe that they have found the killer. "But would he kill and horribly mutilate someone for stealing a few pounds?"

Rina looks quickly up at the camera then bows her head and stares at the tabletop, hiding her face from the lens.

"Ray was not angry with Banjo for stealing money. It was something different. Something to do with stolen mobile phones. I don't know anything else. I only run the café. I'm not a criminal. The café and the phone shop, they are legitimate. But Ray buys stolen phones, mostly from gangs in London. It's big, big money. That's all I know. I swear."

She covers her face with her hands and sobs, her shoulders heaving. Kane waits for her to stop. When she lifts her head, he takes a clean tissue from his jacket and hands it to her.

"You've done the right thing," he says. "We'll need to speak to you again soon but I'll get someone to find you a safe place to stay."

Rina rubs her eyes with the back of a hand. "What are you going to do? I'm scared."

"We're going to arrest Ray Spencer. Then we're going to search his premises. Don't worry. We won't let him anywhere near you."

CHAPTER 32

Granger walks into Ray Spencer's gym. Like every other room in the house, it looks like it's been bombed. The security camera monitors have been smashed, glass fragments scattered across the floor.

The mirrored wall has two large cracks, shaped like lightning bolts, running from ceiling to floor. In one corner, several dumbbells lie entangled in a heap, beneath an upturned padded bench.

Kane enters the room, turns the bench over and sits down. He has dark patches under his eyes and it's still only mid-morning.

"Spencer definitely has an anger management problem," he says.

Granger can't imagine what would motivate Spencer to waste valuable time wrecking his own house when he knows the police are coming for him. For a few seconds she wonders why Rina stayed with him for so long. Then she stops wondering. The man is unpredictable and dangerous.

"No sign of him anywhere?"

Kane shakes his head. "He's not at the café or the phone shop. He clearly knew that Rina was going to come to us.

He'd pushed her to her limit. People like him, they have an instinct about the right time to run."

Kane stands up and walks over to the cracked mirrors, stares at his distorted reflection and rubs his chin. "Even my stubble's going grey."

He sounds downbeat, the excitement generated by Rina's revelation already fading. Granger walks across the room and stands beside him. "We'll get him. We'll find him soon." She hopes she's right. Rina will never feel safe until Spencer is behind bars.

A uniformed constable pops his head through the doorway. "We've got a bunch of journalists gathering outside," he says. "Reporters and photographers. They want to come inside."

Granger walks over to the officer. He's tall and baby-faced. "What's your name?"

He beams at her. "Dev Khan."

"Right then, Constable Khan, I want you to go back downstairs and tell the press that this house is officially a crime scene and anyone crossing the threshold will be arrested."

"You got it," the constable says and hurries back downstairs.

Granger turns back to Kane. "Do you want me to go and deal with the jackals? Throw them some meat to keep them happy?"

Kane shakes his head. "I don't want to give them any details yet. Right now, I want to take a look at the outbuilding around the back."

He leads the way downstairs, along the hall and through the kitchen. They have to watch their step. The floor is covered with shattered crockery, cutlery and smashed wine glasses.

The garden is a wide, lawned rectangle. The flat-roofed concrete outbuilding is set against a rear red-brick wall. Granger peers through one of the building's three tiny square windows. It's too dark to see anything clearly.

"Is there anybody in there?" Kane asks.

Granger shrugs. "Can't see a thing."

Kane approaches the side door and impatiently eyes the lock. Granger guesses he's wondering whether Harry Cannon is inside.

"I think we should wait," she says. "We can get one of the uniforms to bring us a crowbar and jemmy the door open for us."

Kane takes half a step back and eyes the lock again. "I want to get inside now. We don't need to wait."

He swings his right foot up and forward, hitting the door just above the lock and close to the frame. The wood splinters but the lock holds. Without hesitating, he repeats the move and this time the door crashes open.

Granger follows him inside, sniffing the damp air as she goes. She detects a mixture of oil and mould, but no hint of dead body. The sickly sweet smell of decaying flesh is instantly recognisable and hard to forget.

As her eyes gradually adapt to the lack of light, she spots half a dozen large plywood boxes stacked haphazardly against the back wall. Kane pulls the lid off one of them and lets it slide to the floor. He peels away a sheet of soft foam to reveal mobile phones laid side by side on a polystyrene tray. The first of several layers.

"Stolen mobiles. Hundreds of them. I suspect there's more of the same in the storeroom at the phone shop and probably the café."

Granger nods but doesn't respond. Kane gives her a long look and she can tell he's as disappointed as she is. They're not interested in stolen phones.

The detectives retrace their steps through the kitchen, along the corridor, then step out through the front door into the spring sunshine. The reporters and photographers are still there, milling around on the pavement, most of them speaking or texting on their phones.

When they notice Kane and Granger, they surge forward, firing off a barrage of questions, not waiting for answers. Kane holds up a hand until they fall silent.

"Our media office will be issuing an official statement later today. That's all I can say." The reporters emit a collective groan and the huddle parts reluctantly to let the detectives move on. They take a couple of steps toward their car, when a figure blocks their way.

Jack Newman grins. "Is it true that a warrant is out for the arrest of local businessman Ray Spencer in connection with the murders? Is Spencer on the run? When will the public be able to feel safe in their own homes?"

Kane glares at Newman, his lips tight, eyes narrowed. Granger knows him well enough now to spot the warning signs.

She edges forward and turns her body slightly, putting herself in the space between Kane and the reporter. "Please, Jack. We're not ready to release any details yet. As soon as we are you'll be the first to know, I promise."

"All right, then. Seeing as you asked so nicely."

Newman steps aside and Granger leads Kane quickly back to the car. They climb inside and Granger starts the engine.

"That man is so fucking infuriating," Kane says. "He thinks the sun shines out of his arsehole."

"He's just doing his job, I suppose. You can't blame him for that." Granger regrets the words as soon as they have left her mouth.

"We're all doing our jobs. The problem is he acts like he's God's gift to journalism, like he's a Pulitzer Prize winner. And why the hell did you say please? We're murder detectives. We don't need to waste our breath saying please to reporters."

Granger decides it's best not to answer. Silence can be calming. She checks over her shoulder for traffic, ready to pull out. Her mobile buzzes and she studies the screen. She frowns and switches the engine off.

"It's a text from Finch. She says she's sending me a video and she insists it's urgent." The phone buzzes again and Granger opens the video file. She watches for a few seconds then turns to Kane.

"It's a short piece of footage from the amusement arcade security camera. You need to take a look."

Kane leans across and Granger presses the play arrow. The camera zooms in for a close up of the front of Ray Spencer's café. The door flies open and Spencer stalks out, his right arm around a man's neck. Spencer throws him to the floor, kicks him in the stomach and shouts something at him.

After a few seconds, Spencer stands back, his hands on his hips, and watches his victim stumble away along the promenade toward the pier. Another man steps out of the café entrance. Detective Constable Sam Miller grins as he gives Spencer a flamboyant high five.

CHAPTER 33

Ray Spencer pulls the peak of his baseball cap down over his face and sips his coffee. He scans the faces of the people streaming along the promenade, happy parents, smiling children, most of them heading for the pier. Mugs the lot of them. Law-abiding rule followers. Sheep.

That life was never for him. When he started his business, he became Mr Respectable, a local celebrity, a role model for offenders looking to go straight. He conned the lot of them. People who overestimate their own intelligence are often easier to fool than people who know they're dumb.

It was all going so well until that homeless bastard got greedy. The plan was to lie low. Then Rina betrayed him, the bitch. He drains his cup of coffee, crushes the cardboard cup and tosses it into a bin. The game is up. He knows it. But he's not finished yet. The bitch must pay.

He starts walking toward the pier, his head down. He's unshaven and he needs a change of clothes. The owner of the B&B Spencer stayed in last night looked suspicious when he pulled a wad of cash from his pocket to settle his bill. He'll have to find somewhere else to stay tonight.

He hasn't got long. Someone is going to recognise him soon. If he were to leave town, hide out among the teeming hordes of London, he'd have a chance to stay free. For a while at least.

That's not the plan. He doesn't care about his future. There is only one thing on his mind: revenge. The bitch Rina will get what's coming to her. She claims he scares her. Well, that didn't stop her moving into his big house, driving his fancy cars and sleeping in his bed, did it?

He warned her what would happen if she betrayed his trust. She has it coming.

Spencer catches a waft of hot dogs and burnt burgers as he passes the entrance to the pier. The smell triggers a pang of hunger but he ignores it. He hasn't time to eat. He slows his pace as he nears his café. The police have been and gone, leaving crime scene tape sealing off the outside tables and front door.

He descends a set of concrete steps leading down to the beach and sits with his back to the sea wall. He has a good view of the back of his café and the door leading to the kitchens. When she comes, she'll use the back door. She has a key. He's certain she'll come because she'll need money and knows where he stashes it. The police would never find it unless they pulled the place apart.

He'll watch and wait, until it's too dark to see. Then he'll return tomorrow. It's only a matter of time. She won't be able to resist.

When it's done, he'll be done. The police can do what they want with him. Shoot him fucking dead, for all he cares. Whatever happens, there's no way he's going back to prison.

CHAPTER 34

Kane looks at the other two police detectives sitting in the room. They are both wearing grave expressions. One of them is going to prison for a long time.

"Do you want me to delay this interview until we can arrange for you to have a lawyer present?"

Detective Constable Sam Miller shrugs and grunts. "What's the point?"

Kane exchanges glances with Granger. "You don't deny that you have been taking bribes from local businessman and suspected stolen mobile phone exporter Ray Spencer."

Miller shrugs again. "There's no point, is there? I want it officially noted that I'm cooperating fully here. I want to make up for what I've done because I'm sorry and ashamed."

Kane doesn't believe a word of it. This is all about damage control. All judges take a guilty plea and shows of remorse into account when deciding on length of sentence. Miller could slow the whole process down if he decided to deny everything, but he knows they have all the proof they need.

"You've got access to my bank accounts," Miller says. "I am aware how this works, you know. How can I explain all that money away? Well, I can't, can I? I'm well and truly done for and I know it. What I don't understand is why you two are bothering with this. I thought I'd be passed straight on to Professional Standards."

He's right. Kane has no real interest in the fact that Miller is a bent copper. Or that Ray Spencer was exporting stolen mobile phones. What he's desperate to know is whether they are connected to the murders of Banjo and Isabel Anderson and the disappearance of Harry Cannon.

"You'll be questioned by anti-corruption officers as soon as we're finished with you," he says. He sits back in his chair and waits for Granger to step in.

"How was Spencer getting his supply of stolen phones?"

Miller looks up at Granger, surprised to hear her voice. "He's a clever bastard, he is. Totally crazy but far from stupid. He buys the phones from gangs in London. Kids mainly. They roam the streets, some on mopeds and scooters, snatching mobiles. Others steal them in bars and clubs. He pays them a pittance really. They're probably stealing two to three hundred every day."

Granger pulls out a notebook, puts it on the table and scribbles something down. Miller gives loud a snort of derision.

"What they hell are you doing? Nobody uses those things anymore. That's what your force smartphone is for. Anyway, this interview is being filmed and recorded, isn't it?"

Granger leans forward and makes another note. "It helps me think."

Miller shakes his head. "Knock yourself out."

"What does Spencer do with the phones?" Granger asks.

"They're shipped out to Eastern Europe. Romania, I think. He's got technical guys there who strip what personal and financial details they can. After that they're exported to Africa and India, where they can be sold as second-hand phones. There's a massive market for them. Spencer's making a mint."

"And you wanted a share of it."

Miller smirks. "That's true. And I didn't have to do much for it. I was Spencer's pet policeman. I just threw my weight around a bit. Spencer knew that once word spread on the streets that he had me in his pocket then nobody would even think about messing with him."

Granger glances at Kane. It's clear she's disgusted by what she's hearing. Kane guesses it's the first time she's come across a corrupt fellow officer.

"Why throw away your career for a bit of extra cash?"

"It wasn't just the cash. You'll have seen the figures. It was a lot more than pocket money. But that wasn't the only attraction. It's exciting. A kick. Breaking the rules. Being on the other side of the law. Dealing with petty thieves and burglars, day after day, was getting so fucking boring."

Kane has had enough of listening to Miller trying to justify his crimes. There's only one thing worse than a corrupt policeman, and that's a killer policeman.

"Were you involved in the murder of the homeless man known as Banjo?"

Miller flinches, as if he's been slapped. "What the hell are you talking about?"

"Answer the question."

"No. No, I wasn't. What's going on?"

"Where were on the night of March 20?"

"This is ridiculous. I was at home all night. Watched a film. Drank some beer and fell asleep."

"On your own?"

"Yes, I was alone. If you think I'm your killer then you're insane."

Kane pauses. He believes Miller is capable of murder. He has the traits of a hot-blooded killer, someone who could lose control, snap and beat someone to death. The lives of Banjo and Isabel Anderson were taken by a cold-blooded creature. A person who can meticulously plan a murder, then kill and mutilate without hesitation or mercy.

"We have video footage of you high-fiving Ray Spencer after he assaulted and threatened to kill Banjo outside his café. We also know that Banjo didn't steal money from the café."

Miller shakes his head furiously. "No, no, no. You've got this all wrong. Spencer threatens to kill someone almost every week. I reckon he's capable of doing it too, in one of his rages. But even he wouldn't do that. Not the eyes. He's not capable. You'd have to have ice in your veins to do that. And why would he kill that girl jogger? It doesn't make sense."

Kane agrees. He wishes he didn't. It would nice and neat for Spencer to be the killer. He thinks it's a shame that Miller turned out to be dishonest because he has the instincts of a good detective.

"Why did Spencer throw Banjo out of the café and threaten to kill him?"

Miller lets out a long sigh. "It was about the phones. Spencer always wanted more phones, more profit, the greedy bastard. He wanted to set up his own gangs here, in Southend, and other towns in Essex. He put the word around to recruit local villains, including some of the homeless crowd who were eating for nothing at his café. That was a mistake. That Banjo guy was a troublemaker. He thought it'd be a good idea to blackmail Spencer. Said he'd expose him. Go to the press if he didn't pay up. I don't know who killed him. But they did us a favour."

It all makes twisted sense to Kane. Even the threat to go to the press. Banjo probably thought that if Spencer has a local detective working for him then he'd be wasting his time going to the police.

Kane turns to Granger and gives her a nod.

"Where's Harry Cannon?" she asks.

"How should I know? Down some rathole probably."

"When you walked into that interview room he looked terrified. He clammed up. Wouldn't say anything."

"If you say so. I didn't notice anything. But I was the one who arrested him for his beach hut break-ins and got him convicted. I don't suppose I'm his favourite person."

"When did you last see Harry Cannon?"

Miller frowns. "That would have been that time in the interview room when I brought him pizza. I haven't seen the little ratbag since. You can't believe a word he says. He's a natural born liar, that kid. I know he's your big witness but I hope you don't have to rely on him. A jury will see right through him."

Granger stands up and walks out of the room. Miller looks quizzically at Kane, who says nothing. They sit in silence for a few minutes until Granger returns carrying a jacket on a hanger wrapped in see-through plastic.

"Do you recognise this?" she asks.

Miller peers at it through the plastic. "It looks like a jacket."

"When we searched your flat, we found this in the wardrobe in your bedroom."

"I guess it's mine, then."

"We also found some specks of blood on it. On one of the sleeves. Not a lot of blood, but you know we don't need much, don't you?"

"I don't understand where you're going with this."

Granger hands the jacket to Kane, who lays it carefully on the table in front of Miller. "We had the blood analysed and it matches bloodstains we found on the carpet in Harry Cannon's flat. It's Harry Cannon's blood."

Miller drops his head into his hands and massages his temples. "Fuck it."

CHAPTER 35

Sitting in the darkness, Spencer shivers. The breeze coming off the sea with the incoming tide is chilly. He estimates he has no more than thirty minutes before the waves engulf the beach. He checks the time on his phone. It's almost 10 p.m.

Switching his mobile off would make it more difficult for the police to track it but he can't be bothered. All he needs is enough time to make the bitch suffer. He decides to give himself another ten minutes watching the back of his café.

If Rina doesn't show today, she'll definitely turn up tomorrow. The cash is too much of a lure. She won't dare risk leaving it too long in case someone else finds it. Her greed will be her undoing. He knows now that the only reason she was with him was because of his money. He gave her a lifestyle she could only dream of when she lived in her Warsaw hovel.

The beach has been deserted since the sun set, apart from a track-suited woman who jogged past without a glance, her mongrel yapping at her heels. Spencer stands up and stretches his back. Time to find somewhere to spend the night. He's about to head to the steps to the promenade when he hears the crunch of footsteps on gravel.

Straining his eyes, he can make out a figure approaching the back of the café, edging along the sea wall. He lies flat on the ground to keep out of sight. His heart thumps. It's her. The police have no idea. They probably think she's cowering gratefully in the supposedly safe accommodation they moved her to. He knew all along that the avaricious bitch could never resist the pull of easy money.

Rina is closer now. She's wearing a short, hooded jacket, jeans and the £1,000 silver-and-white trainers he bought her last week for her birthday. The rage that's been simmering inside him all day starts to boil. He scans the beach quickly and grins when he spots a pile of driftwood and a ring of large stones where someone has tried to build a fire.

He watches her creep up the wooden steps to the café, use her key to open the back door and step into the kitchen area. He knows how her tricky little mind works. She'll head straight for the cash hidden in a hole in the plaster behind the industrial dishwasher. Money to finance a fresh start, far away from Southend. A new life, without him. He won't let that happen.

He runs to the circle of stones and selects a piece of wood the size and shape of a child's cricket bat. The thinner part fits snuggly in his hand and he waves it around, feeling the weight as he waits for Rina to come back out into the darkness.

"Perfect," he whispers.

CHAPTER 36

Kane studies Miller as a bearded police constable escorts him back to his seat in the interview room. He still has a swagger in his step and is wearing a weary smile. Kane can't imagine why he finds any of this the slightest bit funny.

Miller wipes his lips with the back of his hand. "My mouth is dry. Could I have a coffee, or some water?"

Granger looks to Kane, who shakes his head. "You've just had a twenty-minute break. You could have asked for a drink in your cell."

"I was trying to sleep. It's late. Way past my bedtime."

Kane wonders whether Miller was born a smart-arse or whether he's had to put in a lot of work to get to this level.

"We were talking about Harry Cannon. Why is his blood on your jacket?"

"I didn't intend to hurt him. I meant to frighten him, that's all."

"Why would you want to do that?"

"To warn him to keep his mouth shut. To zip it."

"About the mobile phones?"

Miller nods. "He knew what Spencer was trying to do. We wanted the kid to run one of the new gangs. He'd steal mobiles every now and then, when he wasn't robbing beach huts. He was good at it too."

"But he refused?"

"He did. Claimed he was going straight. When I heard he was your murder witness, I panicked. Thought he might start mouthing off about me and Spencer."

Kane pauses to think. No wonder Harry clammed up when he saw Miller at the police station. He knew what was coming his way.

"You went to his flat and roughed him up."

Miller gives Granger a sheepish look. "I did. To warn him. Not hurt him. He started getting aggressive with me and I had to put him in a chokehold. He wouldn't keep still and I had to choke him harder than I meant to, then he blacked out. I let go and he fell to the floor. He broke his nose, I think, because it was bleeding. He seemed to be breathing but I put him in the recovery position just in case."

Kane glances at Granger. She looks as sick as he feels. He can't believe that this sorry excuse for a detective is expecting a pat on the back for putting a kid he choked out into the recovery position.

"Spencer wanted him silenced and you ran off and left him for dead."

Miller screws up his face to show his feelings have been hurt. "I wanted to frighten him, no more than that."

"Where is Harry now?"

Miller throws up his hands and shrugs. "How would I know? Last time I saw him he was out cold on the floor in his flat."

Kane looks up at the bearded uniform standing with his back to the door and beckons him over. "Get him out of my sight," he says. The constable crosses the room and waits for Miller to rise from his seat before marching him back to his cell.

When they're gone, Granger stands up and slips her notebook into her pocket. "Do you think he's telling the truth?"

Kane shifts his chair around to face her. "Most of it sounds true. Not everything. The story about Harry worries me. Spencer wanted him silenced and it's possible Miller did exactly that and then disposed of the body. It's almost impossible to prove murder without a body."

CHAPTER 37

Jack Newman bounces out of bed, brushes his teeth and dresses quickly. No time for a shower this morning. This is a momentous day. A day he'd always hoped for but never thought would come.

He smiles to himself as he imagines the look on Dawn Brady's face when he tells her. It's taken his news editor a while to realise how lucky she is to have joined a newspaper with a ready-made star reporter on its staff. Now, just when she's come round to appreciating his talent and has stopped treating him like a novice, he's going to tell her where she can stick the job.

His plan is to get into the office early, announce to Dawn Brady in the middle of the crowded newsroom that he's off to London to cover crime for the newspaper of his dreams, then celebrate with a slap-up breakfast at the posh new hotel near the pier. He can afford it now.

He couldn't believe what was happening when the editor of the *Daily News* called and virtually begged him to join his newspaper. Made him an offer he couldn't refuse. Twice the salary and twice the glory. It's all he ever wanted.

He takes a moment to check himself in the mirror, adjusting the collar of his white shirt and dusting flecks of fluff off of the lapels of his black jacket. Very smart, if he says so himself. He'll need a whole new wardrobe when he's up in the big city, of course. Image is important when you're mixing with the big boys and girls.

Newman leaves the flat, stepping into the fresh morning sunshine, and heads downhill toward the seafront. He has a sudden urge to stop everyone he sees and tell them his good news, but then they wouldn't understand.

He passes a young woman in a smart trouser suit carrying an expensive-looking briefcase and flashes her his warmest smile. She blanks him. How ignorant. If only she knew who he was, what he's done and has yet to achieve. If only.

His new status means he'll probably be even more popular with women than he is already. He'll have to show restraint, not get distracted. It's important that he puts all his energy into his new role. There's no way he's going ruin all his hard work.

At the end of the road, he crosses on to the promenade and heads west. He's decided to take the scenic route to the office. It'll add at least ten minutes to his journey. Who gives a damn? What's Brady going to do, sack him? Walking along the seafront, breathing in the salty air, is one of the few things he'll miss when he's gone.

As is the way of the world, when you're successful, some of your colleagues will be envious. Most of them, probably. Whatever they think, nobody at the *Herald* will be able to deny that he deserves this new job. Everyone agrees that his coverage of the See No Evil, Hear No Evil murders has been nothing short of exceptional. It's even made him a bit of a celebrity in his own right.

The seafront is quiet. It's still early and it's a school day. Passing the manicured greenery of Cliff Gardens, Newman notices a flurry of activity in the distance, close to the Shingles Café — people milling around and several cars parked on the promenade.

His reporter's instinct kicks in and he increases his pace. As he nears the spot, he notices two police constables guarding the access down to the beach.

A third uniformed officer is busy running crime scene tape from the sea wall to the promenade railings, sealing off a large area. Newman fishes his press card from his pocket and waves it until he catches the police constable's eye.

"I'm Jack Newman, the *Herald*'s crime reporter. I need you to tell me what's going on."

The policeman pulls another stretch of tape across the promenade and wraps around an ornate lamppost. "Please stay outside of the tape, sir," he says. "This is a protected area."

"But I'm a reporter. What is happening here?"

The police officer shakes his head slowly and walks away. Newman knew he was unlikely to get anything out of him but it's always worth asking. What's the worst that could happen?

A white van pulls up and parks at an angle in front of the café. A man and a woman climb out, open the back door and pull hooded crime scene suits over their clothes. They duck under the tape and slip shoe covers and masks on before descending the steps.

Newman runs over to the sea wall, hoists himself up and peers down at the beach. The police have already put up a small white tent on the shingle. The two forensic officers head straight for it, push the flap aside and step inside.

Newman remembers the first time he was assigned to cover a local murder. A drunken day-tripper stabbed someone for flirting with his girlfriend. It was the sight of the crime scene tent in the middle of the street that set his heart racing. All these years on, it's still a big thrill. The tent sits halfway between the back of the café and the lapping waves. The forensic team will have to work flat out to get their work done before the tide sweeps in.

He calls Dawn Brady. She answers straight away. "Where are you, Jack? You're meant to be in the office for our editorial meeting."

Newman considers telling her there and then that he's leaving her local rag but he wants the satisfaction of seeing her face drop when he does it.

"Never mind the meeting," he says. "I'm on the seafront near the Shingles Café and I need you to send a snapper down here as quickly as you can. We've got another murder to write about."

CHAPTER 38

Kane and Granger don't say a word to each other during the ten-minute drive from the police station to the Shingles Café. Granger breaks the silence while they're putting on their forensic suits.

"How much do we know?" she asks.

Kane gives her a blank stare. "Not much. We have a dead body found on the beach by a schoolteacher out for a jog before work. According to the police constable who was first on the scene, it's a violent death."

They walk toward the cordoned area and Kane pushes the tape down for Granger to step over. Before he can follow, he feels a light tap on his shoulder.

"You took your time," Newman says with a grin.

Kane glares at him. He shouldn't let the reporter get under his skin but the man has a gift for it. "You again," he says. "You're always hanging around, like a bad smell."

Newman feigns offence. "That's a bit harsh. I'm just doing my job. Maybe you should start doing yours, Inspector?"

Kane twists away and follows Granger to the steps and down to the beach. They walk side by side toward the white tent. The sea is calm and freakishly blue. A rippling mirror reflecting the cloudless sky.

At the entrance to the tent, Kane acknowledges the uniform on guard with a nod. Granger pulls back the flap and stoops to go inside. Kane touches her gently on the forearm to stop her.

"If this is victim number three, the tongue is going to be cut out and I'm well and truly gone. Out of here. Off the case. Finished."

Granger straightens up. "You don't know that for sure."

"Yes, I do. Dean has already given me a final warning. I'm supposed to have the case sewn up. Instead, I'm checking out another corpse on the beach."

Granger shrugs. "This hasn't been a straightforward case. If Superintendent Dean asks me, I'll tell her you're doing everything possible."

"Thanks, but I doubt she'll be seeking your opinion."

Kane enters the tent and Granger follows. The body is lying face down in the shingle. The back of the skull is a sticky mass of tangled hair and blood. He looks at Granger. Her eyes are moist as she nods agreement.

A bead of sweat runs down the back of Kane's neck. He's lost count of the number of dead bodies he's seen over the years, but it's different when you know the victim.

One of the forensic officers is on his knees, studying the woman's right hand. The other is tapping information into a smart tablet and Kane recognises her.

Obi Musa, the local crime scene manager, looks up from the screen and acknowledges the detectives with a businesslike "Good morning."

Kane wants to insist that it's a terrible morning. He forces himself to look down at the body again. The blood in the hair and staining the shingle around the head hasn't fully dried.

"Can you give me an estimated time of death?"

Musa shuts her tablets. "I'm sure you can see for yourself that it's not been long. The pathologist is on his way. He'll give you the definitive answer. If I had to guess I'd say eight to twelve hours."

Kane feels claustrophobic in the small tent. He tugs at the collar of his shirt and loosens his tie.

"Blunt trauma to the head," Musa continues. "Beaten repeatedly until the skull caved in. There are what look like defence wounds on the hands. There is one strange thing. Look, her shoes have been taken."

Kane wants to get out of the tent and breathe in some fresh air, but there's one question he needs to ask before he can leave.

"Are there any signs of facial mutilation. Is her tongue still intact?"

Musa open her tablet and starts tapping away again. "Your guess is good as mine. We can't touch or move the body until Martin Carter gets here, and even then, he won't be able to tell you that until he does the autopsy."

Kane and Granger hurry out of the tent. When they reach the stairs to the promenade, Kane stops and sits on the bottom step and stares out to sea. Granger hesitates, then sits beside him.

"She was supposed to be in hiding, in safe accommodation," Kane says.

"She was taken to a refuge last night. She would have been safe if she'd stayed put. She knew Spencer was out to get her. She told us he'd kill her. What was she doing coming back here?"

Kane doesn't know the answer. He's asking himself what he could have done to have prevented her death. If he'd locked her in a holding cell for a couple of days, she'd still be alive. Perhaps he should have sent a uniform to watch over her at the refuge. The only thing he can do for her now is find Spencer.

"We need to put officers at the railway station and the airport. We also need to alert the Coastguard to keep an eye out for a boat taking him over to France."

He turns to face Granger. He can see she feels as sick as he does. He wants to say something to make her feel better but he can't find the words.

"Are you all right?" she asks.

"No, I'm not."

"It isn't your fault."

Back on the promenade, a small crowd of murmuring onlookers has gathered around the cordon, hoping for free entertainment. Newman is among them, with a blonde wearing jeans and a leather jacket and brandishing a camera. The reporter points to Kane and Granger and the photographer starts taking pictures.

"Ignore them," Kane says. "Not a word."

They hurry to the car and pull off their forensic suits, keen to get away from Newman and his snapper. With the image of Rina Krol's bludgeoned body still fresh in his mind, Kane doesn't trust himself to stay calm.

He gets into the car and slams the passenger door shut, with seconds to spare. Newman raps his knuckles on the window.

"Is this a third victim? Have you identified the body and has the tongue been cut out?" He presses his face close to the glass and shouts again. "Will you be taking responsibility for your failure and stepping down?"

Kane clenches his jaw, unclips his seatbelt and grabs the door handle. Granger reaches across, gripping his wrist.

"Take a deep breath," she says. "You told me to ignore him."

Kane sits back in the seat and fastens his seatbelt, silently giving thanks that Granger is with him. A police siren screams in the near distance. Kane's mobile rings and he snatches it out of his pocket.

"We've got a report of a sighting of Spencer," says Detective Constable Finch.

CHAPTER 39

Ray Spencer strides along the wooden walkway running parallel to the pier train track. He feels more content than he has for a long time. Whoever it was who said revenge is sweet was one smart bastard.

Up ahead, he can see the Lifeboat Station and a dozen or so people sitting at tables outside the tearoom — drinking, eating and enjoying the sunshine.

He has no idea what he's going to do. He only knows that he's not going to run. There's no point. His face is bound to be plastered all over the newspapers and featured on every TV news bulletin. He has nowhere to hide.

When he reaches the end of the pier, Spencer walks straight to the railings and stares down at the sea. The water, glistening in the sunlight, looks strangely peaceful.

He hears voices murmuring behind him and turns around. A group of grey-haired pensioners sitting outside the tearoom are abandoning their table, throwing him nervous glances as they shuffle off.

Spencer puts the plastic shopping bag he's carrying on the floor and looks down at himself. His jeans and T-shirt are spattered with blood.

The pier train stops at the terminal, the doors slide open and four uniformed police officers jump out, followed by two plain-clothes officers. Spencer recognises them straight away. Kane and Granger walk slowly toward him, while the uniformed officers lead startled members of the public and tearoom staff into the train carriages, ready for evacuation.

Spencer sighs. He wishes he could lie down, close his eyes and make all this go away. He didn't get a wink of sleep last night. Killing is such an adrenaline rush.

He holds up a hand. The detectives stop.

"Don't come any closer, or I'll jump."

CHAPTER 40

"Stay right here," Kane tells Granger and takes two steps forward. Spencer is about thirty feet away, his back pressed against the railings. Behind him the sea stretches to a hazy horizon.

"I told you to keep back!" Spencer shouts. "I mean it!" Kane can see that his clothes are flecked with blood. Blood that only hours ago flowed through Rina Krol's veins.

Kane considers rushing him. Why should he care if Spencer falls? Instead, he takes a step back. "All right, I hear you. But an armed response unit is on its way. They won't give you a choice. They tend to shoot first and ask questions later."

Spencer laughs but there's no humour in the sound. "What choice have I got? A bullet in the brain or a slow death in a prison cell. Which would you choose?"

Kane can't believe the man is feeling sorry for himself, fishing for sympathy. "Why kill her? She didn't deserve to die like that."

"Oh, but she did. She really did." Spencer bends down and pulls a pair of white-and-silver trainers from the shopping bag and hurls them over the railings. "I rescued her from the gutter, gave her everything she wanted and, in the end, she betrayed me. Then she tried to steal from me."

He grabs the bag and tips it upside down. Several thick wads of cash fall on to the floor.

He kicks them under the railings into the sea.

Kane recalls the fear in Rina's eyes when she came to the station to tell them about Spencer's mobile phone gangs and how he forced her to give him an alibi for the night that Banjo was killed. In his book, she was a courageous woman.

"Did you murder Banjo? Did you kill Isabel Anderson?"

Spencer puts both hands back and hoists himself up until he's sitting on the top of the railings. He takes a nervous look down at the swirling water, sweat popping on his forehead.

"That cheating bastard Banjo tried to blackmail me. Said he'd go to the newspapers if I didn't pay him £5,000. He was going to ruin everything I'd built. I'm glad he got what was coming to him."

Spencer looks up, startled by the *whoop-whoop-whoop* of a police helicopter. The movement tips him off balance but he manages to stop himself falling.

"Wow, you called a chopper out for me. I'm flattered. I'm starting to feel like I'm in one of those big cop movies."

Kane edges forward while Spencer is distracted. He's near enough to take a run at him but he hesitates. There's a risk his momentum could take them both over.

"The armed officers will be here any minute. Why don't you give yourself up? Tell us everything. Get it all off of your chest."

Spencer looks him right in the eye. "I'm bored with this cesspool."

He lets go of the railing and leans back.

CHAPTER 41

Bailey Granger unlocks her front door and steps inside. It's the first time in two weeks that she's been home before dark.

She takes off her jacket, drapes it on the back of the sofa and goes straight upstairs. In the bathroom, her mother is drying Daisy with a towel and the little girl is giggling because it tickles.

"Look who's here," her mother says, lifting the child up and placing her gently into Granger's arms.

"Hello, gorgeous, Mummy's going to put you to bed tonight. Won't that be fun?"

Daisy rests her damp head on Granger's shoulder and squeezes tight. "Can I have two books tonight, Mummy? Two stories, please?"

Granger hugs her daughter close, her heart swelling with joy. "Let's get your pyjamas on, then," she says. "Which ones do you want? Your unicorn ones or the dinosaur ones?"

Three stories and thirty minutes later, Granger is standing in the dark next to Daisy's bed, watching her sleep the sleep of the innocent and wondering what she's done to deserve to be so blessed.

It's at times like this that the doubts creep in. Should she be doing a job that means she's rarely home before Daisy's bedtime? Police work has its dangers. Seven hours ago, she came face to face with a killer and watched him throw himself off the pier. If anything were to happen to her, how would her daughter cope?

Granger pushes those thoughts away and creeps out of the room. She's pursuing a career she loves, and that can only be a good choice. She wants to show her daughter that nobody should be scared to be ambitious, that positive energy and hard work can get you where you want to be.

Downstairs, her dinner is ready for her on the table. She counts her blessings again. Her life would be so much more difficult if she didn't have her mother's love and support.

She's sitting alone, devouring her chicken stew, when her mobile vibrates in her pocket. She considers ignoring it in case it's work. She can't face going back out there. Not tonight. She looks at the screen. It's a text from Kane. *Hi, I'm outside. Can we speak?*

Granger wipes her mouth with the back of her hand, walks quickly down the hall and opens the door.

"What's going on? What are you doing here?"

"Can I come in?"

She ushers him inside. He sits down at the kitchen table and looks at her half-finished plate of food. "I'm sorry, I didn't realise you were eating."

Granger sits and pushes her food to one side. "Don't worry about it, I'm done."

Her mother bustles into the kitchen. She beams when she sees Kane. "So good to see you, Edison. What a lovely surprise. Would you like some stew?"

Kane smiles back. "Thanks Naomi, but I've already eaten. This is more a work visit than a social one."

Granger gives her mother a nod and she gets the message. "I think I'll take the opportunity to have an early night," she says and hurries out of the room.

Granger gives Kane a quizzical look. "Come on, then. Don't keep me in suspense."

"I received an email from Helen Dean this evening," he says. "She congratulated me and summoned me to a meeting in her office tomorrow morning."

"Congratulated you for what?"

"Haven't you seen the news tonight?"

Granger shakes her head. "I've had enough excitement for one day, and anyway, I've been busy with Daisy. What's happened?"

"Ray Spencer's body washed up on Thorpe Bay Beach a couple of hours ago. The autopsy will be done tomorrow but it's looking like his head hit one of the pier's metal struts on the way down. He was unconscious when he hit the water, didn't stand a chance."

Granger doesn't believe in karma. She does believe that every so often some people get what they deserve. "We know he killed Rina. There's no doubt about that, is there?"

"There isn't. But the media is already putting two and two together and making five. They're speculating that Ray Spencer was the See No Evil Killer, that Rina Kroll was his third and last victim and that he chose death to avoid the humiliation of a trial. The problem is, I think Dean is tempted to believe that too. She's desperate to get this case cleared up and off her desk."

Granger remembers Spencer's icy stare just before he plummeted into the sea.

"Is it possible he was our man after all? He threatened to kill Banjo. He lied about his alibi. He brutally murdered his girlfriend."

Kane grimaces. "I wish I could say I really believe he killed Banjo and Isabel Anderson. The evidence is weak and all of it is circumstantial. Spencer doesn't fit the profile. He was undeniably a dangerous man, a brutal killer in the end. But the previous victims were mutilated. Eyes and then ears taken for trophies. That's a calculating, cold evil. Rina's murder doesn't fit that pattern."

Granger takes a moment to think. What Kane is saying makes a lot of sense. His record shows he knows what he's doing when it comes to catching killers. But Detective Superintendent Dean is no novice either.

"What is it that you want me to do?"

Kane stands up and rests his hands on the back of the chair. "Come with me to the meeting with Dean tomorrow. She's not going to like what I have to say. I thought you could back me up, help her see sense. I don't want the case closed just to placate the media when there's a good chance the killer is still out there."

"Won't that become obvious to everyone if and when he kills again?"

"That's what I want to avoid. Do you really want to wait until another person dies? I don't."

Granger nods slowly. "I'll come. Maybe together we can persuade her to keep the case open."

Kane manages a grateful smile. "Thank you. I'll leave you to get on with your evening."

"Why don't you stay? You can have the sofa and we can leave for the meeting together."

"That's kind of you but no thanks. I'll sleep better in my own bed."

Granger stands on the doorstep and watches her boss climb into his car and drive away. She knows for sure that he was lying about one thing. There's no way he'll be getting any sleep tonight.

CHAPTER 42

Detective Superintendent Helen Dean pulls her reading glasses down and peers over them at the two detectives sitting on the other side of her desk.

"I don't remember asking Detective Constable Bailey to attend this meeting."

"I wanted her to come," says Kane. "I thought it'd be useful to have her here."

"Thought you might need an ally?"

"Do I?"

Dean picks up a sheet of paper from a red plastic tray marked 'inbox', scans the text quickly and signs it on the bottom, then places it in black tray marked 'outbox'.

"I called you here in the hope that you're able to tell me your little sojourn on the coast is over. I've read your report on the latest murder and I must say I'm disappointed. The newspapers are reporting that this killer you were hunting has topped himself and that the good people of Southend can once again walk the streets without fear. You appear to have left that bit out."

Kane knew this was coming. If he doesn't tell Dean what she wants to hear, then he's finished.

"I don't believe that Ray Spencer killed the other two. He was running legitimate businesses to cover the fact that he was exporting stolen mobile phones. When his girlfriend came to us to inform on him, he killed her. There is no real evidence to suggest he murdered Banjo or Isabel Anderson."

Dean rests her elbows on the desk and steeples her fingers. "This is not looking good, Edison. The newspapers disagree with you. They seem convinced that Spencer's suicide brings this troublesome case to a neat and tidy end."

Kane wants to ask her exactly when the press was given the power to assess evidence and make judgements on guilt or innocence.

"The newspapers always want simple solutions. They don't like stories that don't have endings."

Dean sits back in her chair and folds her arms across her chest. "What about you, Detective Granger? Why don't you tell me what you think?"

Granger looks at Kane. She's nervous and he feels a pang of guilt. He wishes he hadn't had to drag her into this mess.

"I agree with DI Kane," she says. "The only evidence we have linking Ray Spencer to the other murders is circumstantial. We could close the case now and have another body on our hands next week."

Kane is heartened by Granger's loyalty. A lot of people in her position would think twice before supporting a colleague who was about to be declared unfit for duty.

"Whatever you decide, I want to put it on record that Detective Granger has been an asset in this inquiry and has always performed to the highest level. She's a highly competent investigator."

Dean looks at Granger then back at Kane, her expression solemn. Kane guesses she made her mind up well before the meeting started.

"This is an extremely sad day, Edison. You have a long, distinguished record and I feel for you. But I did give you some warning and now I have no choice but to act. I'm putting you back on compassionate leave while we consider your future."

Kane doesn't react. He focuses his gaze on the wall a fraction above Dean's head. He doesn't want her or Granger to see how he's really feeling. If he's banished again, there will be no future to consider. His life as a murder squad detective will be over.

"The last time we spoke, you gave me seven days to achieve a breakthrough. That was four days ago. I'd like to take the next three days to tie up a few loose ends around the Sam Miller corruption case. I'd really appreciate it. Miller was part of my team and I want to make sure everything is watertight before I hand him over to the anti-corruption mob. I don't want to give him any chance of avoiding prosecution."

Dean looks surprised. She removes her glasses and takes a moment to think while wiping the lenses clean.

"I see no harm in that," she says, slipping her glasses back on. "It'll give me the chance to find a suitable replacement." She turns to Granger. "Whoever the new senior investing officer is, he or she will be reviewing the murders, including the killing of Rina Krol. As you've already been working on the case, I'd like you to stay on and assist."

* * *

Kane and Granger agree to have breakfast before driving back to Southend. The café is bustling with office workers and shop staff tucking into bacon sandwiches, coffee and cakes before starting their shifts.

The detectives sit opposite each other at the only vacant table. Granger takes a bite of her blueberry muffin. "Are you sure you don't want something to eat?"

"I'm not hungry."

Kane is not in the mood for eating or talking. His head is spinning. His stomach is in knots. Three days, then he's forced into the wilderness. For good. There will be no way back, unless he's prepared to return to investigating muggings and burglaries. He can't bear the thought of that. He wonders whether Lizzy, wherever she is, knows what a complete mess he's made of his life since losing her.

"I wish I could do something to help," Granger says, blinking back tears. "You don't deserve this."

Kane should be the one who's weeping, but tears are a waste of time. That's one of the hard lessons he learned after Lizzy's murder. Three days, seventy-two hours, then it all ends.

"The last thing I want is for you to feel sorry for me. I'd rather you were angry at me. I am."

Granger puts her coffee down on the table. "What do you mean?"

The fog in Kane's mind clears. Three days' grace. Three blinks of an eye. One more last chance. That's all he needs.

"Come on, then. Let's finish what we started."

CHAPTER 43

Jack Newman reads the message for a third time, puts his mobile back down on his desk and punches the air in triumph. This will be the perfect way to bring the story to a satisfying end before he moves on to bigger and better things.

His readers are going to lap up this latest insight into the mind of a murderer. It will be a fitting last exclusive for the *Herald*. The final words of a killer, a blood-soaked mystery solved. Brady is not going to believe her luck when he tells her.

He stands up, pauses and sits down again. Why should he go running to his news editor? The right thing to do is summon her to his office. He's the high-flyer. He's the man at the top of the food chain.

"What do you want, Jack?" Brady snaps on the other end of the line. "I'm extremely busy."

"Come on now, Dawn. There's no need to be like that. Just because I'm leaving you. I understand you're heartbroken but let me make it up to you. I have another big story. A parting gift you're not going to believe."

Brady ends the call abruptly, and Newman smiles to himself. She'd love to tell him where to stick his story but she's not that stupid. If he says it's big then it's going to be too good to miss.

When she arrives in his office, her breathing is ragged and her face is flushed. She gives a long, exasperated sigh and pushes her fringe out of her eyes.

"The lift is out of order again. Of course, you already knew that. This better be as good as you say it is, Jack."

Newman laughs. "Oh, it's good all right. In fact, it's fantastic. I've had another message from the killer. And this one's a cracker." He slides his mobile across his desk. "See for yourself."

Brady picks up the phone and studies the screen. After a few moments, she looks up at Newman, wide-eyed with excitement, then carries on reading.

> *It's done and so am I. This world's full of evil, more than you can ever understand. She was judged and executed. Killing comes naturally to me now. Am I mad, a beast, a monster? I know the truth. I'm an ordinary human being with an extraordinary sickness. Nobody can stop my descent into the darkness. Death is the only cure.*
>
> *See No Evil, Hear No Evil, Speak No Evil.*

Brady places the phone down carefully on the desk. "This stuff is absolute dynamite, Jack. Bloody amazing."

Newman smiles broadly at his news editor's enthusiasm. "It is, isn't it?"

Brady stares reverentially at the phone. "It's Ray Spencer. He's telling the world that he's had enough and he's going to kill himself, isn't he?"

Newman agrees. "That's exactly how I read it too. He batters his girlfriend to death and decides enough is enough. Instead of fleeing or going into hiding, he takes himself off to the pier, where he knows there's a good chance someone's going to recognise him, and waits for the police to arrive. It's a brilliant story, and there you go. I've even come up with the headline for you: 'The Last Confession'."

"I love it. You've always been a proper pain in the neck, Jack, but I'm going to miss you when you've gone."

"I know you will."

Brady frowns. "Wait a minute. The timing's got to fit. When exactly did you receive this message? Spencer's been dead for twenty-four hours."

"It pinged on my phone about fifteen minutes ago. But it's simple to write an email and then set the date that you need it to be sent. He obviously didn't want this to arrive until after his death."

Brady nods. "That makes sense, I suppose. Can you start writing it up? Right away. I want to get this on our website as soon as possible. I guess we'd better let the police see it before we publish. That's what we agreed, isn't it?"

She's right but Newman doesn't see the point of honouring an informal agreement designed to help the police when there's no need for the investigation to continue.

"Don't worry about that. This message confirms what we already thought. Ray Spencer lost his mind and went on a bloody rampage, killing Banjo, then Isabel Anderson and Rina Krol. We'll never know what triggered it but he's clearly publicly confessing his crimes here. Detective Inspector Kane has spectacularly failed and we've done his job for him."

CHAPTER 44

Back in Southend, Kane asks Granger to drive straight to Thorpe Bay. She parks on the coastal road and they walk down to the beach where Harry Cannon witnessed the killer dragging a body across the shingle.

Kane is aware that the first of his three days is flying by. It's already almost midday. With a sense of urgency, he leads Granger down to the waterline, passing a couple enjoying a picnic with their curly haired toddler, and a group of teenage girls and boys, who should be at school, flirting in the spring sunshine.

Kane points to the nearest beach hut. "That's where Harry Cannon was when he saw the killer. The body was dragged to where we're standing. It was in the early hours of the morning and still dark, but Harry's young, his eyesight's sharp."

"You think he'd recognise the killer if he saw him?"

"I do. If he thought it was Ray Spencer, he would have told us, wouldn't he?"

"Not if he was scared. We know he was terrified of Sam Miller."

Granger points to the steps they had used to get to the beach. "Harry heard the victim being dragged past the beach hut. The killer must have used those steps. He must have brought the body here in a vehicle and would've had to have parked close."

They are going over old ground, but that's exactly what Kane wants to do. They must have missed something.

"We checked all the traffic cameras in the area, didn't we?"

"We did. Finch and Miller did it. They drew a blank."

Kane shakes his head slowly. That was before they knew they had a corrupt cop on the team.

"We can't trust anything Miller did. The footage will have to be reviewed again. Quickly."

"I'll ask Finch. If she's already heard that you're being replaced she might be reluctant."

Kane can't afford to lose the only other detective in his team. "I'll speak to her. Until my replacement is named, I'm still the senior investigating officer in this case."

They trudge up the beach back to the car. As they pass the brightly painted huts, Granger stops dead.

"I've just had a thought," she says. "About Harry."

Kane finds himself thinking about the kid all the time. Is he still alive? If so, where the hell is he?

"Go on, then. Don't keep me waiting."

"We know Harry has a long history of breaking into beach huts and there are hundreds along this piece of coast. If he wanted somewhere to lie low, he'd have plenty to pick from."

It's a good suggestion, but a systematic search of the area's beach huts would be time-consuming and labour-intensive.

"You could be right, but my priority is catching the killer, not finding Harry." When they arrive back at the station, Granger heads for the squad room to find Finch. Kane goes straight to his office. He sits at his desk and calls up the autopsy reports on Banjo and Isabel Anderson.

He reads them again, the details confirming his view that they were not killed by Spencer. Rina Kroll was battered to death with a blunt instrument, her killer consumed by a murderous rage, unconcerned about being covered in her blood.

The other two victims were dispatched by a single thrust of a knife, puncturing the heart, then their bodies mutilated. Both killings would have involved careful planning. The murderer must have ice in his veins.

At that moment, Granger bursts into the office. "Come quick, you need to see this." Kane doesn't ask why. He gets up and runs.

In the squad room the four detectives on duty and two uniformed offices are bunched around a TV screen in the corner watching a news bulletin. When Kane joins them, they part to give him a better view.

Half of the screen is taken up by a shot of the *Southend Herald*'s website. Kane sees the main headline: 'The Last Confession'. The newsreader, an animated brunette wearing a floral blouse, is summing up the story with relish.

"According to the town's local paper, the killer terrorising the seaside town sent their crime reporter an email confessing to the murders and revealing that he was planning to take his own life. Two days ago, businessman Ray Spencer killed his girlfriend and died after throwing himself off Southend Pier after being cornered by the police."

In unison, the detectives watching the broadcast turn to Kane, eager to gauge his reaction. He pushes his way to the front, grabs the remote control and switches the TV off.

"Bullshit," he says. "Total bullshit."

* * *

Back behind his desk, Kane brings up the *Herald*'s website and reads the story for himself. He's still reading when Granger comes in and he gestures for her to sit down. When he finishes, he slams the laptop shut.

"I thought Newman agreed to show us any messages before he publishes."

"He did. He assured me he would."

"I knew that snake couldn't be trusted. We need to call the paper's editor. Make an official complaint."

Kane takes a deep breath. He needs to calm down, think clearly. He can't waste time and energy on Newman.

Granger leans forward and hands him two sheets of paper. "I printed out the story and the message separately. Thought it would be easier for us to read."

Kane gives her a smile and a nod, then focuses on the message. "Newman is making a lot of assumptions. No way does the writer of this email, whether it's Spencer or not, say anything about killing Banjo and Anderson. Also, the paper wouldn't sit on this story, so it must have been sent after Spencer jumped."

Granger points to a paragraph in the news story. "It says here that the message arrived on Newman's phone this morning but would have been written after Rina was killed and before Spencer died. You can set an email up to be sent later."

Kane looks up. "Can you? I didn't know that. I've only just worked out how to attach a photograph. I doubt the paper can prove when the email was written and sent, only when it was received. We need his phone for the tech team to look at. See what they can find. Will you chase him? Tell him we need his mobile urgently."

Granger gets up. "I'll go to the *Herald*'s offices right now."

"Once you've done that, you might as well go home to your family."

Granger smiles. "Are you sure? I'm happy to work late. Daisy will be asleep before I get home anyway."

"Thanks, but no thanks. Just get Newman's mobile to our tech team then go."

Granger reaches for the door handle, then pauses, a frown creasing her brow. "What about Ray Spencer's mobile? There was no mention of it in the reports. If he sent the message from his phone the evidence would be there."

Kane realises she's right. It won't tell them who the killer is but it could prove that Spencer didn't murder Banjo and Isabel Anderson.

"It doesn't make sense for him not to have a phone on him," he says. "He ran a mobile phone shop. It's a long shot but I want a diving unit to search the seabed around the pier at first light."

CHAPTER 45

Bailey Granger checks the clock on the wall as she approaches the reception desk at the *Southend Herald*. It's 7 p.m., which means she'll be handing Newman's mobile over to the tech team's night shift.

Behind the counter, a woman with dark hair and pale skin gives her a tired smile. "Good evening. I'm Tina, how can I help?"

Granger flashes her ID. "Detective Constable Granger. I need to speak to Jack Newman, and please tell him it's urgent."

Tina perks up at the mention of the reporter, her smile brighter. "Can I tell Jack what the request is in connection with? He's a busy man. Especially at the moment."

Granger gives her a cold-eyed glare. "No, you can't and, let me stress, this is not a request. I want to speak to him immediately."

Tina's cheeks redden. She picks up the telephone and punches in an extension number. She lets it ring for a while before ending the call.

"I'm sorry, officer. Jack isn't at his desk at the moment. If you like I can get him to call you as soon as he has a moment."

"I don't like," Granger says. She marches around the reception desk and through a door into a dark, square room with access to a lift and a staircase. She takes the stairs, and after two flights comes to swing doors bearing the sign 'Newsroom'.

She pushes her way in and is immediately assailed by a cacophony of keyboards clicking, voices yelling, phones ringing and the babble of TV news channels.

Granger spots a woman striding purposely down the middle of the room toward her. She assumes it's someone in authority who's had a warning from reception.

The woman, who's wearing dark trousers and a loose, pale-green sweater, sweeps her fringe to one side. "Welcome, Detective. I'm Dawn Brady, the news editor."

Granger is not in the mood for small talk. "Where's Jack Newman?"

Brady throws up her hands. "I've no idea and to be honest I don't really care."

"I need to speak to him urgently."

"Follow me," Brady says. "Let's go somewhere quieter."

She leads Granger out of the chaos, along a battleship-grey corridor into an empty room with a large rectangular glass table and eight chairs.

"This is one of our editorial conference rooms. It's where we decide what's going into the newspaper and what's not. Please, take a seat."

Granger assumes she's supposed to be impressed. She isn't. "I'd rather stand. It's important that I speak to Newman."

"You're too late, Jack's gone. He doesn't work here anymore."

Granger thinks she must have misheard. "I know he's busy but it's imperative that I talk to him right away. We believe he's in possession of important evidence, and withholding it is an arrestable offence."

"I told you, he's gone. For good. He resigned and we let him go straight away. Got a big offer in London. Today was his last day and he certainly left with a bang. He's a real story magnet, but to be honest I'm not that sad to see him go. The man's a maverick with a rampant ego."

Thrown off balance, Granger takes a moment to absorb the news. "He's still in town?"

Brady shrugs. "As far as I know."

"Then you're going to have to get your human resources department to give me his address. Pronto."

* * *

Thirty minutes later, Granger is driving along the north boundary of the town's Cliff Gardens and turns left into Marine Avenue. She pulls up outside Newman's ground-floor flat, the lower half of a large, white-rendered 1930s house.

It's a moonless night, but the street is well lit. Granger presses the doorbell and steps back. The door opens almost immediately and Newman emerges on to the threshold. He's dressed casually in faded jeans and a black polo shirt.

"Detective Granger, what a pleasant surprise. Is this a personal or official visit?"

Granger has always found it hard to tell whether Newman is being sarcastic or serious.

"I'm here to pick up your mobile phone. We need to get our technical experts to try to trace the source of the new message."

Newman steps forward on to his doorstep. "Isn't that a waste of time? Your so-called experts have tried before and failed spectacularly."

"I'm not here to argue with you. I need your mobile now."

"Explain to me why I should just hand over my personal property. Have you got a warrant?"

Granger can't fathom why the reporter would refuse to cooperate. She's glad Kane isn't with her. He'd be losing it by now. The best way to handle Newman is not to rise to the bait.

"I can get a warrant if that's how you want to play this — come back in the morning with a couple of enthusiastic colleagues to confiscate your phone and search your home from top to bottom. How's that for an explanation?"

Newman crosses his arms and tilts his head. "Seeing as you've made the situation so clear, Detective, why don't you come in while I fetch my phone?"

Granger follows him along a short corridor into a large, uncluttered living area. The only furniture is a low-slung leather armchair and a marble-and-oak coffee table. On one of the walls is an unframed, off-white oil painting. Brush strokes spiral from the centre.

"What do you think?" Newman asks. "It's one of mine. A black hole. Their centres are so dense not even light can escape the pull of gravity. That's why they're not black at all. They don't have any colour. They're invisible."

Granger isn't sure what she thinks about it as a painting. But she's surprised. She would never have guessed that Newman had an interest in modern art.

"I didn't know you like to paint."

"There are a lot of things you don't know about me."

Granger is starting to realise how true that is. "Your news editor told me you've left them for a fancy new job in London. Why the big secret?"

Newman grins. "It's no secret. I told the people who need to know. I don't like to brag about my success. I've been made a brilliant offer and the truth is I deserve it. There's no reason for me to tell you lot I'm moving on. I'm not suspected of any crime."

He's right, he's not a suspect, but he is guilty of being a conceited prick. "You should have told us about the new message before you made it public. There's something not quite right about it. Detective Inspector Kane is far from convinced that Ray Spencer killed the first two victims."

"Oh dear, I'm sorry if I've been a bit of a naughty boy," Newman says, not looking in the slightest bit apologetic. "I do admire your loyalty to your boss, but you've got to admit that he really hasn't got a clue what he's doing. He cracked up after his wife was killed and he's never recovered."

Granger wants to leap to Kane's defence but stops herself. She decides the best way to undermine Newman's criticism is to ignore it.

She holds out a hand. "I'd like your phone now, please."

Newman puts his hands on his hips and gives her a silent stare for a few seconds then breaks into a smile.

"All right, take a seat. I'll be back in a second."

Granger walks over to the window and looks out on to the street. The lights are on in the property opposite and she can see images flickering on the screen of a wall-mounted TV.

A few minutes later Newman hasn't returned. Granger paces impatiently to the door and back again. Daisy will be fast asleep by the time she gets home. Her mother too. Kane believed he was giving her the chance to finish early. It was a kind thought.

Still no sign of Newman. Granger wanders over to the door again and peers out. No movement. No sound. She walks slowly down the hall and into the kitchen. It's square, with white and chrome fittings, and surgically clean.

She moves on along the hall toward the two rooms at the end. Both doors are slightly ajar but the one on her right is framed by light. She creeps nervously toward it. She can't hear Newman moving around. The silence is eerie. It feels as if she is the only person in the flat.

Granger puts her hand on the door and calls out. "Jack, are you in there? I'm in a hurry."

She tells herself there's no reason to be afraid. It doesn't calm the fluttering in her stomach. She pushes the door open and steps inside. The windowless room is a study. All four walls are covered by wooden shelves groaning with books. At the far end is a small desk with a vintage adjustable lamp on it.

Granger's eyes are drawn to the whiteboard fixed to the wall above the desk. Pinned along the top are newspaper cuttings of Newman's front-page stories on the murders of Banjo and Isabel Anderson. Below them are photographs of

Ray Spencer and Sam Miller, both with arrows drawn in red felt-tip pen pointing to the cuttings.

At the bottom of the board is a headshot of Edison Kane and next to it a smaller photo. Granger steps closer to see who it is. It's her.

Her heart is beating hard and fast. She's not sure why. This could simply be the work of an obsessive reporter doing his research, couldn't it? In her head, an urgent voice tells her to run. To get out while she can. Instead, she walks over to the bookshelves.

She runs her finger along the spines. The books on this shelf are all about notorious serial killers. *I'm the Yorkshire Ripper*, *The Jeffrey Dahmer Story*, *Understanding Fred and Rose West*. Granger turns away, a sickness in her stomach. She scans the other shelves and every book, hundreds of them, appear to be about murder or murderers. The psychology of murder, the world's worst serial killers, secret psychopaths, the sexual motives of thrill killers . . .

The temperature in the room seems to dip. Granger shivers. She hears someone breathing behind her and twists around. Jack Newman stands in the doorway. He doesn't look like Jack Newman. His lips curl into a sneer. His eyes are cold and empty.

"Welcome to my darkness."

CHAPTER 46

Harry Cannon pulls the peak of his baseball cap down and slips through the late-night convenience store's automatic doors. He knows exactly where to turn his head away from the security cameras. They're always in the same places — inside the entrance, at the end of each aisle and above the cash tills.

Picking up a plastic shopping basket, he makes his way to the shelves stocked with fresh vegetables and fruit. It's almost 10.30 p.m. and the store is quiet. Harry guesses he's one of half a dozen shoppers wandering around the store. He can see two staff members on the tills and another one refilling shelves.

He picks up a bag of potatoes and drops them in the basket. Next, he selects a large cabbage and studies the leaves for signs of pest damage. He's hardly eaten for two days and is so hungry his stomach feels like it's digesting itself.

Out of the corner of his eye he spots a security guard emerging from a doorway and heading for the alcohol aisle. The woman has short grey hair, her uniform tight around her hips and chest.

Harry crouches and busies himself retying one of his laces until she is out of sight. He pulls the zip of his jacket down to his navel and walks quickly down the biscuit and confectionary aisle. By the time he reaches the end, he has two large bars of milk chocolate and a packet of cheese crackers tucked away, and his jacket zipped up to his neck.

His mouth is already watering at the thought of devouring his haul. He's so desperate he doesn't bother to check if he's being watched. He drops the basket of vegetables on to the floor and sprints for the exit.

Outside, Harry turns left, and takes a quick look over his shoulder to make sure he's not being followed before slowing to a jog. He passes a busy Chinese takeaway, the smell making his stomach growl.

He stops and sits down on a step in the doorway of a children's shoe shop. Unzipping his jacket, he lets his goodies fall onto the chequered tiles and snatches up one of the chocolate bars.

He rips away the paper wrapping and the silver foil, snaps off a block of squares and stuffs them into his mouth. The jolt of sweetness and the velvety texture of the chocolate makes him moan with pleasure and he closes his eyes.

When he opens them, he findings himself staring at a pair of shiny black boots. He looks up, his mouth still full. The store security guard looms over him, a determined expression on her round face.

Before he can even think about getting up, she grabs the scruff of his neck with both hands, throws him face down on to the pavement and straddles him, pressing down hard on his shoulders.

Harry tries to wriggle free even though he knows it's hopeless. Her weight is crushing his chest, making it almost impossible for him to breathe.

"That's it, boy," she says. "Don't waste your energy, you're going nowhere. The police are already on the way."

CHAPTER 47

Kane watches the three divers slip smoothly from the boat into the water and disappear. It's 6 a.m., and the beach is deserted. To his right is the haphazard network of metal beams and struts beneath the pier. Behind him, the Adventure Island amusement park is eerily silent.

It's a windless morning, the sea calm as a millpond. The conditions will help the underwater search but Kane knows the chances of success are low.

He checks his mobile, hoping for a message from Granger to say she's on her way. He sent her a text last night asking her to meet him before the dive started. He understands its early but his nerves are jangling. One day gone already. Someone has pressed the fast-forward button and time has become his enemy.

Half a mile out to sea, two of the police divers resurface and climb back on to the boat. Kane walks down the beach, watching carefully for a wave or a thumbs-up from the unit supervisor, Shona Collins. There's no signal but the divers will go again, once they've had a rest and rechecked their equipment.

Five minutes later, the third diver appears, holding one arm up and waving it around. Collins helps pull him back aboard the boat and they give each other a high five. By the time Collins is back on the beach, the mobile phone is already safely inside a sealed evidence bag.

She hands it to Kane, grinning from ear to ear. "We got lucky. The mudflats are so extensive here, the water is no more than ten feet deep."

Kane holds the evidence bag up and examines the phone. It's smeared with mud, a single strand of seaweed wrapped around the cracked screen.

"Brilliant, Shona. You've done your job, now it's up to our tech unit."

Collins walks up the beach to the promenade, where her divers, already out of their gear, are drinking steaming hot coffee from a flask.

Kane's phone rings and he checks the screen. He's expecting it to be Granger and is surprised to see it's Detective Constable Finch. He answers it with a feeling of dread.

"We've had a call from Detective Granger's mother. She says she didn't come home last night. She went to bed assuming her daughter was working late again and it wasn't until she got up this morning that she realised Granger's bed hadn't been slept in."

Kane is already running up the beach to his car. "I'm on my way back right now. The last time I saw her she was heading to the *Herald* to pick up Jack Newman's phone. Find out where he is and bring him in."

When he arrives back at the station, Finch is waiting for him in his office. On the drive back he'd been praying that he'd find Granger there too, apologising and explaining that her mother had made a mistake.

"Is Jack Newman here yet? Did he see Granger last night?"

Finch shakes her head. "I've spoken to Dawn Brady, the paper's news editor. She confirmed that Granger was at the newspaper's offices at about 7 p.m. She told her that Newman doesn't work for the *Herald* anymore and Granger asked for his address. I've sent a patrol car to bring him in."

Kane is only half listening. He should never have sent Granger out on a job on her own. He should have gone too, or at least sent a uniform with her. His desperation to save his own skin clouded his judgement. Finch is watching him closely. He has to hold it together, stay calm and focused. For Granger's sake.

"Newman's left the *Herald*?"

"That's what Brady said. Apparently, he's being paid big bucks to write crap for one of the London papers."

Kane grabs his phone and calls Granger's number. He gets a 'not available' message. The room suddenly seems unusually warm. His shirt is sticking to his back. He can't sit around and wait. He has to do something. "Come with me," he says to Finch. "We're going to Newman's flat."

As soon as Finch starts the engine and pulls off into the heavy traffic, Kane calls Granger's mother. She answers immediately. "Please tell me you've found my girl. Is she all right?"

"Naomi, this is Kane. We haven't found her yet, but we will soon. I promise." Kane wishes he really felt that confident.

Naomi isn't saying anything. She's crying softly into the phone. She sounds broken and Kane desperately wants to fix her.

"I know how worried you must be, but can you think of any reason she might have made a spur-of-the-moment decision to visit someone, an old friend, or an ex-boyfriend?"

Naomi sniffs loudly. "Bailey would never stay out overnight without letting me know first. Never ever. She knows Daisy would be asking for her. Maybe she's been in an accident, a car crash? We need to call the hospitals."

"We're doing that already. You sit tight in case she calls you."

"Please bring my girl home."

"I promise, we're doing everything we can."

Kane ends the call as Finch turns into Marine Avenue. A patrol car is parked halfway down the street and she pulls up behind it. One of the uniforms is busy telling a small crowd attracted by the police presence that there's nothing for them to see.

The constable, tall and fresh-faced, greets the detectives with an enthusiastic nod and introduces herself. "PC Rani Desai," she says. "It doesn't look like there's anyone in the flat. Nobody's answering the door. My colleague, PC Dines, is having a look around the back."

Kane takes a look at the building. It's a large, white-fronted semi-detached house, with a red-tiled roof. "Stay here and keep an eye on the front door," he says and leads Finch briskly through the side gate.

The back garden is small, laid to lawn and well-kept. PC Dines is standing close to the back door, peering hard through the glass panel. He's stocky, with a greying, neatly trimmed beard.

"Can you see anything?" Finch asks.

PC Dines looks round, startled. He recognises the detective constable and gives her a rueful smile. "Afraid not. No sign of life at all."

Kane doesn't like his choice of words. He walks up to the back door and takes a moment assessing the quality of the lock. "We need to get inside. Quickly."

PC Dines throws Finch a questioning look. "Go in without a warrant?"

"This is my boss, Detective Inspector Kane. If he wants to go inside, then we're going inside."

The more Kane works with Finch the more he likes her. "If we have reason to believe that someone's life might be in danger, then we don't need a warrant."

The police constable shrugs, takes a couple of steps back and shoulder-charges the door. Kane can tell he's done this before. He crouches low, making sure the impact point is close to the lock. The plastic around the lock shatters and the door swings in. Momentum takes PC Dines with it.

Kane and Finch follow him into the kitchen. It's spotlessly clean. Kane guesses that Newman relies more on takeaways than home cooking. "Let's spread out. Try not to touch anything."

He leaves the kitchen and walks slowly down the narrow hallway. Finch and the uniform head in the opposite direction toward the living area.

At the end of the hall, Kane finds two rooms. He pushes one of the doors open and steps inside. The bedroom is as pristine and uncluttered as the kitchen. A double bed that doesn't look as if it's been slept in, a pine wardrobe and a standing full-length mirror.

Kane leaves the room and checks out the other one. It's a second bedroom that Newman uses as an office. The walls are covered in bookshelves, roughly half of which are empty. Kane checks out some of the books. They're a mix of commercial crime paperbacks and true crime hardbacks. Above the small desk is a blank whiteboard. For an investigate journalist, Newman doesn't seem to make many notes, Kane thinks.

He walks back along the hall into the living area, where Finch and the uniform are waiting for him. Finch shakes her head. "Nothing to see here. No sign of anything untoward."

Kane is both disappointed and relieved. It's possible that Granger never got to see Newman, that she was never here. He needs to speak to the reporter to clarify that. But can it be a coincidence that he goes off the radar at the same time as Granger vanishes?

Finch's phone rings and she digs it out of her jacket. She listens intently for a moment and holds up a hand to attract Kane's attention. "Are you sure it's him?" she asks. "Okay then, bring him over to the station." She ends the call and steps closer to Kane. "That was Shoeburyness police. They arrested a youth for shoplifting last night."

Kane is thinking about his next move in the hunt for Granger. It makes sense to ask the Automatic Number Plate Recognition control room to see if they can pick up her car.

"Why on earth would we be interested in a shoplifter?"

"The youth they arrested says his name is Harry Cannon."

CHAPTER 48

Granger draws her knees up to her chest, rounds her back and rolls on to her side into the foetal position. Her legs are taped tightly together at the ankles, her hands bound at the wrists. Several strips of tape cover her mouth and nostrils, making it almost impossible for her to breathe.

The boot of her car is dark and cold. She catches a whiff of petrol, then something much more subtle, more personal. The smell of her fear.

The back of her neck throbs. Pain shoots across her scalp. She can't remember the blow being struck and has no idea how long she's been unconscious.

The car isn't moving. Newman must have found a hiding place. The chances are it's somewhere he's used before. Kane will track her down. She's sure of that. He knows she was on her way to see Newman.

But she knows she can't afford to wait to be rescued. Newman is a merciless psychopath. When he decides to kill her, he'll do it without hesitation and with relish. She must do whatever it takes to survive. Daisy needs her mother.

Granger hears footsteps approaching and her courage fades in an instant. The boot opens and Newman takes a long look at her, as if he's studying a specimen in a laboratory jar. He reaches down and rips the tape from her mouth, tearing patches of skin from her lips. She twists her head in pain and groans.

"What are we going to do with you, Detective? You shouldn't have started wandering around my flat. Now I have to deal with you. It's not personal. In fact, I like you. I've always thought you came across as an extremely agreeable woman."

Granger tries to clear her head, stop her thoughts racing. She needs to concentrate, pick her words carefully, if she wants to stay alive. If she's to have any chance of convincing him not to harm her, she needs to sweeten the lie with a dusting of truth.

"Please, let me go. I won't say anything, I promise. If you untie me and let me walk away, nobody needs to know about this. I'll be content just to still be around, to live to see my daughter grow up. That's what matters most to me."

Newman crouches and examines her face. "Oh dear, your lips are bleeding. Sorry about that. I didn't mean to hurt you."

His words send a shiver down Granger's spine. There's something truly diabolical about a person you know is a cold-hearted killer pretending to be kind. She twists her head to try to get a clue where they are. She catches a glimpse of a decaying timbered ceiling, and guesses it's some kind of farm outbuilding.

"I mean it, Jack. If you let me go, I'll keep my mouth shut. I will. I'll resign from the police, do something completely different. All I really want is to be able to live my life and look after my family."

Newman laughs softly. "You're not a bad liar, I'll give you that. But I can't be fooled that easily. I'm a master of untruths. You're too weak, too normal, to let someone like me escape justice. Your conscience would never let you live in peace."

He starts to close the boot, then pauses. "I haven't decided what I'm going to do with you yet, so don't give up hope. By the way, don't bother screaming. We're pretty remote here. There's nobody around for miles."

The boot slams shut and Granger is engulfed by darkness again. She takes a deep breath, sucking in air. At least she's not going to suffocate. She tests the strength of the tape around her wrists, straining every muscle and sinew in her arms and shoulders. She gives up after a few seconds.

Granger wriggles to the side of the boot until her head is level with the edge of the board she's lying on. She knows that under the board is a spare tyre and tools, including a jack and a bolt wrench.

She sticks her tongue into the tiny gap and tries to lever the board up. She tries a few more times before realising that even if she could get her teeth around the edge of the board, her bodyweight would make it impossible to lift.

She rolls over on to her back and thinks about what Newman said. Of course, he's right, and the reverse applies. There is no way he can consider letting her go. The only chance he has of getting away with what he's done is to make sure she dies.

She blinks hard, fighting back tears. She imagines Daisy standing by a freshly dug grave, holding a single red rose. Granger shakes her head, angry with herself. She has to get a grip. This isn't over until she draws her last breath.

She lifts her hands and strains her eyes to look closely at the tape wound round her wrists. She spies a loose edge, moves it to her mouth and starts to chew. After a few minutes, she gives up, her jaw aching, her lips rubbed raw. The tape is slick with her saliva but shows no sign of tearing.

Time is running out. Newman won't hang about once he's figured out his next move. There's no way he's avoided detection for so long without meticulous planning. When he's ready, he'll come for her. She lifts her feet and kicks hard against the boot lid. The metal clangs but the lock holds fast. She kicks again and again, until she has to rest her legs.

She has a sudden overwhelming urge to shout for help, to yell at the top of her voice until her lungs are bursting, until someone comes to save her. But she knows she'd be wasting her breath.

She's shackled and locked up in the middle of nowhere, at the mercy of a murderer who mutilates his victims. She can scream her heart out if she wants. Nobody will hear.

CHAPTER 49

Newman sits in the kitchen at the table where he sat a thousand times as a morose little boy, and later as a sullen, spotty-faced teenager. Two decades of dust covers every surface, the cupboard doors are warped by damp and cobwebs hang from the ceiling like fluffy streamers.

Stone Cottage is his childhood home. He owns everything in it, every inch of the acre of land it sits on, and he hates it with a vengeance. On the day he found out his mother had left the place to him, he vowed never to live there and never to sell it.

He loves the idea of leaving it to rot, to have the satisfaction of knowing that time, the elements and the inevitable process of decay would inflict a long slow death on the home his mother loved.

At least the place has turned out to be useful. He has nowhere else to go, nowhere to hide. Despite this latest setback, he's confident that all is not lost. If he's smart, and he definitely is, he can emerge unscathed and unsuspected.

Newman's confident that the police won't be able to track him down. He destroyed Granger's SIM card and tossed her mobile into a ditch on the way out of town. He stayed clear of main roads, sticking to country lanes to cut the risk of being snapped by surveillance cameras.

Sometimes he genuinely wishes that the average level of intelligence of senior police detectives was higher. It would at least make the game a little more challenging. Newman takes his mobile out of his pocket and finds Edison Kane's number in his contacts. At some point he should call the detective, express his surprise and heartfelt concern about Granger's disappearance.

His finger hovers briefly above the call button. He changes his mind and puts the phone away. It'll look much better if he makes his way back to town and turns up at the police station, making it clear he's willing to do all he can to help Kane find his missing colleague. It's an hour's walk to the train station followed by a twenty-five-minute train journey. He'll be back in Southend by mid-afternoon.

Newman stands up, brushes the dust off the back of his trousers and the sleeves of his jacket, and walks to the moss-stained window above the sink. The barn is decaying from the inside out. It won't last more than another one or two winters. From where he's standing, he can see two large holes in the roof and he knows there are more.

He turns his back on the barn and the bad memories. He needs to focus his mind on deciding how Granger is going to die.

Newman can't deny that he's tempted to complete the Three Wise Monkeys theme. One stab of a knife, remove the tongue. The mere thought thrills him. He never imagined that killing could be so addictive.

Making Granger victim number three has practical benefits too. It would give him the chance to send another message. That would surely delight his new bosses at the *Daily News*. The idea appeals but it has its dangers. He'd have to drive the body back to Southend and leave it somewhere he can be sure it'll be found.

The longer he plays this game, the greater the chance that Kane will get his act together or simply get lucky. All the serial killers he's studied, the ones that got caught, made the mistake of not being able to stop when they were winning.

He'd like to say that he feels some sympathy for Granger but he can't. Her death will mean he can start his new life in London, working with reporters who can at least come close to matching his talent and ingenuity.

If he simply leaves the detective where she is, she'll die soon enough. Nobody can survive without water for more than a few days. Her body can stay hidden in the boot of her car. It can rot along with everything else. He's the master of Stone Cottage and there's no reason for anyone else to visit this damned place.

CHAPTER 50

Kane strides down the corridor, a coffee in one hand, his phone in the other. Every detective and uniform that can be spared has been assigned to the team looking for Granger. He can already hear excited chatter coming from the squad room.

When he enters, the volume drops to an expectant murmur. All eyes swivel in his direction, the weight of leadership heavy on his shoulders.

This is a team talk, not a briefing. He needs to pitch it right. A sense of urgency but no hint of panic, though inside he's jittery. He has to bring Granger home safe and sound.

"You all know what you have to do. It's important that you do it swiftly and efficiently. At this moment we have no idea what has happened to Detective Granger. Has she been in an accident? Unlikely. Every hospital within twenty miles has been checked. Is she being held against her will? It's possible. What we do know is that as every hour goes by the chances of her being found alive reduce. Let's get going. Do your jobs properly and let's bring her home safe and sound."

In response, the room buzzes with a mixture of excitement and determination. Kane watches the officers form into their set groups and file out. He's hoping that the door-to-door inquiries around the newspaper office will turn something up. That's the last place Granger was seen before she disappeared. Officers will also be calling on residents in Marine Avenue, in case she did drive to Newman's flat.

Kane is on his way back to his office when Finch calls out to him. He spins around to see a handcuffed Harry Cannon flanked by the detective constable and a burly, shaven-headed uniform.

Harry looks a little thinner and a lot dirtier than when he last saw him. His jeans are grimy, his sweatshirt stained and the mop of unkempt hair under his baseball cap is greasy.

"Take the cuffs off. I want to talk to him in my office."

* * *

Kane perches on the edge of his desk and waits for Harry to sit down. Finch hovers in the doorway.

"Do you need me to stay for this?"

Kane realises the detective's wondering why he isn't doing this in an interview room, where everything can be properly recorded. He can't tell her it's because he doesn't want what he's going to say on any official record.

"That's all right. You go. Why don't you chase up the number plate recognition inquiry? We put an urgent request in hours ago and should have heard something by now. This isn't going to be a formal interview. There's no need for that yet. We're just going to have a casual chat, sort a few things out."

Finch hesitates and frowns but doesn't question him. She gives a curt nod and leaves, closing the door as she goes.

Kane looks down at Harry, shaking his head slowly. "Where the hell have you been? We've all been worried sick."

"I'm going back to prison, aren't I?"

Kane still hopes that can be avoided, but the kid's arrest has made the situation more complicated.

"Have you been formally charged with shoplifting?"

Harry's bottom lip quivers. Kane guesses he hasn't cried for years, but the prospect of a long spell in jail has reduced many a hardened criminal to tears.

"I don't think so, not yet. I'm sorry, yeah? I was starving. I haven't eaten for ages. I didn't know what else to do."

Kane thinks he sounds genuinely contrite. He's a habitual thief. Circumstances have made him what he is. How else is he supposed to survive?

"Where have you been hiding out and why did you go?"

Harry glances furtively over his shoulder. "I've been staying in a few different beach huts in Shoeburyness. Loads of them are empty out there. The beaches are much quieter. I had to leave my flat. I was scared."

"Don't worry. We know all about Sam Miller. He won't be able to hurt you ever again. He's given us a full confession. He'll be going to jail for a long time."

Harry takes his baseball cap off and uses it to dry his eyes. "He came to my flat. He warned me to keep my mouth shut then choked me until I blacked out. I woke up, blood pouring from my nose. I was frightened. Shit scared. I thought if I told you what was going on, he'd kill me and make it look like an accident or suicide."

Kane understands the kid's reasoning. Miller is a vicious bully, a corrupt police officer. He took money to do dirty work for a local criminal. Why wouldn't Harry assume that all police officers are bent?

"There's a good chance we can prevent you going back to the young offenders' prison. Detective Granger has already smoothed things over with your probation officer, and I can suggest to the police at Shoeburyness that they don't press charges for the shoplifting because you're an important witness who's helping us with our inquiries."

Harry sits up and straightens his shoulders, his eyes wide, his expression less crestfallen. "I don't get it. Why help me?"

Kane considers explaining that he and Granger know his background and feel sorry for him, that they both believe he's not inherently bad and that he deserves at least one good break in his life.

"Why not?" he says.

Harry puts his cap back on his head, a smile tugging at his lips. "Where is Detective Granger today? She's cool, considering she's a copper."

Kane is unsure whether to tell him that Granger has disappeared. He's hoping she'll be back soon and he won't have to. At that moment Finch bursts into the office.

"Jack Newman walked in the front door five minutes ago. He says the *Herald*'s news editor called him to tell him that the police wanted to speak to him. I've put him in interview room one."

CHAPTER 51

Newman wonders whether coming to the police station voluntarily was a good idea after all. He doesn't appreciate being marched straight to an interview room to be guarded by a twitchy police constable who looks more like a boy scout than an officer of the law.

What would happen if he stood up and announced he'd had enough of being treated like a criminal? Would they handcuff him and throw him in a cell just to teach him a lesson? He can't image they'd treat a respected news reporter like that.

He's warming to the idea of testing out his theory when Kane arrives. The detective inspector doesn't appear to be enjoying his time on the east coast. His shoulders are tense and he's a little more haggard around the eyes than when he first arrived.

Before Kane can sit down, Newman takes the chance to go on the offensive. "Why am I being treated like a suspect? I came here as soon as I heard about Detective Granger. I'm willing to do whatever I can to help, but I expect to be treated with respect."

Newman detects a flicker of doubt in Kane's eyes and suppresses a smile. His outburst has done exactly what it was designed to do.

"The last time anybody saw Detective Granger she was on her way to your flat in Marine Avenue to request that you to hand over your mobile phone."

Newman is prepared for this. He's been rehearsing his answer all morning. The most annoying people are often the most predictable. "As far as I know, Detective Granger never came to my flat. I never set eyes on her that night. I hope she hasn't come to any harm, I really do."

He reaches into his pocket and pulls out his mobile with a flourish. It's not the phone he used to send the killer's last message to himself. It's the one that received it.

"Here you are, take it. You're more than welcome to get your experts to examine it. They've done it before and never found anything. I have nothing to hide. If Detective Granger had come knocking on my door, I would have handed it over to her. Why wouldn't I?"

He places the phone carefully on the table and slides it across. Kane doesn't even look at it. The detective is wearing his poker face. He needs to work on it. Newman can see his left cheek twitching nervously and sense his desperation. He takes a guess that the events of the last few weeks have not been good for the detective's career prospects.

"You broke our agreement," Kane says. "You were supposed to let me see any messages from the killer before you put them in your newspaper."

"There didn't seem any point this time. The message proved Ray Spencer was the killer. Then he killed himself with his entertaining little end-of-the-pier show. Case closed. My news editor was pressuring me to get the story on the paper's website as soon as possible."

"We don't believe Ray Spencer was the killer. He murdered his girlfriend. Not the others. That monster is still out there. I won't rest until we get him."

Newman shrugs. It seems to him that the one thing Kane needs, more than anything else, is a long rest. He's not going to bother trying to convince him that he's made a mistake.

He's sure the detective's bosses will be pulling the plug on his failed investigation pretty soon.

"Where were you last night?"

"Didn't I already say? I was at home. I had an early night. If Detective Granger did make it to my house, and I don't believe she did, I didn't hear the doorbell. I must have been asleep. I'm a notoriously heavy sleeper. You know, she could turn up at any moment, safe and sound, with a good explanation for her absence. I hope she does. Her family must be going out of their minds. Have you checked out her girlfriends or ex-boyfriends?"

Kane ignores the question. Newman isn't surprised. Nobody likes being told how to do their job, especially when they think they know what they're doing.

"Where were you this morning? You weren't at the flat."

"I told you I had an early night, and that was because I had to get up early. I went to London. Spent the day checking out areas I might want to move to. I suppose you've heard about my new job?"

Kane doesn't look interested. Jealousy is an ugly emotion. Just because his career is in freefall it's churlish not to congratulate someone who's heading for the top.

"While I think of it, when I got back from London, I was a bit dismayed to find my back door had been smashed in and then badly boarded up. I'm going to need that replaced and paid for before I move out."

Newman is tempted to question the legality of the police forcing entry into his flat without a search warrant but chooses to leave it, at least for now. He's not the sort to kick a man when he's down. Not unless he has to.

Kane looks down as if it's the first time he's noticed Newman's phone on the table. He picks it up gingerly with his thumb and forefinger and slips it into his jacket.

"Let me get this right," he says. "You're claiming that Detective Granger never went to your home?"

Newman knows he needs to tread carefully. It's possible that one of his neighbours saw Granger's car parked outside his flat.

"I never said that, and you know it. Don't put words into my mouth. I didn't see her. If she did come calling, I have no knowledge of it. I would have been in bed, fast asleep."

"Can you prove that?"

"Can you disprove it? I don't believe you can. I want leave now. Unless you're going to arrest me, I'm going to go."

Newman can tell that Kane is torn. He's not happy with the way the interview has gone but he wants to get on with trying to track down Granger.

"You can leave," Kane says. He nods at the young police constable standing with his back against the wall next to the door. "This officer will escort you out."

Newman stands up, turning his head to hide his smile. "Please pass my best wishes on to Detective Granger's family. I hope you find her soon. You know, I have a feeling she's going to turn up unscathed."

He walks down the corridor toward the lift, the police constable by his side, feeling pleased with himself. Coming here was the right decision after all. Kane has nothing on him, not a single piece of evidence linking him to the murders, or to the mysterious disappearance of Granger.

The police constable leans forward, pressing the button to call the lift. While they're waiting, a door at the end of the corridor swings open and a middle-aged woman strides out and heads off down the corridor. Newman recognises the detective's miserable face. He's seen her moping around at crime scenes with Kane but he doesn't know her name.

His eyes are drawn to the open door. A scruffy looking kid, about sixteen years old, maybe seventeen, is sitting at an interview table, chewing hungrily on a slice of pizza. He turns his head and looks straight at Newman. The kid stops chewing, blood draining from his face.

Newman takes a step closer to the open door. "Is everything all right? You look like you've seen a ghost."

The lift arrives with a ping. The police constable steps in and Newman follows.

CHAPTER 52

Granger's throat is dry, her tongue sore and swollen. Her energy is fading fast. She remembers reading somewhere about the Survival Rule of Three. *You can survive without oxygen for three minutes, without water for three days, without food for three weeks.*

Lying in permanent darkness, drifting in and out of sleep, makes it almost impossible to judge the passing of time. Her best guess is she's been locked in the boot of her car for one and a half, maybe two days.

She lifts her wrists to mouth and chews on the tape for what seems like the hundredth time. Her jaws ache with fatigue. Her lips are bruised but have stopped bleeding. She knows that isn't a good sign. As dehydration worsens, the blood thickens. The flow around the body slows until the organs, including the brain, are deprived of nutrients and eventually fail.

As the hours pass, Granger finds it hard to think clearly. Her head aches, her brain engulfed by waves of dizziness and confusion. She can't work out why Kane hasn't tracked her down. If only he'd come. She'd be able to tell him that Jack Newman is a secret psychopath.

She takes a break from trying to tear the tape with her teeth. It's hard to keep it up for more than a couple of minutes at a time. She's so dehydrated, she can't produce saliva. Her eyelids droop. They're heavy, sticky. She lifts her head slightly and lets it fall with a thump. She can't afford to sleep. Sleeping is giving up. Sleep is a practice run for death.

Daisy will never forgive her if she doesn't make it. Granger can't bear the thought of her daughter believing she didn't fight hard enough to stay alive. She chews the tape again. This time she twists her head one way and then the other, like a savage dog tearing at flesh. Pain shoots through her jaw, a tooth jerks loose, and she hears the wonderful sound of ripping.

Granger rolls on to her back. She's breathing heavily, the side of her mouth throbbing. She looks at her wrists and despite the pain she gives a triumphant squeal. The tape at the base of her right thumb is torn, flapping loose. She tries to pull her wrists apart and this time she can feel the binding give. She yanks again and though it gives a fraction more, it's not enough.

She's close to succumbing to her exhaustion but tells herself that she has a chance to escape. She's going to get out. What she needs first is a short rest, a minute or two, no more, to gather her strength. She closes her eyes, takes a long slow breath and falls asleep.

CHAPTER 53

"Granger's car was picked up by a number plate recognition camera heading north out of town at 10.30 p.m.," Finch says. "The bad news is that there was no other sighting of it and the image isn't clear enough to identify the driver."

Kane gets up from behind his desk and paces frantically back and forth across the room. The door-to-door inquiries haven't turned up anything useful either. In less than thirty-two hours he's going to be unceremoniously kicked off the case, with Granger still missing and the murders unsolved.

Finch is watching him with a concerned expression. He stops pacing. "What about the mobile phones?"

Finch shrugs. "The tech team say it's impossible to trace the origin of the message sent to Newman's phone. What they can confirm is that it didn't come from Ray Spencer's."

Kane has always been confident that Spencer wasn't their man. He was a rage killer.

"Once Harry has been fed and watered, I'd like you to take him back to his flat. Let him clean himself up, get a change of clothes and then bring him back. We'll put him in a cell overnight but make it clear that it's for his safety."

Finch nods and stands. "How did it go with Newman?"

That's a good question. Kane's not sure how to answer it. The reporter's account of the night Granger disappeared is credible. But something about it doesn't ring true. The news that he's leaving to start a lucrative new job in the city is unsettling. The only person who seems to have profited from the murders is Jack Newman.

"He reckons Granger probably never got as far as his flat. He says he went to bed early and slept through."

"You think he's lying?"

Kane has a feeling that the reporter is always lying about something. "Telling lies comes more naturally to pathological liars than telling the truth. Sometimes everything you think you know about them is a complete fabrication."

Finch turns to leave, hesitating at the door. "I don't know if this is important or not boss. When we were trying to find Newman the other night, I spoke to a few of his colleagues at the paper to see if he had any relatives nearby. One of the receptionists said he once told her he had an aunt in Great Wakering, a village along the coast."

* * *

It takes Kane fifteen minutes to drive the four miles east to the marshland village. The pale-pink thatched cottage stands on the edge of common land. From the doorstep Kane has a good view of the creeks snaking their way to the sea.

He knocks twice and waits patiently, aware that the woman he's come to see may take a while to make her way to the door. After a couple of minutes, he knocks again, this time with more force.

The door opens slightly. A wrinkled face peers up at Kane over a pair of half-moon spectacles. "What do you want?" The woman's voice is raspy, hardly more than a whisper.

Kane shows her his warrant card, holding it up long enough to make sure she gets a good look at the photograph. "I'm Detective Inspector Kane. I take it you are Violet Pearse?"

"I might be."

"I called you about an hour ago to tell you I was coming. You said it would be all right."

The woman frowns, furrowing her deeply lined brow. "Did I really? How strange. In that case, you better come in." She slides the safety chain out of the catch and opens the door.

Kane walks past her, straight into the living room, stooping to avoid hitting his head on the ceiling beams. The woman hobbles after him. She's stooping too but not for the same reason. Her spine is so severely curved, she looks in danger of toppling over.

"You know, I used to be tall once upon a time," she croaks. "A tall, elegant young woman. Now look at the state of me. A bent old crone."

Kane is not sure how to respond. He sits down on a floral-patterned armchair angled to face a grubby tiled fireplace. He guesses the chair has been in the same room, in exactly the same place, for at least half a century.

The woman gives him a curious look. "Why don't you take a seat, inspector? Oh, I see you already have." She sits in a similar armchair on the other side of the hearth, pulls a tartan blanket over her legs and gazes at him expectantly.

"Thank you for seeing me at such short notice, Ms Pearse. I appreciate it."

She lifts a bony hand and waves it dismissively. "I'd prefer it if you called me Violet. I don't get many visitors these days. It feels good to hear someone saying my name. Reminds me who I am, and I do need reminding some days. Violet has always been my favourite colour. It's derived from the word *viola*, which means purple in Latin."

"All right then, Violet. I explained on the phone that I wanted to speak to you about your nephew, Jack Newman?"

"Of course. I know I look decrepit but I'm not senile yet. I haven't seen young Jack for years. He's my sister's boy. What's he done now?"

Kane shifts forward in his seat. "What makes you say that?"

"Always in trouble, he was, which was a shame because he was smart. Expelled from school several times. Cheating in exams, bullying classmates."

None of this surprises Kane. The man is still sly and arrogant but that doesn't mean he's a killer.

"He works as journalist now, a newspaper reporter specialising in crime."

Violet nods, then shakes her head. "I did hear something about that. What a shame. Iris would be so disappointed. My big sister had plans for her only child. Wanted him to follow in her footsteps and take over her veterinary practice. I told her that was never going to happen. He hated animals."

"What about Jack's parents? What were they like?"

Violet wrings her hands, closing her eyes briefly to help her concentrate. "I loved my sister but she wasn't an easy woman to be around. She could be demanding and extremely stern, and she became worse after Joseph, her husband, killed himself. Nobody could work out why. Jack was thirteen. He found his dad. He'd hanged himself in the barn."

Kane never imagined he'd be in a position where he'd feel sorry for Newman.

"That must have been tough for them both."

Violet sighs. "Nobody had any idea why Joseph did it. Jack took it into his head that his mother was to blame. Time is supposed to heal but he never forgave her. He left home as soon as he possibly could and never returned. Not even when Iris was diagnosed. The cancer took her quickly. Jack never even came back for her funeral. I must say I thought that was wicked of him. She left him everything. The cottage and the land."

Kane had no idea that Newman was a property owner. As far as he knew, the reporter rented a flat in the town centre and lived modestly.

"Where is this cottage? Is it local? Does he rent it out?"

Violet's eyes narrow suspiciously. "What's with all these questions? Are you a policeman or the taxman?"

"I showed you my warrant card at the door, remember? I'm a detective inspector and I'm investigating a serious crime. I'm hoping you can help me."

"Is my nephew in danger?"

"No, I don't believe so."

"Is he in trouble?"

"I think he might be."

Violet gazes down at the mottled skin on the back of her hands. She closes her eyes for a few seconds, as if gathering her strength. "Stone Cottage is only a couple of miles from here. Just outside a village called Barling. It's the place where Jack grew up, where his mother's veterinary practice was based. I believe it's empty now and it's decaying quickly. A bit like me."

Kane stands up, impatient to get away. He wants to drive over to Stone Cottage before it gets dark. Newman may have abandoned the place but it needs to be checked out for his own peace of mind.

"Thank you for your help. I appreciate it, but I have to go."

Violet's face crumples in disappointment. Kane realises he's probably the first person she's seen in days, maybe even weeks.

"Have I really helped? I do hope I haven't got young Jack into more trouble. He's not that bad, you know. Not really. It's just that his brain works a little bit differently than most people's, that's all. That's what Iris always said."

CHAPTER 54

Granger opens her eyes, blinking rapidly. It takes her a moment to remember why she doesn't have to rush to make Daisy's packed lunch and get her ready for school, why one side of her mouth is throbbing, why her throat is raw and her stomach cramping.

She lifts her wrists close to her face, her heart fluttering in her ribcage like a frightened bird. She balls her hands into fists and twists them back and forth, grunting with effort. Each time the tear in the tape gives a little more.

She stops to catch her breath. The thought crosses her mind that the last time she hugged her daughter before sending her off to school could turn out to be the *actual* last time. Granger shakes her head, unwilling to accept that as a possibility. She twists her fists again, while summing up her last ounce of strength to pull them apart. To her astonishment, the tape finally gives, ripping in two.

A rush of adrenaline gives her weakened body renewed strength. She lifts her knees to her chest, reaches down and claws at the tape around her ankles, freeing her legs. Working quickly, she twists on to her front, wriggles the fingers of both hands down the edge of the boot floor and yanks it back. A six-inch strip of the plastic snaps clean-off. She slides her right hand into the gap.

Her fingertips brush the rubber tread of the spare tyre, then the cold metal of a car jack. She shifts forward a few inches to force her hand deeper, scrambling around until she cries out in triumph, her fingers curling around the handle of a screwdriver.

Granger knows she mustn't stop, even though she's exhausted. Newman could return any moment. She rolls on to her back and jams the point of the tool into the latch, twisting it one way, then the other. The boot springs open.

She struggles to her knees and climbs out, her limbs stiff and heavy. The barn is as dark as the car boot, the air rotten. She's still gripping the screwdriver tightly, half expecting Newman to jump out of the shadows.

Granger tries to lick her scabbed lips but her tongue is too swollen and dry. She has no idea how far away the nearest inhabited dwelling is but she knows that finding it is the only way she's going to get help.

She walks slowly to the barn door, still unsteady on her feet, and is relieved to find it unlocked. She shoulders it open and staggers out. The night is moonless, the air fresher. The black bulk of an unlit cottage looms on the other side of an overgrown lawn.

Newman would only have brought her to this place because he knew for sure that it was abandoned and isolated. She wonders whether he's asleep in the cottage dreaming about killing her, or lying on his back staring at the ceiling, planning in gory detail how he's going to mutilate her body.

A nagging voice in the back of her mind urges her to run, to flag down a passing car, knock on the door of the nearest house and beg for help. That would be what any sensible woman with a child waiting for her at home would do. Granger considers herself sensible. But she's much too weak, too dehydrated to run anywhere. She can't hear any passing traffic or see a single light nearby.

Perhaps she should have trained to be a doctor. She almost did. Her mother had tried hard to guide her down that path. Her brothers would be proud. They'd probably even still speak to her. Doctor Bailey Granger has a ring to it. At least she wouldn't be putting her life in danger, wouldn't be risking her daughter's future.

She raises the screwdriver, brandishing it in front of her like a weapon, and wades through the knee-high grass toward the building. As she draws closer, she realises the cottage is derelict. Several windows are broken and large patches of thatch are missing from the roof. She decides it's unlikely that Newman is inside and heads for the back door, praying that the building still has running water.

The door is locked. The mechanism looks almost new. That surprises her. Why bother securing a building that's been neglected for years? She shoves the point of the screwdriver into the keyhole, tries to force the lock open but gives up after a few minutes.

She moves quickly to the nearest window and has more luck. The wooden frame is crumbling, the glass pane cracked down the middle. Granger uses the screwdriver to lever out a length of the frame, removes the two sections of glass, and clambers inside.

The kitchen is small. The square table in the centre of the room is the only thing not covered in dust and cobwebs. She walks quickly over to the sink and twists both taps. The pipes gurgle and shudder violently. Granger bows her head, more in frustration than in despair. Even if she wanted to cry, she'd be too dehydrated to produce tears.

She sighs and swallows hard, wincing at the rawness of her throat. Straining her eyes in the gloom, she spots a light switch on the opposite wall. She flicks it. No power. Beside the switch is a small pantry door. Granger presses an ear against it, wondering if her mind is playing tricks. She can hear a faint electrical hum.

She opens the door tentatively, stooping low to step inside. The space is more like a large cupboard than a small room. It's empty except for a shiny new mini refrigerator, slightly larger than the ones you'd find in a hotel room. A green light on the fridge door confirms that it has power.

What is a fridge doing here? Granger can't work it out. All she can think about is a long drink of chilled water. She drops on to her knees and pulls the door open. Her heart sinks when she sees the shelves are empty. She opens the small freezer box, already imagining cubes of ice melting on her tongue.

She slides out the tray, stares down at it for a few seconds before placing it carefully on top of the fridge. Bile rises in her throat and she lurches forward, her empty stomach retching.

The last thing Granger wants to do is look again, to have to see what she'll never be able to unsee as long as she lives. But she can't stop herself. The black silicone tray contains four king-size ice cubes. Two of them are staring back at her. Two frozen eyeballs. Beside them, a pair of ice-encased ears.

Granger covers her mouth and retches again. She takes a few seconds to let her stomach settle, then reminds herself that the cottage is a crime scene. She needs to be careful about contamination, but the ice cubes mustn't be allowed to melt. She picks the tray up again and puts it back into the freezer box, relieved that it's out of sight.

She gets off her knees and reverses back through the pantry door, her hunger pangs, even her desperate thirst, fading. Her priority now is to find the nearest person with a mobile phone, contact Kane and get him to send a full forensic team.

Granger walks across the kitchen to the window and prepares to climb out. She freezes at the sound of a car engine, ducking out of sight as a pair of powerful headlights slice through the dark.

She catches her breath. Newman has returned to finish her off. She should have got as far away as possible when she had the chance. Panic flutters in her chest. He'll go straight to the car, she tells herself. Why wouldn't he? She decides to wait until he's inside the barn, then run.

The engine noise dies, a car door slams shut. Granger backs away from the window, crouching behind the wooden table. Her hand trembles slightly as she pulls the screwdriver out of her jacket.

She holds her breath and listens for footsteps. The only sound she can hear is the thudding of her heart. A figure looms at the window, hesitates briefly, then climbs inside.

Granger gets up from behind the table as the figure approaches. She sees his face and wants to cry out but she doesn't. She stands tall and straightens her shoulders. She doesn't want Kane to see her at her weakest.

"Thank God," he says. "You're alive."

Grangers drops the screwdriver on the table. "And kicking."

CHAPTER 55

"I ain't done nothing wrong," Harry Cannon says. He can hear the fear in his voice and hates himself for it. When he's scared, he panics, and when he panics, he always ends up getting into big trouble.

"Where's your boss? He told me I wouldn't have to go back to prison. He fucking promised me."

Harry can't believe he was so easily taken in. He's been let down numerous times by people who said they'd help him. You can't trust anyone. He should have learned his lesson by now. Everyone lies to get what they want. That's the truth.

The door of his flat is open. Detective Constable Finch stands on the threshold, her hands on her hips, her nose wrinkled as if she's detected a bad smell.

"How many times do I have to explain this to you?" she says. "Detective Inspector Kane has decided that you should be held overnight at the station for your own safety. You are not going back to prison. Not this time, anyway. We'll find you somewhere more comfortable tomorrow. Put whatever you need in a bag and let's go."

Harry still isn't convinced. He's never considered a police station a place of safety. Not for people like him. "I need to talk to your boss. I got something big to tell him. If he knows, he'll understand."

Finch sighs. "Tell him what? Listen Harry, I'll let Kane know that you want to speak to him and that it's urgent. But you need to come with me right now. I'm under strict instructions to keep an eye on you until you're safely tucked up in one of our cells. You'll be warm, fed and watered. It'll be like staying in a hotel."

Harry has never stayed in a hotel. He has been in a cell and he didn't like it. He thinks about telling Detective Finch about the man he saw waiting for the lift at the police station. How he recognised him straight away despite the fact that it had been dark that night on the beach and he'd only caught a glimpse of his face. It was easy because he'd seen the man before. Close up. In broad daylight. And Banjo had told him that the man was a reporter willing to pay a lot of money for information about the detective on Ray Spencer's payroll.

But then he'd have to explain why he never admitted that he knew Banjo, confess that he called the police to tell them what he'd seen that night only when he found out that the body being dragged down the beach was Banjo's.

"Okay then," he says. "I'll be a couple of minutes. You can come inside if you want. It's not as bad as it smells."

Finch eyes the stained sofa with undisguised disgust. "I'd rather wait here, thanks, but get a move on. It's late and my shift was supposed to have ended an hour ago."

Harry goes into his bedroom, closing the door behind him. Most of the space is taken up by an unmade single bed. His spare clothes are stashed haphazardly in two cardboard boxes.

He rifles through them quickly and puts on a fresh pair of jeans and a hooded jacket he stole last week from a bag outside a charity shop. It's at least a size too big for him but he's hoping to grow into it.

Harry walks over to the window and opens it slowly and silently. He leans on the sill and stares into the darkness, wondering whether he's making a big mistake. It's a habit he can't break. When things get difficult, his first instinct is to run.

The detectives Kane and Granger seem like decent people, for coppers. But they're outsiders. Once this case is tied up, they'll be gone. Then what? Harry can't recall a single time when getting involved with the police hasn't ended badly for him.

CHAPTER 56

Jack Newman puts his hand in his pocket and curls his fingers around the handle of the knife. He can see the detective standing in the doorway, her back to him. A perfect target.

He crosses the narrow road and slips between two parked cars. The black sky is moonless, the street lamps casting pools of yellow light on the pavement. Newman knows what he must do.

Kane's prime witness saw him, clearly recognised him, and it's only a matter of time before the kid destroys everything Newman has worked for. He can't let that happen, even if it means two more deaths, two messy murders.

He needs to keep calm. Killing in cold blood is always the most efficient way to snuff out a life. It takes a lot of self-control. Deep inside he's raging. The See No Evil Killer is his creation. His pride and joy. Every detail planned to perfection. Now he's being forced to kill in a hurry and that's risky.

As he moves closer, he can hear the detective talking. He can't make out what she's saying but the conversation is keeping her distracted. He scans the street quickly. There's nobody in sight. His last two steps are fast and forceful. The knife flashes in his hand and, before the victim knows what's happening, before she can twist away or cry out, it's done. Silent, swift, deadly.

Newman shuts the door behind him. Detective Finch lies face down on the floor, blood bubbling from the wound in her back. If she's not dead yet she'll be gone in a matter of minutes. He looks down at her still body, his gaze devoid of pity. She's collateral damage. Nothing more.

The room is a mess. Stains on the sofa, dirty dishes piled up in the sink and empty food packaging scattered around the base of an overfilled waste paper bin.

Newman watched the detective and Harry Cannon arrive together. The kid must be here somewhere. His eyes flick to the two doors on the far side of the room. One is slightly ajar. He grips the handle of the door that is shut and pushes.

Harry Cannon is standing beside an open window, eyes wide and fixed on the bloodstained knife. Newman walks across the room and shuts the window. The kid backs away.

"Please don't hurt me."

"I don't want to hurt you. I just want to kill you."

The boy is trembling. He's eyeing the door, weighing up his chances of escape. Newman allows himself a smile. Fear makes you feeble. Freezes your brain. Newman is in total control. He holds the power of life and death in his right hand, and the boy knows it.

"Get into the other room."

The boy does as he's told, his legs buckling, when he sees the detective on the floor, blood pooling beside her. Newman shoves him hard in the back, directing him toward the sofa.

"For God's sake, sit down before you fall down."

The boy takes a seat, wiping beads of sweat from his face with the sleeve of his hoodie. "Have you killed her?"

"I hope so."

Newman considers taking Finch's car and driving the boy back to Stone Cottage but dismisses the idea immediately. He's not planning to pass these murders off as the work of his creation. These deaths, like Granger's, are simply a case of tying up loose ends, clearing the way for him to start his new life in London. The police will draw their own conclusions and if their performance so far is anything to go by, they'll probably be wrong.

The boy drags his eyes away from Finch's body. Newman knows what's coming next. He's going to waste his last minutes on this earth pleading for mercy, begging to be allowed to live. Newman will listen because, you never know, it might be entertaining.

"Please don't kill me. I won't say nothing to nobody. I'll leave Southend. Leave the country even, if you want me to."

Newman wishes the boy was telling the truth. Not because he wants to spare him, but because he wasn't expecting to have to kill people as himself. The thrill is the same but that was never the plan, and it's dangerous when a plan goes awry. His murderous creation was a masterstroke. It made him the author of his own story.

The boy is waiting for him to say something, maybe even give him a glimmer of hope. Newman can't do that.

"I swear I won't go to the police. They don't know the truth. Please don't kill me. I'll won't say a word. Please, I promise."

Newman looks down at the boy with contempt. He's a pathetic creature who doesn't deserve to live. Banjo was the same. They'd agreed a price and the story was going to be big. Big enough to give Newman's career a much-needed boost, even attract the attention of the national newspapers. Then Banjo got greedy, threatened to tell Spencer and Miller unless Newman tripled the payment. He couldn't afford to pay up but he couldn't put his life in danger either. Instead, he created his own story. A much bigger story. About a killer with a taste for mutilation. And Banjo made the perfect first victim.

The kid is still whingeing. Newman has had enough. Time to get the job done. He raises the knife.

CHAPTER 57

Kane puts his phone back in his pocket and looks across at Granger, who's gulping down a bottle of mineral water she found in the glove compartment. Considering what she's been through, she doesn't look too bad.

He starts the engine and pulls out on to the dark country lane. "I'm going to drop you off at the nearest hospital. You need looking at. Maybe an intravenous drip to get some fluid and vitamins into you."

Granger shakes her head. "We haven't time for that. I'm not feeling that bad, honestly. Nothing a good feed and a long sleep won't fix. We need to make sure Harry's safe, then track down Newman before he can harm anyone else."

Kane is loath to take risks with her health but he is worried about Harry. "I asked Finch to take the kid to his flat earlier this evening, to pick up a change of clothes. Then she was supposed to bring him back to one of our cells for the night. Nobody at the station has seen either of them since."

Granger drains the last drop of fluid from the bottle and puts it back in the glove compartment. "That settles it, then. We'll drive straight to Harry's flat. I reckon Newman sees that things are starting to unravel and he's losing control. Anyone posing a threat to him is in real danger."

Kane knows she's right.

"As soon as we're satisfied that Harry is safe, I'm taking you to hospital."

As they reach the edge of town, two patrol cars speed past them, blue lights flashing and sirens wailing, followed by a more sedately driven white van.

"I've tipped forensics off about what they're going to find in the ice cube tray," Kane says. "It must have been quite a shock."

He feels Granger shudder beside him. "If you don't mind, I'd rather not talk about that right now."

Kane isn't surprised. He's seen plenty of blood and gore in his time but nothing as horrific as that. He makes a mental note to suggest to Granger that she considers booking a few sessions with the force's trauma counsellor.

He gives her a sideways glance. Her eyes are closed, her head tilted back. They're going to be arriving at the flat soon. He might as well let her rest until then.

Ten minutes later, Kane accelerates down the deserted coastal road, braking sharply as he nears Castle Avenue. He steers carefully around the patrol car parked across the entrance to the street and pulls up. Six uniformed officers wait for him on the pavement.

He leans across to give Granger a nudge but she's already unclipping her seatbelt. Kane gets out of the car and walks to the uniforms. The tallest officer, a dark-haired woman with three stripes on her arm, moves forward to introduce herself.

"Sergeant Alison Grey," she says. Kane acknowledges her with a nod.

Grey points to a car parked fifty metres down the street. "We've confirmed that the vehicle outside Harry Cannon's flat is Detective Finch's. We've called her mobile several times. She's not answering. As you instructed, we haven't approached the flat yet. Lights are on inside but we haven't seen anyone enter or leave the building.

"What about a back door?"

"We have two officers in the alleyway behind the flat."

Kane turns to Granger. Her lips look painfully sore, the whites of her eyes bloodshot. "Are you sure you're up to this?"

"Don't worry, I'm doing okay. Come on then, let's go get this done."

The two detectives walk briskly toward the flat. The uniformed officers follow, positioning themselves in a line along the pavement, facing the building. Kane tries the door. It's unlocked. He opens it a fraction, gives Granger a nod, and they step inside.

The scene in the flat is worse than either of them could have imagined. Detective Finch lies face down in a slick pool of blood, a knife wound in her back. Harry Cannon cowers on the sofa. Newman looms over him, a long-bladed knife in his hand.

The reporter grabs Harry's hoodie, drags him to his feet, wraps his left arm around the boy's neck and turns to face the detectives.

"Stay back or I'll kill the kid. You know I'll do it. You've seen the autopsy reports. Through the back and straight into the heart. Quick and effective."

Kane looks to Granger. He wants her to take the lead, start the talking, give him a chance to assess the situation. She gets the message and holds up her hands.

"Please stay calm, Jack," she says. "Nobody's going to rush you, I promise. We don't want anyone else getting hurt. Not Harry and not you. Just take a minute to think about what you are doing."

"I know exactly what I'm doing," Newman says, grinning as he tightens his hold on Harry's neck. The kid's eyes bulge as he gasps for air.

"I knew I should have finished you off when I had the chance. My first big mistake. Now everything I've worked for is ruined. The life, the recognition I deserve, gone."

"Please let him breathe," Granger pleads, wincing at the pain on Harry's face. "You're crushing his windpipe."

"Does it matter? The boy's going to die anyway."

Granger takes a small step forward. Newman notes the movement with a tilt of his head but doesn't react.

"Why would you bother killing him now? There's nothing to gain from his death. We know everything and we have plenty of evidence. There's no way out of this for you."

Newman's grin disappears. It's replaced by a malevolent grimace. "Maybe I'll simply kill him out of spite. For fun. Just to see the look on your faces. What have I got to lose?"

Kane studies the reporter's expression, fascinated by his first glimpse of the real Jack Newman. A secret psychopath unmasked. Trying to make him feel sympathy or guilt is a waste of time. Kane knows that. But there is always a way to get someone as self-obsessed and narcissistic as Newman to listen.

"You certainly fooled us all. I have to give you credit for that."

Newman twists to face Kane, pulling Harry around with him. "Well, well. There he is, the big man. Detective Inspector Edison Kane. I'd be lying if I said fooling you and your team was a difficult task. It was all so depressingly simple. Killing is surprisingly easy if you set your mind to it. And you know what surprised me most? It gets easier every time."

Harry's face is scarlet, his eyes brimming with tears. Kane wants to tell him to hang tough, that he won't let anybody hurt him and that everything is going to turn out fine. He can't. Newman is teetering on the edge.

"Writing those emails to your newspaper, then sending them to yourself, that was probably your most impressive move. A masterstroke. My tech unit couldn't work it out."

Newman nods in agreement. "It was a great idea, wasn't it? A stroke of genius, really. It placed me exactly where I wanted to be, right at the centre of the story, while at the same time it put me above suspicion. Technically, it wasn't difficult to do. All it took was a handful of burner phones and a few temporary email addresses."

Kane can hear the pride in Newman's voice and knows he's on the right track. "You played us perfectly, right from the start."

Newman takes a deep breath and sighs loudly. Kane senses that the reporter is starting to relax, relieved that his brilliance is being recognised. Harry feels it too, and twists his head to squirm away. Newman whips the knife around and jams the blade against Harry's throat. The edge splits the skin and blood trickles down the boy's neck on to his hoodie.

"Keep perfectly still, Harry," Granger says. "Try to breath slowly, and do not move a muscle."

Newman lifts the blade a fraction. "Listen carefully to the lady detective, kid. That's extremely good advice."

Granger exchanges a knowing glance with Kane. "This will turn out better for you if you let him go, Jack," she says. "You're going to prison for a long time whatever happens, but you're still going to be at the centre of the story, aren't you? The nationals love a super-smart killer. You must know that better than anybody. You almost got away with it, and the papers and news channels are going to lap that up, make you a celebrity. If you murder this boy now, when you're in a position to show him mercy, it's too messy."

Newman's eyes widen when he hears the word *celebrity*. There is silence as he lets Granger's plea sink in.

Kane estimates he's about eight feet away from the reporter, Granger a little closer. They could rush him if they had to. If it was the only chance of saving Harry.

Newman nods in Granger's direction. "You know what, Kane? You better watch your back. This woman will probably have your job soon. She talks a lot of sense."

"I'm fully aware of how smart she is, and she knows I value her highly."

Granger risks taking another step forward. This time Newman jabs the knife at her. "Stay back. Don't push me. I need space to think. I created this killer. This isn't how my story is supposed to end."

Granger takes two steps back. "I'm sorry," she says. "I know things haven't worked out the way you wanted them to, but for a while you outwitted everyone. I don't know how this all started but letting Harry go would be a way to show that you're not a total monster."

Newman looks at Kane, then back at Granger. He drops the knife on to the sofa and releases his hold on Harry, who slumps in a heap on to the floor.

"I want people to know that I'm not evil," Newman says. "That's important to me. I'm not crazy either. Everything I did, I did it for a good reason. I have no interest in killing anyone if I don't benefit from it."

CHAPTER 58

Granger rolls on to her back, the tape around her wrists rubbing the skin raw. The darkness smells of decay and death. She bends her knees, kicks as hard as she can and the car boot pops open. Dazzled by the light, she snaps her eyes shut. When she opens them, Kane is looking down her, an awkward smile on his face.

"Sorry, I didn't mean to wake you. How are you feeling this morning?"

Granger sits up, raises her knees and pulls the starched white sheet up to her neck. She's desperate for a pee. They must have dripped gallons of fluid into her vein. She decides she can hold it in until Kane leaves.

"I'm feeling pretty good considering. A little drowsy. They gave me something to help me sleep."

She reaches over to the bedside table and checks the time on her mobile. It's 7.30 a.m. "It's a bit early for a visit, isn't it? How did you persuade them to let you in?"

"The usual way. I flashed my badge. I wanted to check how you were before I start preparing to interview Newman."

The reporter's name triggers a flutter of panic high in Granger's chest. Memories flash through her mind, like stills from a horror movie. Detective Finch lying dead on the floor.

Rivulets of blood streaming down Harry's neck. Eyes frozen in ice cubes, staring up at her accusingly.

"Like I said before, I'm feeling all right. I'm assured there's nothing to worry about. No permanent damage. I've been thoroughly examined by a variety of medics. Mum and Daisy are coming in after I've had breakfast to take me home."

Granger isn't thrilled by the prospect of taking time off work. Not yet. She can tell by the wry smile on Kane's face that he knows why.

"I think it's makes sense that you spend today at home with your family. You deserve it. Take the chance to relax and rest up. If you're feeling up to it, you can join me in the interview room tomorrow. How about that?"

It's a reasonable suggestion and she's desperate to make up for lost time with Daisy. The problem is, she's not feeling the slightest bit reasonable. After everything that's happened to her, she wants to look Newman in the eye and listen to him try to explain why he murdered three innocent people.

"What time do you think you're likely to be starting the interview today?"

Kane drags a chair to the side of the bed and sits. "I'll take a couple of hours to prepare. Newman will have to be given time to speak to a lawyer if he wants legal representation. We have a lot of detail to go through but I'm hoping he won't make things difficult for us. I reckon we'll be able to get going at noon. You saw what he was like last night. As long as we show interest, he's going to love telling us he's a criminal mastermind, how he almost got away with murder."

Granger suppresses an urge to yawn. "Noon is perfect," she says. "When Mum and Daisy arrive, I can take them out for coffee and a milkshake, let them see how well I am. Once they're reassured, I can get to the station in plenty of time to join you."

Kane falls silent. Granger can tell he's torn but she's confident he's going to relent. He'll understand the importance of seeing this case through to end. He must feel the same. She needs to see justice done, for the victims, for their families, and for her own peace of mind.

Kane stands up and pushes the chair back against the wall. Granger assumes that means that he has made up his mind.

"My problem is that I don't want to take any risks with your health. Physical and mental. You did an amazing job talking Newman down last night. There's no denying that he likes you, in a weird sort of way, and I admit that could be useful. But I'm worried about you."

Granger doesn't believe that being liked by a serial killer is something to be proud of. In fact, she finds it disturbing. "How many times do I need to say it? I'm fine. The doctors have given me a clean bill of health. You can speak to them yourself if you want to. There is no need for you to worry. What I do need you to do is let me do my job."

Kane looks at her, his expression blank, turns and walks to the open door. For a moment, Granger wonders whether she went too far. Maybe she should have been more subtle. Picked her words more carefully.

Kane turns back to face her. "Enjoy your coffee. Take your time and treat yourself to some cake. Just make sure you get to the station in plenty of time to be briefed."

CHAPTER 59

Newman sits on the edge of the bed, a grey blanket around his shoulders, spooning the last of the baked beans into his mouth. His first night in a cell turned out to be more comfortable than he expected. He'd slept soundly, the deep sleep of the innocent, which is funny if you think about it.

Last night, they took his fingerprints and a mugshot and swabbed the inside of his cheek for DNA. What a waste of police time and resources. He did it, he murdered three people and he's not going to deny it.

He stands, raises both arms and stretches, wondering what his first day in police custody is going to bring. It never crossed his mind that, one day, the police would catch him, but why should he be fearful of the future?

Newman folds the blanket and places it neatly on the end of the bed. If all had gone to plan, he'd be viewing penthouse flats to rent in East London today. Instead, he'll soon be swapping the police holding cell for a permanent residence in one of His Majesty's prisons.

He paces across the cell, pondering the alternatives. Maybe suicide would be an option. Is killing yourself easier or harder than killing a stranger? The idea doesn't frighten him but he's not ready to take that path yet.

An idea pops into his head. He stops pacing and sits back down on the bed. If he can convince a shrink that he wasn't in his right mind when he went on his killing spree, he could end up in psychiatric care.

Receiving treatment for a mental illness rather than punished for being evil appeals to him. Perhaps he's destined to join the ranks of some of the crazy serial killers he's spent so much of his time reading about.

The cell door opens and the custody sergeant enters. He's a fleshy man with greying ginger hair and a permanent smile on his face.

"Good morning. I trust you had a good night's sleep in our humble hotel. Make sure you give us a five-star review on TripAdvisor."

Newman guesses he's supposed to laugh. Instead, he responds with a cold stare.

"Suit yourself, buddy. Most of my guests think it's funny. Anyway, you're entitled to legal representation and we have a duty lawyer available now if you'd like to speak to her."

The sergeant's smile widens as he waits for an answer. Newman can't recall seeing anyone enjoy their job so much. Who knew locking strangers up could be such fun?

Five minutes later, he's wearing his shoes again minus the laces, and sitting across a table from the duty lawyer in an interview room. Newman estimates that Ms Kemp is in her late twenties. He'd hoped for someone with more experience, but when she speaks it's clear that she knows what she's talking about.

"You're facing three charges of murder and I'd recommend that at least during this first interview you answer all questions with a no comment. It'll give you more time to consider how you want to plead when you appear in court."

Newman nods slowly. "I know all about my right to remain silent. I'd rather not waste anyone's time. I'm guilty and they have plenty of evidence to convict me. I know this might offend you but I'm not ashamed of what I've done. In fact, I'm proud."

Ms Kemp blinks hard as she struggles to keep her expression blank. Newman chalks this up as a little victory and celebrates with a smirk. He's always enjoyed unnerving people.

"Naturally, it's your right to say whatever you want in an interview, Mr Newman. I can only advise."

"I've been thinking about pleading not guilty by reason of insanity. A good move?"

Ms Kemp sits back in her chair and gives Newman a curious look. He wonders whether lawyers are trained to assess a client's sanity by appearance alone.

"It's possible but not easy. Your defence counsel would have to prove that at the time of the murders you were suffering from a defect of reason as a result of a disease of the mind."

Newman nods thoughtfully. "I like the sound of that. It seems like it's doable."

"I wouldn't advise it," Ms Kemp says. "It's an extremely complex defence and difficult to win. That's why it's so rarely used. Another option, which is more common, would be pleading not guilty to murder but guilty to manslaughter due to diminished responsibility."

"Claiming that at the time of the murders I was temporarily out of my mind and didn't know what I was doing?"

"Correct, more or less. If successful you'll be sent to a secure psychiatric hospital."

"For how long?"

"Until the doctors are convinced that you're ready to be released back into society." Newman thanks the lawyer for her help and is escorted back to his cell. After what he's heard, he's even more confident that he won't be serving a maximum sentence in a hellhole prison.

He lies on the bed, puts his hands behind his head and stares at the ceiling. How difficult can it be to convince experts that when you killed three innocent people you didn't understand it was wrong? If anyone can do it, he can. The ability to persuade has always been one of his talents.

A psychiatric hospital is his best option. You're a patient, not a prisoner. As long as you're co-operative you get the chance to play table tennis, stroll around the gardens, attend arts and craft classes. He's always considered himself creative. He'd be crazy not to go down the insanity route.

CHAPTER 60

"Is it true that before you killed the homeless man known as Banjo, you'd been working with him on a news story in which you were planning to expose Detective Sam Miller as a corrupt police officer?"

Newman looks across the table at Kane, lifts his right hand and points to Granger. "I'd prefer it if she asked the questions now. We've been at this for at least half an hour and your voice is starting to grate."

Kane is tempted to send Granger out of the interview room and replace her with one of the local detectives. He's worried that Newman is showing signs of obsession.

"I'd like you to answer the question."

"And I'd like Detective Granger to ask the question."

Kane looks across at Granger. He doesn't want her to do anything that will make her feel uncomfortable. She gives a nod of assent.

"What was your connection to Banjo?" she asks.

Newman sits up straight and claps his hands. "Bravo. Take note, Detective Inspector. That is a much better way of putting the question. I was never working with Banjo. He was simply supplying me with information. He came to see me at the *Herald* a few months ago, saying he knew about a local detective who was in the pocket of a crooked businessman. He wanted paying. A thousand pounds, he said."

"You agreed to pay for the information."

"I did. He told me about Ray Spencer's mobile phone gangs and that Sam Miller had been recruited to help. I thought it'd make a fantastic story, that it would be big enough to attract the attention of the London papers and help me make a name for myself. I was prepared to pay him myself. The *Herald* has a policy of never paying cash for stories. It's considered vulgar."

Newman glances at the camera in the corner of the interview room. "Is this being filmed?"

Kane places his hands flat on the table and sighs. Psychopaths get bored easily. He's seen it before. They need constant stimulation. If they're not getting it, they create their own drama.

"I told you at the start of this interview that it was being digitally recorded and filmed. You said that you understood."

"Did I?" Newman says, rolling up the sleeves of his white shirt and smoothing his hair with his hands. "Don't remember the bit about it being filmed. If I knew I was going to be on camera I'd have dressed up."

"Let's get on with the interview."

Newman nods at Granger. "By all means. Go ahead."

"When did you decide to kill Banjo?" she asks.

"When he got greedy. He was using cocaine. Did you know that? Desperate for money to feed his habit. We met on the seafront near the pier and I gave him a first instalment of five hundred pounds. His eyes nearly popped out of his head when he saw the cash. Then he told me he wanted three thousand pounds or he'd tell Spencer and Miller that I was about to expose them. Not only was he threatening to ruin my big story, he'd be putting my life in danger."

"So, you murdered him."

"Not there and then. I went along with it. Arranged to meet him at my flat that night to hand over the cash."

"Then you murdered him."

Newman pauses, staring blankly into space. "It's all a bit of a blur now. Though I remember at the time everything seemed perfectly clear to me. This man was destroying my best chance to boost my career. He was putting me in danger. For years I'd been reading and researching everything I could about the phenomenon of murder and serial killers. I hoped it would give me an edge in my job. The truth is, I think I became obsessed, got drawn deep into the darkness. What was it that the philosopher Nietzsche said? If you gaze long enough into an abyss, the abyss will gaze back into you."

Kane holds up a hand to stop Newman going on. It sounds as if he's already trying to lay down the basics of some kind of defence.

"That's when and where you killed Banjo, wasn't it? That night, in your flat."

Newman keeps his eyes on Granger, deliberately ignoring Kane. After a moment, he relents.

"You're right. That's when I did it. I'm not sure what came over me. I desperately wanted a big news story and there's nothing bigger than a killer stalking the streets. I don't know where it came from, but the idea of creating a killer was suddenly there and Banjo was the perfect first victim."

Kane stands up, slips off his jacket and drapes it over the back of his chair. Newman is giving them a full confession. At the same time, he's lying.

"Why did you murder Isabel Anderson? She didn't pose any threat to you. She didn't even know you existed."

Newman shrugs. "I needed a second victim to keep the story going, that's all. She was in the wrong place at the wrong time. It wasn't personal."

Kane can't believe what he's hearing. Not personal. Tell that to her parents, to her boyfriend. Tell that to Linda Finch's family.

He takes a deep breath and sits back down next to Granger. "You mutilated Banjo's body, took the eyes. Then you took Isabel Anderson's ears. Can you explain that?"

Newman bows his head and gazes down at the table. It's a posture of remorse but Kane has no doubt that it's fake.

"I needed to do something juicy to make my story more sensational. Something eye-catching." He lifts his head and grins at his sick joke.

"Have you heard of the American serial killer Charles Albright? He murdered three women in the 1990s in Texas. He cut out their eyes and took them with him. He was obsessed with eyes."

"You thought it was a good idea. A fun thing to do."

Newman shakes his head. "I didn't say that. It wasn't fun. It was necessary. I was creating a monster. A lot of serial killers take trophies."

Kane stands up and picks up his jacket. He needs a break and is sure Granger does too. He's forgotten how draining spending time in the presence of evil can be.

"You're going back to your cell for now," he says. "In a day or so you'll be transferred to prison, where you'll stay until your trial."

Newman looks up at him. "Just so you know, I'll be pleading not guilty by reason of insanity."

Kane knows he shouldn't rise to the bait, that he should walk away. But he can't. "Psychopathy isn't considered to be a mental illness. It's simply how people like you are. How you're born."

Newman's eyes darken. "I've told you. I became obsessed with murder and murderers. I thought it would make me better at my job but it drew me in. Twisted my mind. I didn't kill for the sake of killing. I dreamt up the See No Evil Killer to achieve a goal."

Kane can't believe what he's hearing. The man genuinely thinks he was just *pretending*, that the killer came out of his imagination.

"You murdered those people in cold blood then mutilated their bodies. You did it. You didn't create a killer. You *became* one. You *are* your killer."

"I'm not evil. I'm not a psychopath."
"I believe you are both of those things."
"Are you medically qualified?"
"No."
"I rest my case, your honour."

CHAPTER 61

Granger carries the drinks back to the booth and sits down opposite Kane. He takes his beer and stares into the amber liquid. He's been unusually quiet since the interview.

"Don't worry," she says. "He's admitted everything. He's going down for three murders. They're going to lock him up and throw away the key."

"I hope so."

He doesn't sound convinced. "You should be celebrating. The case is solved. Newman is behind bars. He can't hurt anybody else."

It's early in the evening but the Dolphin is filling up with drinkers starting their weekend a day early.

Kane sips his beer and gives her a half-smile. "He still worries me, though. He's one of the most dangerous human beings I've ever met. I don't believe he's as clever as he thinks he is, certainly not a genius, but he's cunning and extremely manipulative."

"You reckon he could fool the forensic psychiatrists?"

"It's possible. It's not unheard of."

Granger picks up her glass and downs the rest of the lemonade in one go. She has no idea whether Newman is insane, an out-of-control psychopath or simply plain evil. But something deep in her gut tells her that for someone to even consider doing what he did to his victims, they'd have to be more than little bit crazy.

"What will happen to him now?"

"He's going to have a session with a psychologist tomorrow and in a couple of days he'll be transferred to Chelmsford Prison, where he'll be examined by at least two psychiatrists before his trial."

Granger finishes her drink. "I have to go. I want to put Daisy to bed tonight. Mum says she's been a bit anxious since, well, since . . . you know."

On the way to the pub, she'd felt sorry for Kane having to spend the evening on his own in his hotel room and was tempted to invite him around for a meal again. In the end she chose time with her daughter.

Before she can leave, Kane waves hand. "Would you mind staying for a moment? I won't keep you long, I promise." Granger checks her mobile, decides she can spare a few minutes and sits back down.

"I just wanted to say that considering this was your first murder investigation, you've done a great job and I'll be pointing that out to Superintendent Dean in my report. I also want to say that I'm sorry for what you went through. You must have been so scared. I really am sorry."

Granger is surprised by the emotion in Kane's voice. She wants to reach over and squeeze his hand. She doesn't. That would be too weird.

"I admit it was pretty frightening. There were moments when I thought I wasn't going to get out of that car boot alive. It wasn't your fault, though. I don't blame you at all, so stop beating yourself up. It's been a good experience working with you and I wouldn't hesitate to do it again."

She smiles, stands up and heads for the door, weaving her way through the crowd of rowdy drinkers. Before she reaches the exit her mobile rings. She answers it and listens, turns and walks slowly back to the booth.

"That was Suri Kumar, Harry Cannon's probation supervisor. He's vanished again. She temporarily placed him in a town centre hostel but the manager says he's disappeared. Kumar says he's run out of chances. When he turns up again, he's going back to prison."

Kane shrugs. "What more can we do? We tried out best. The boy's got demons to deal with. Perhaps he's not ready to be helped. You did everything you could. You go home now and be with your child. Go on, she needs you."

CHAPTER 62

Kane sits on the edge of the bed and kicks off his shoes. The hotel room is airless and claustrophobic. It's probably smaller than the cell Newman is spending the night in.

He stands up and switches the kettle on. The instant coffee the hotel provides is cheap and nasty. He's had to get used to it. He knows he shouldn't be going anywhere near caffeine at this time of night but he won't sleep anyway.

His head is still full of Newman's lies, of dead people, mutilated bodies, the grief of mothers, fathers, brothers and sisters. He needs more time before he can gather it up and file it all away.

If all goes to plan, the reporter will be moved to prison in a day or two and Kane will be able to go home. The thought should be a happy one but he's dreading returning to that house. Their house. He and Lizzy loved their home. Now it's full of emptiness, the heart ripped out of it. Sometimes he lets himself imagine that he can hear her footsteps or her laughter in one of the rooms upstairs. It helps a little.

The house will never feel, smell or sound the same again, and Kane has considered selling up and moving. He finishes his coffee, sits on the edge of the bed and stares at a brown stain on the worn carpet. He's not ready, not yet, to abandon the house that brought him and Lizzy so much joy, even though living there alone brings him nothing but misery.

* * *

Kane lifts a hand to stifle a yawn as he steps out of the lift. As expected, sleep had evaded him for most of the night. He takes three strides along the corridor toward his office and stops dead. He wants to turn and walk the other way but it's too late. Granger has seen him. He stays rooted to the spot, letting her and the woman with her come to him. As they approach, Granger says something and the other woman smiles in response. Rebecca Baxter is dressed more formally than usual, her dark grey trouser suit smart and androgynous.

"This is Detective Inspector Kane, who led the investigation," Granger says. "Ms Baxter is here for Jack Newman's psych assessment."

Kane nods. He'd been expecting a forensic psychologist but it hadn't crossed his mind that it might be Baxter. He moves to offer a handshake, then pulls back.

"Good morning. Nice to, er, see you, Ms Baxter."

The psychologist nods. "Thank you, Inspector, and please, I'd prefer Rebecca."

Kane throws Granger an uncomfortable glance. "If you could arrange for Newman to be brought up to the interview room, I'll brief, er, Rebecca, in my office."

Granger eyes the psychologist and then looks back at Kane. "Will do. I'll give you a shout when he's ready."

When she's gone, Kane leads Baxter to his office and they both take a seat. "These chairs aren't as comfortable as the ones in your consulting room, I'm afraid."

"They'll do, but you're looking more than a bit uncomfortable yourself. I take it you weren't expecting to see me."

"No."

"Well, you have nothing to worry about. I'm here to do my job as a forensic psychologist, that's all. Now, you said you want to brief me?"

Kane wishes he hadn't made things awkward, hadn't panicked when he saw Baxter with Granger.

"That's right. Jack Newman is a ruthless killer. A grade-A psychopath. He's going to try to convince you that he wasn't in his right mind, that he needs treatment, not punishment."

"I have done this before, you know."

Kane holds up a hand in apology. "I'm sure you have. I'm not suggesting otherwise. I just want to warn you. Let you know what you're dealing with. Newman is a cunning bastard. A master manipulator."

Baxter stands up, her cheeks flushing. "You know, it sounds like *you're* trying to manipulate me. I'll do my job to the best of my ability and, of course, you'll get a copy of my assessment. I'll wait in the corridor."

CHAPTER 63

Jack Newman smiles broadly at the forensic psychologist when she enters the interview room. He's spent all morning alone in the holding cell and he's desperate for some fun.

The woman smiles back, sits down and puts her mobile, a beige folder and a laptop on the table. "Good afternoon. I'm Rebecca Baxter. I'm here to ask you some questions. Your answers will be recorded and I'll be making notes as we go along. Is that all right with you?"

She isn't what Newman expected but it's a pleasant surprise. For some reason he'd pictured a middle-aged male wearing a suit and tie.

"Go ahead and ask me whatever you want. You've a job to do and I'll try to be as honest as I can."

Baxter opens the laptop and taps away. "That's good to hear, but I'd prefer it if you did more than just try to be honest."

"I bet you would." Newman can't see her fingers but he can hear them fluttering over the keyboard. He'd love to know what she's writing. She hasn't asked him a single question yet.

"I understand that you've been charged with three counts of murder and you don't intend to deny that you killed the victims."

"That's right. I killed them. There's no point denying it, is there?"

"Can you tell me how that makes you feel?"

Newman knows he can't tell her the truth. He can't tell her that he never wastes energy thinking about the people he killed. They had to die. It's as simple as that. He gave the killer life and the killer had to kill. Predators need prey.

"I don't know what to say about the victims. I wish they weren't dead. If I could snap my fingers and bring them back I would. But I can't."

Baxter's eyes narrow as she starts typing again. Newman gets the feeling that she suspects he's lying, and that unsettles him. He's always been a good liar. It's a skill he's honed over the years.

"And what about the victims' grieving families? If you were given the chance, what would you like to say to them?"

Newman bows his face and covers his face with his hands. He wants to be careful, subtle. This woman is sharp.

He sits up straight and looks her right in the eye. "That's not a question I feel I can answer right now. It's too much for me to handle. I'm sorry, but my mind won't let me go there. Not yet."

Baxter pulls her ponytail forward, flicking it over her right shoulder. She sits back, slides her hands away from the keyboard and steeples her fingers.

Newman takes this as a good sign. He's making her think hard about what he's saying.

"Staying on the subject of families," she says. "I read a little about yours. I understand that your mother brought you up on her own after your father died."

"After my father killed himself. Do you think she'd be proud at the way her boy turned out?"

"Why don't you tell me about her? What was she like?"

Newman doesn't ever talk about his mother. He hasn't mentioned her in conversation, hasn't uttered her name, for years.

"She was a vet. She spent her life treating animals. I don't know why because she didn't like them at all. She was cruel."

"Was she cruel to you?"

"No."

"Was she cruel to your father?"

"I don't know."

"Why do you think he killed himself?"

"Because he didn't like living."

Baxter pauses. Newman knows where this conversation is going and he decides to put a stop to it.

"I'd like to say on the record, and you should note this down, that I did not kill those people because my mummy was horrible to me when I was a little boy. She never liked me and I never liked her. That's just the way it was. I know what you're thinking, but I assure you I haven't got a mother complex."

Newman watches as Baxter taps away on her laptop. When she finishes, she gives him a curious look and he knows she doesn't believe him.

"Well then," she says. "Why do you think you murdered those people?"

Newman shakes his head in frustration. "Why can't anyone understand? It's a simple concept. The killer was a character I created. A cold-blooded murderer I could use to achieve my ambitions. But a fictional character can't kill anybody. That's why I had to do it."

"Just like that?"

"Just like that. It was easier than you might think. I've spent all my working life studying crime, particularly murder and serial killers. I got to know how killers think, how they crave the power, the thrill of it. When I decided to kill, it was no big deal for me. A blade straight through the ribs. It was a simple thing."

CHAPTER 64

Kane walks to the interview room, relieved that Rebecca Baxter has gone. He's also happy that this will be the last time he has to speak to Newman for a while.

As he enters the room, Newman looks up from his chair and smiles like he's greeting an old friend. Kane doesn't sit down. He'd rather keep his distance.

"You know that you'll be appearing in court this afternoon, don't you?"

Newman drums his fingers on the table. "I do. I'm looking forward to it. I've had the pleasure of chatting with the wonderful Ms Baxter this morning. She seemed to understand me. I think I struck lucky there."

Kane ignores him and continues. "Once you return from your court appearance, you will be transferred by van to Chelmsford Prison, where you will await trial."

"You're assuming that I'm going to be declared sane enough to stand trial. From what I could tell, the gorgeous Ms Baxter might have a different view. She's very astute. You know, I've had a lot of time to reflect and wonder how anybody who wasn't insane at the time could do what I did. I must admit, it does make me feel a bit better about myself, knowing that I wasn't in my right mind."

Kane is fully aware that Newman is toying with him. "It's easy for you to talk like this, but it's not going to be easy to dupe the forensic psychologists and psychiatrists who will be reporting to the court. They know what they're doing."

Newman nods. "I'm sure they do. And so do I. I know you might find this hard to believe, but I want the outcome to be right and just. If there's something wrong with my mental state, then I deserve to have treatment."

"I don't know what you're hoping for. Life as a patient in a top-security psychiatric hospital is no picnic. Those places can be grim."

Newman leans back in his chair and grins. "But I'm going to have you visiting me regularly to cheer me up, aren't I? That will give me something to look forward to. I don't agree with what people say about you. I think you could be fun if you put your mind to it."

Kane glances sideways at the shirt-sleeved constable standing beside the door. The young officer raises his eyebrows. Perhaps, Kane wonders, Newman is crazy after all.

"What the hell are you talking about?" He pulls the chair back from the table and sits, annoyed with himself for being drawn into Newman's games. "Why on earth would I ever want to visit you? You're deluded."

Newman gives the police constable a wary look, then lowers his voice to just above a whisper. "You'll come to visit me because you're desperate to find the man who drugged, sexually assaulted and killed your darling wife."

Kane's heart jolts in his chest. "What are you talking about?"

"I'm saying that I can help you. I know how it's eating you up. Gnawing at your insides. I can imagine how you feel. You'll never rest until you find the killer. I have information."

"You're lying."

"Are you going to risk that? I can do it, Inspector. I can give him to you. If I want to."

Kane's stomach is churning. He is close to throwing up. "This isn't funny."

"I'm not joking. I'm a good — no, I'm a great crime reporter. I've been obsessed with murder cases for years. I research, I have contacts. I know things the police will never know."

Kane is sweating. He wipes his brow with his sleeve. He needs it to be true because he wants nothing more in life than getting his hands on the monster who murdered Lizzy. He needs it to be a lie because he can't let a monster like Newman have power over him.

"This is a sick fantasy."

"Is ketamine and ecstasy a fantasy?" Newman says with a smile.

Kane stands up. He puts a hand on the table to steady himself, turns to say something to the uniform, but he can't speak. He walks out of the room, runs down the corridor and into his office, slamming the door behind him.

He can recite Lizzy's autopsy report word for word. Ketamine and ecstasy were found in her blood. Her killer used them to spike her drink. Details that were never made public.

THE END

THE JOFFE BOOKS STORY

We began in 2014 when Jasper agreed to publish his mum's much-rejected romance novel and it became a bestseller.

Since then we've grown into the largest independent publisher in the UK. We're extremely proud to publish some of the very best writers in the world, including Joy Ellis, Faith Martin, Caro Ramsay, Helen Forrester, Simon Brett and Robert Goddard. Everyone at Joffe Books loves reading and we never forget that it all begins with the magic of an author telling a story.

We are proud to publish talented first-time authors, as well as established writers whose books we love introducing to a new generation of readers.

We won Trade Publisher of the Year at the Independent Publishing Awards in 2023. We have been shortlisted for Independent Publisher of the Year at the British Book Awards for the last four years, and were shortlisted for the Diversity and Inclusivity Award at the 2022 Independent Publishing Awards. In 2023 we were shortlisted for Publisher of the Year at the RNA Industry Awards.

We built this company with your help, and we love to hear from you, so please email us about absolutely anything bookish at feedback@joffebooks.com

If you want to receive free books every Friday and hear about all our new releases, join our mailing list: www.joffebooks.com/contact

And when you tell your friends about us, just remember: it's pronounced Joffe as in coffee or toffee.

Made in the USA
Columbia, SC
08 October 2024

43985694R00171